BLOOD MAGIK

BLOOD MAGIK

Meri Elena

PROSPECTIVE PRESS
Winston-Salem

PROSPECTIVE PRESS LLC

1959 Peace Haven Rd, #246, Winston-Salem, NC 27106 U.S.A.
www.prospectivepress.com

Published in the United States of America by PROSPECTIVE PRESS LLC

TRADEMARK

BLOOD MAGIK

Copyright © Meri Elena, 2022
All rights reserved.
The author's moral rights have been asserted.

Author photo by Guinevere Nease

Cover and interior design by ARTE RAVE

ISBN 978-1-943419-60-9

First PROSPECTIVE PRESS trade paperback edition

Printed in the United States of America
First printing, April, 2022

The text of this book was typeset in Alegreya
Accent text was typeset in Aquifer

PUBLISHER'S NOTE

ACKNOWLEDGMENTS

For The Clump. And everyone who patiently waited.

Prologue

Jasmine knelt in the middle of the cave, with only a small ball of purple light in her hand to illuminate the sunless room. The spellwork to temporarily weaken the boundary was complete. She had dismissed all her attendants and closed and locked the door behind her. This was for her eyes only. A painful prickling crawled over her skin, telling her that her masters were breaking through the barrier. Her pitch-black hair ruffled in a sudden breeze. Of course, there couldn't naturally be a breeze several hundred feet below ground. It was a ripple in the fabric of space, caused by the Infinites pulling themselves up through a mass of interdimensional "stuff," the stuff in which the Guardians had imprisoned them ages ago.

The tear opened a meter in front of Jasmine. As soon as she noticed the world beginning to split, she closed her eyes. She hadn't forgotten the first time an Infinite had appeared to her, nearly a decade ago. She had been thrilled beyond measure to lay eyes on an Infinite and the flesh of the world from which it would emerge. She was so young then, so naïve. She never for a moment thought that the sight of the universe's entrails might be too astonishing for her mortal brain. Jasmine saw the inside of the rip for scarcely a heartbeat before the image of boundless space, time, and energy overwhelmed her. The Infinite was obliged to smack her a few times to rouse her from unconsciousness, yet another experience Jasmine would rather not repeat. So, this time, as with every time since, she kept her eyelids shut until the click-clack of claws on stone told her that one of her masters had arrived and closed the rift behind it.

When early humans saw Infinites, they called them dragons. They certainly were a reptilian species, quadruped and scaly, though tailless. Like the Chinese dragons of lore, Infinites were not limited by any standards of size. The one standing before Jasmine appeared as only four feet tall to accommodate the small chamber. Scales no bigger than dimes covered the Infinite's surface, everywhere except the translucent, gelatinous eyes and the gleaming black claws and teeth. As it opened its maw to speak, Jasmine could see scales lining the inside of the mouth, paving the surface of the tongue, and extending down the throat into darkness.

"This past cycle wasn't as successful as we had planned," the Infinite said. Its voice sounded like two hunks of granite grinding a sheet of sandpaper between them.

"No, my lord," Jasmine said. The two young Guardians had wriggled free from her grasp at every turn. Jasmine—and the Infinites—had no one to blame but herself, although she would happily reduce Kell to ash if the deal with Daemonicus went sour.

"We have considered how to address your failure and have decided that your power and loyalty make you too valuable to destroy in this critical time. However, we also concluded that we would give another of our acolytes a chance to prove his worth. You will continue with your plans while he goes forward with his. Whoever has made more progress by the time your moon has made ten revolutions will earn the right to live and continue his or her offensive against the Guardians." The four black spheres in each of the Infinite's eyes coalesced into single pupils to stare Jasmine down.

She wanted to argue. She wanted to tell him that, this time, the plan would work. She would engineer an army more potent than any this world had ever seen. But the effort would take more than ten months, Jasmine was certain of that. If she was to convince the Infinites that she was more reliable than this other person, whoever the hell *he* was, the schedule would have to be amended and sped up. It was going to get messy. Jasmine wasn't ready to state her case yet, not without reworking a good chunk of it, so she merely nodded to the Infinite in acceptance and swallowed her ire.

Jasmine exited the cave with slow, stiff steps, trying her best to contain her anger and frustration. The Infinite had wanted to know about her latest scheme. She glossed over many of the details, knowing that she would have to fill in the blanks later, once she was sure what to put in them. She had expected the brilliance and ingenuity of her plan, even when explained only vaguely, to impress upon the

Infinite that no other acolyte could match Jasmine's talent. Yet when she boasted that no one had ever successfully combined magic and the sciences in the way she was going to, the Infinite responded with a hint of condescension that there was someone who had been doing much the same for longer than Jasmine had been alive. And she was working for the other side. Jasmine's masters were not as impressed as she'd expected.

"Doctor" Kitch had a knack for thwarting Jasmine at every turn. Half the time without even trying. Jasmine's upper lip curled. What was the good doctor's stake in all this? Jasmine couldn't tell that she had any. It was probably just something entertaining for the little cotu princess to do—a nice adrenaline rush. Jasmine had pledged her allegiance almost fifteen years ago and sank everything into this, all for the promise that justice would be done. She had abandoned her home. She'd killed two of the old Guardians with her own hands, no simple task for someone who'd never even been taught how to squish a spider. Meanwhile Sally Kitch stayed holed up in her nice, cozy palace and waited for not one, but *two* Guardians to just fall in her lap so they could all play a big game of keep-away.

Ultimately, though, Jasmine had to admit that she probably would not have thought of this pseudo-scientific plan of attack had she not spent the past year parlaying with Sally. Delving into the woman's body of work had not just helped Jasmine understand her, it had been unexpectedly inspiring. Perhaps the Kitch clan could be made a means of enacting Jasmine's justice, rather than an obstacle. The corners of Jasmine's mouth twitched into a momentary smile at the thought. But this was no time for fantasizing. There was work to do. She had two hours before her phone meeting with Daemonicus, and she didn't intend to let the time go to waste. By the end of the night, Jasmine was determined to know exactly how she was going to wrest a Guardian from Sally's clumsy cotu claws in ten months *without* disrupting the rest of her work.

1

Brunswick

"Sally, can you explain it to me one more time?"

Sally and her brother, known to her as William but to many as Jack, were in the library in the basement of Kitch Manor. Sally sat on the cool, wooden floor, her laptop resting on her crossed legs. She leaned back against the well-worn velvet armchair she'd bought at an estate sale the week before. Sally had intended only to peruse the deceased's book collection, but she made the mistake of bringing her very impulsive elder sibling with her. They returned from the sale with six books, an ornate bird cage, a mediocre landscape painting, and that stylish but completely unneeded chair. William must have sensed her annoyance, because he promptly set about putting their extra purchases to use to justify their presence in the house. He touched up the painting himself, bought a parakeet for the bird cage, and was currently sitting in the velvet chair as he read the trashy romance novel he had coerced Sally into buying. The bottle of bourbon at his feet, however, he had somehow acquired on his own, despite not having a penny to his name.

"What is it you want me to explain?" Sally asked, flicking her gaze at William. His large lime-green eyes and softly angular jawline were almost identical to hers.

"The whole Guardian situation. I'm just not really comprehending it."

Sally set the laptop aside, reminding herself to be patient with William. It had been a long time since the two of them had shared a living space, but Sally had not forgotten that communication was a struggle for him.

"Okay. There are creatures called Infinites," Sally said. "We don't really know what they are, only what they did. The Infinites made themselves masters of much of the universe, once, a long time ago, possibly before humans appeared on this planet. They enslaved the intelligent lifeforms under their command to ensure their material comfort and insisted on being given blood offerings to slake their thirst for violence. When it wasn't enough, they would go on hunting safaris of their own.

"After quite some time, twelve Earthlings decided to stage a coup of sorts. They called themselves Guardians, or rather the equivalent of the word in their native tongues. The Guardians performed a ritual to banish the Infinites between the worlds, somehow managing to gain immortality themselves in the process, or so the story goes. The Infinites didn't appreciate that, so they keep trying to come back into the world. The only way that can happen is if all the Guardians are killed.

"Now, almost all the original Guardians are dead at the hands of the Infinites and those loyal to them, so whatever force has sustained the Guardians thus far is calling new Guardians. A sort of passing of the torch. Does that help?"

"If there are twelve, why are there only two?" William asked.

"Huh? Oh, there *are* twelve, somewhere. We just haven't found the other ten of them yet. That's my mission—to figure out where they are. While simultaneously not letting anything happen to the two I already have."

"That sounds difficult."

"It is. Increasingly," Sally agreed, "but I don't have to handle it alone. My colleagues and I may not always get along, but we are united in purpose. And you've been some help too. I understand Richie would be dead if not for you. At the least, he wouldn't be here, where he's marginally safer."

"Just 'marginally'?"

"Sorry. I learned my brutal honesty from you. Richie is safer here than anywhere else, as is Jason, but they aren't really safe anywhere. So, marginally." Sally shrugged. There was nothing more to it. She had sworn to do anything she must to protect the new Guardians, but she had to accept that it might not be enough. The danger wouldn't subside until the Infinites were beaten, years down the road. Sally waited a few moments to see if William had any other questions, but he didn't say anything, just stared off towards the far wall. Sally picked up the laptop and resumed typing. The estate sale had furnished her with several good books, just not the one she was looking for. She had noticed that Richie's powers of prophecy were increasing as the rest of the world's prophets began to lose the Sight. There had to be an explanation. She was sure Kandrik's treatise on prophecy had the answer, if only she could find a copy—

"Sally? Do you think Richie hates me?"

Stifling a frustrated sigh, Sally again placed the computer on the floor and turned her attention to her older, but more childlike, sibling.

"William, you know my understanding of people is only barely superior to yours."

"Surely you have a theory," William asked. "You have a theory for everything."

"I suppose that's true." Sally chewed her tongue for a moment while she considered the data. "Well, he's certainly been avoiding you ever since he found out that you neglected to tell him you're my brother. That seems to me a rather silly thing to hold a grudge over. I suspect that Richie is simply deflecting onto you his anger at the universe for cursing him with prophetic dreams, or his anger at me for not making the nightmares stop, or maybe some sense of self-loathing—"

"Self-loathing? How? Why?" William sounded genuinely shocked. "He's smart. He's independent. He knows what to do in a fight. What's not to like?"

"He is a killer now, or so I hear," Sally said, reminding him. "Many people can't stand to have blood on their hands, especially social animals or those raised among them. Think Lady Macbeth. And isn't that the reason you're here, anyways? Because you feel guilty? Why else would you bury your pride and ask your baby sister for help? Again. You despise feeling dependent." William averted his eyes. His left heel started thumping the floor anxiously.

"You mean, you already know?"

"Not everything. But I've heard the rumors. I know enough. It can't have gotten any better after Lily." Sally said the name of their murdered sister softly, hoping to lessen the impact on William's nerves. Still, he winced, as though physically wounded by the word. Sally reached up and took his hand with a comforting squeeze. His alabaster skin was chilly to the touch.

"I'm a physician, not a psychiatrist, honey," Sally said gently. "I can't help you like you want me to, not really. But I will always be here, if you need to talk, for whatever my advice is worth. Right now, though, I think the best thing you can do for yourself is figure out this quarrel with Richie. You may find he's fighting much the same feelings that you are."

"You ran away from my glorious medieval castle to live here, Alexandru? This woman's little Gothic Revival bauble is in such poor taste," Vlad Dracula said and sniffed. "And the mattress is made of cardboard."

"Whatever you say, Father," Alex replied, chuckling lightly. He had forgotten how entertaining the Count could be in certain moods. Alex folded the last of his father's many dark-colored dress shirts and plopped the stack into the suitcase. The senior Dracula had been moved into a makeshift spare bedroom two floors up from the treatment room about a month ago. His brush with werewolf venom had been harrowing, but he was plenty healthy even before he took up guest residence. He continued to fabricate a variety of lingering symptoms, however. Alex knew Sally was a little insulted that Vlad really thought she didn't know what he was doing. However, even Sally had enough sense of family to know that Vlad had a right to prolong his stay with his only son if he wanted to. Besides, he had been polite to almost everyone. Every once in a while, Sally would feel the need to remind him that she had saved his life, and while his vast knowledge of synonyms for the term "prostitute" was quite impressive, he had best keep them to himself. Alex could see both sides. He knew his father was exceptionally rude to Sally at times when he ought to be grateful. On the other hand, Alex suspected that Vlad considered the day Alex left with Sally one of the worst in his very long life. That was a stain of guilt Alex would never outlive.

"Is this the last one?" asked Scarlet, coming in the room in a whirl of tie-dye t-shirt and cool, blue-green aura. Vlad stiffened almost imperceptibly. Even after several weeks in her friendly presence, he was still wary of her, as she was a werewolf, and it was a werewolf excretion that had so lately crippled him and obliged him to seek Sally's medical expertise. Werewolves and vampires infamously did not get along as each was toxic to the other, but Alex had long ago learned to live happily and harmoniously with Scarlet.

"That is, indeed, the last one," Vlad said, edging ever so slightly away from the door to keep at a safe distance from the boisterous wolf girl. Scarlet, oblivious to Vlad's quiet nervousness, nodded and bounced on the balls of her feet as she waited for Alex to finish packing so she could take the suitcase out to the VW bus. The Count had a flight out of Asheville Regional in a few short hours. Alex was sure that he didn't want to return home, despite his complaints about the accommodations, but he said he couldn't trust his minions to run the estate unsupervised for long, and Alex knew his father to be a bit of a homebody. He had made Alex promise to write to him at least once a month, in code if he had to, or Brunswick would be flooded with Dracula's hypnotized servants. Alex didn't doubt that for a moment.

"We'll miss you," Scarlet said, taking the suitcase. Alex knew she meant it too, even if she hardly knew Dracula and he didn't much care for Scarlet. Deception was completely alien to Scarlet, and everyone who wasn't her enemy was her friend.

"Thank you, Scarlet," the elder Dracula replied, softening a smidgen. "I will miss most of you as well. If I don't see Richie and Jack—William, rather, before we leave, make sure to give them my regards. And tell them…well, tell them not to lose heart. Those boys could use some encouragement, especially the Scotsman."

Scarlet nodded, and then she was gone, leaving the Draculas alone in the room. Alex swallowed. In a few minutes he would drive his father to Asheville and see him off in the chaos of the airport. This might be their last chance to really talk before going their separate ways again. They stared at each other awkwardly, neither man sure how best to address the other. At length, Alex dredged up from his memory the one thing he hadn't yet told his father about their time apart. He hadn't told anyone but Sally, preferring to save it for a moment when he would be one-on-one with the person whose wisdom he trusted most.

"Father," Alex began slowly, "something has happened. Something odd. I want your take on it." He sucked in a fortifying lungful of air. "My visions are gone." Alex had always known his father to be a man of muted facial expressions. Only a slight tightening of the muscles and widening of the Count's eyes told Alex just how shocked he was.

"When? How? Who has done this to you?" Vlad demanded with an edge of aggression. The Dracula patriarch would gladly devise a most cruel death for whoever robbed his son of the gift of prophecy. However, his distress would have no such outlet.

"Sally thinks it has to do with the Guardians rising, but that's really just a guess. We don't know why it's happening. It started about two years ago," Alex said. "The visions became blurrier, less frequent, and finally stopped altogether. The last one was this past winter, and it was so distorted I couldn't comprehend it. I can still read minds, use telepathy, and read auras. I think I can still hypnotize, although I haven't tried lately—"

"Who else knows?" Vlad said, interrupting Alex's confession.

"Only Sally, but even she doesn't know I've lost the Sight completely now. I can't bring myself to admit that. She has promised not to tell anybody else, and I trust her. So it's just the three of us."

"Good. Keep it that way. Not a soul is to know that you have acquired this weakness. Understood?" Vlad held Alex's gaze firmly, taking hold of his shoulder for emphasis. The grip was a fraction tighter than it needed to be, a rare sign of fear.

"Of course," Alex said. "But I'm not the only one this has happened to. Sally says other prophets are fading now, as well. Father…have you any idea what it might mean?" The Count shook his head in bewilderment.

"I do not know. The world is changing in ways unprecedented, at least in my time. Never has a prophet lost his vision before without it being stolen. Perhaps I shouldn't leave."

"No, it's fine. You have things to take care of back home, and I'm okay. I need to be here. And you aren't comfortable. I can tell. What's more, I can handle myself well enough," Alex replied. Vlad hesitated, throat tensed to speak even as his brain debated what to say.

"You are right. My place is not here. But I *will* return, and soon, I swear it. And if anything else troublesome occurs, you *will* alert me immediately."

Alex nodded. Then, overwhelmed by an impulse, he closed the gap between himself and his father and flung his arms around the Count. Vlad tensed at the touch. In the old, aristocratic world in which he raised Alex, emotional displays were improper if not taboo. Awkwardly, he placed one arm across Alex's back and gave him a couple of uncertain pats. Alex released Vlad at last and reminded him that he had a flight to catch. The two headed down the stairs to make the trek to the airport.

"No, no, no, no, no, you hold the bow the *other* way, Richie."

"What other way?"

Scarlet, in her boundless patience, confiscated the longbow, flipped it horizontally, and situated it back in Richie's fumbling hands.

"I don't see why I have to learn how to shoot sticks," he said in complaint, struggling in vain to nock an arrow. "I mean, I can throw fireballs, as soon as I get the hang of it. What use is this thing to me?"

"Well, if nothing else, it might help improve y'all's hand-eye—"

"Hey, imagine if you could shoot *flaming arrows!*" Cameron said.

"Or that." Scarlet smiled and rolled her eyes. At least someone was excited. "Maybe not today, though, okay?"

Cameron stood on Richie's right, wrestling with the longbow much as Richie had been all morning. He had taken off his shirt under the steamy summer heat, and thin ribbons of muscle imparted a grotesque animation to his scars, an echo of the Black Dog's claws. Since his injury and Jose's death, Cameron had healed faster than expected, in mind and body. To Scarlet, his way of coping had the suggestion of revenge: he asked Sally to let him train with the young Guardians so that he could someday take the fight to the genies, and she agreed. Scarlet wasn't sure Cameron should be in on the fighting, or if Sally really intended to let him be, but if there was a chance this would do the poor boy some good, it was worth a try.

"Not even Jason can make an arrow spontaneously combust," Tyler said. He stood by Cameron's other side, leaning on a crutch and stubbornly trying to adjust his grip on the bow to accommodate his injury. Sally didn't want him to be out and about yet, but after eight weeks of bed rest the cabin fever was fixing to shred his sanity. Tyler managed to convince her that one low-impact training session wouldn't aggravate his damaged skeleton too much.

"How did Jason learn? Is that his 'Guardian gift' or whatever?" Richie asked. His fellow trainees emitted a general murmur of confusion.

"You mean like your gift of prophecy," Alex said. He lounged in the grass behind the line of Scarlet's students, watching their antics with some amusement. "No, Jason doesn't have anything like that. He's got a talent for the bow, but if he has a magical 'gift,' it hasn't shown itself yet."

"Hey, where is Jason anyway?" Cameron glanced in Scarlet and Alex's general direction without lowering his bow.

"Doctor's appointment, I think." Scarlet shrugged. "He doesn't really need to be here for this, anyway. No offense to you guys. Everyone has to start somewhere." Richie tried to loose an arrow and managed to weakly launch it backwards over his shoulder. Scarlet stifled a sigh.

"Alex, if Jason isn't magic Robin Hood, and he doesn't have any other gift you know of, then how do you know that he's a Guardian?" Tyler said. He gave up on the bow and leaned it against his crutch, training his gaze on Alex.

"His aura," Alex answered. "It's bright and…yellow." Richie raised an eyebrow at him. "Look, it's hard to explain. Just go with me on this one. Yours looks exactly the same, Richie."

"I glow yellow?"

"Um, yes. It's not as unmanly as it sounds, I promise."

"So what about the rest of us? You said there are twelve, right? What are you going to do, travel the world looking for yellow, glowy people?" Richie had lowered his bow as well, more interested in interrogating Alex than in the lesson. Only Cameron remained engaged in the task at hand, doggedly shooting arrows into the sky in short, wobbly arcs. Scarlet was thankful that he at least was taking the lesson seriously. Although she couldn't really blame Richie for having questions about his unwanted fate.

"Well, yeah, sort of. I don't know." Alex shrugged. "Sally and Hope have been arguing about our strategy for years. As soon as they agree on something, I'll be happy to tell you what the plan is."

"Alex, you might be waiting a long time for that," Scarlet said. She hoped it came across less exasperated than she felt about all that drama. "Now come on, this isn't Story Time with Alex. Pick up your bows, boys. Richie, you're holding it wrong again. Like *this*."

"It's good that Richie's fitting in so well, now that he's finally outside," Jason said, sitting down on a fallen log. Out in the field, Richie and Robin were trying to steal the soccer ball from each other. It had taken a few weeks for Richie to decide to participate in Soccer Sundays. At first, he spent his days moping inside the Manor. Jason had finally resigned himself to his Guardianship, because it was his nature to take life as it came. Richie, however, was resentful and of no mind to accept his fate. He came to Sally to ask her to take the supernatural out of his head and discovered that he was destined never to be normal again. At last, he was starting to bounce back and take an interest in Jason's soccer buddies. Jason encouraged him to come, hoping that some sport would get Richie out of the funk he had been in—a mood that made developing friendships difficult. The plan hadn't been entirely successful, but at least Richie was out of the house.

"He's an excellent player," Tyler said. "Even if he insists on calling it football."

Jason grinned. Richie made a great show of his foreignness, mostly because the girls in town ate it right up. They swooned anytime they heard that Scottish brogue, and Richie loved it.

"You know, you should be out there with him," Tyler pointed out.

"I just didn't feel like playing today," Jason said. He felt Tyler's gaze on him but kept his own looking straight forward. Sammy, who had so recently been Jason's best friend, had bested both Richie and Robin and taken hold of the ball to drive it down the field. Jason struggled to remember the last time he'd said more than a few words to Sammy. Not that Sammy hadn't tried. But he hadn't been able to keep Jason's Guardianship a secret for a week, and Jason found that impossible to get past.

"No," Tyler said, "you don't want me to be the only one sitting here watching on the sidelines." He stretched his legs out in front of him, causing the components of his leg brace to clink together. Jason flinched at the sound. "You don't have to do this, you know. Although I can't say I'm not grateful."

"I don't mind. Besides, I really *don't* feel much like playing." Jason forced himself to look at Tyler's broken form. His skin had healed from the worst of the scars. He had his werewolf genes to thank for that. And Sally, of course. If it hadn't been for her, Tyler would never have survived. But she could only do so much, and his right leg and pelvis were beyond repair, especially since they had begun to knit together before the pieces could be put back in place. When Tyler had bitten the Black Dog, he'd gotten a mouthful of magically toxic blood, which had scrambled his werewolf healing and, to a lesser extent, morphing powers. Tyler, the fastest, sportiest kid in Brunswick, who had always sworn he would be a professional basketball player, might never walk unaided again. At first, Jason just blamed himself, but with Alex's help, he had begun to direct his emotions toward the one who really caused all this distress—Jasmine.

That name. It had been bouncing around all over the Manor for four months, ever since the Black Dog had revealed it to Alex, but no one knew anything about the genie behind it. She was even more elusive than the Dog had been. The girls had been researching her nonstop, in every vein they could imagine. They had little to show for their efforts. It wasn't that there were no genies named Jasmine in the history of the world, but nothing linked any genie they could find to what was going on now. It didn't help that the scientific jury was still out on the length of a genie lifespan. Should they look for this woman in twelfth century folklore, or were newspaper articles from the 1980s too old?

"Any new developments?" Tyler asked, interrupting Jason's train of thought.

"Not really. The genies have been quiet ever since we burned up their pet. Sally's been trying to figure what set the genies off, but she's been pretty distracted lately."

"Oh, yeah, I guess I've been kind of in the way, huh?"

"What? No! That's not what I meant," Jason said. "I meant with Richie and Dracula and her brother."

"What's William got to do with anything?"

"I don't know. I thought he would just move in and do his own thing, but instead he spends all day following Sally, and I think it's distracting for her. I mean, I try not to judge, but he seems very needy."

"And Sally puts up with it?" Tyler raised his eyebrows. "I find that hard to believe."

"Well, she does get impatient with him, but he's her brother, and they have a lot of catching up to do. And it's not like he's totally messing stuff up or anything. He does things around the house to give everyone else more time to research, and he volunteers to keep guard over me or Richie so that Alex and Scarlet don't have to split up to watch both of us."

"If he's so clingy, what is Sally going to do with him when she goes back to school with you?" Tyler said. "Or is she going back to school?" Jason paused to think. He couldn't remember Sally mentioning school one way or the other. Cleaning up the mess left over from the spring kept her occupied. She would take Jason to the library once a week or so, but otherwise they rarely crossed paths.

"I hadn't really thought about it," Jason replied. "I guess I should ask."

The next morning, Jason walked over to the Manor. He was allowed more freedom these days, since there hadn't been any direct threats on his life for several months. A responsible adult still had to be within shouting distance at all times, but Jason didn't have to cower in his house anymore. He tried his best to take advantage of the liberty while it lasted.

He found Sally in the library with William. They both spent a lot of time there as of late. Sally was immersed in a thick, fabric-bound text. William was sprawled on his back on the floor with a ratty paperback. Sally sat up when Jason opened the door, eyebrows raised in a classic picture of surprise. She always seemed astonished when Jason came to the Manor of his own volition.

"Hey, Sally, I was hoping I could talk to you?"

"Sure thing." She slipped an envelope, as a makeshift bookmark, into the volume and looked up at Jason expectantly. William ignored them both. Apparently, he shared his sister's obliviousness to subtext. Well, Jason supposed there wasn't a problem with William listening in. He joined them on the floor.

"I was wondering, are you and Alex coming to school with me this year?"

"Alex is. I'm not," Sally said with her customary succinctness.

"Why not?" William asked, setting his book on his chest.

"An excellent question," Jason added. Sally glanced at William, then apparently chose to ignore him and focused on Jason.

"It's a waste of time, really. I thought I would come by the first day to make sure there aren't any issues with Alex's schedule or anything, but that's as much as I might be needed. I hope. Alex has proven that he can protect you just fine by himself, and I'm not very likely to run into another Guardian in the same school. Besides, I'm sure you would rather I stay out of your way, wouldn't you?"

"Out of his way of what?" William asked, but Jason knew what she meant. It had been a point of tension from the moment Sally told him he was a Guardian: where was the line between keeping Jason safe and preventing him from having a life?

"Sally, you don't have to do that," Jason said, a sort of knee-jerk re-action of politeness. "We all know I can't have 'normal' anyway." If he were honest, he didn't value his illusion of normalcy over his safety like he used to, now that he'd had a taste of the dangers.

"It's fine. Really, my energies are best expended elsewhere. This Guardian search is like five amoebae looking for twelve mouse hairs in a haystack." She poked a finger at her collarbone. "This amoeba has a lot more haystack to cover."

"Um, all right. So what are you going to do, then? Scope out a different school?"

"Yes. There have been some odd events in part of rural New York, so I'm going to portal over there for several hours every weekday, ostensibly as a college student, and peruse the area. We're trying to branch out a little in our search pattern."

"Oh, is Hope going to make a portal for you?" Jason knew that cotus could make portals themselves, but it took a lot of energy. Witches like Hope could channel that sort of magic more easily.

"No," Sally said. "Well, probably not. Maybe. I haven't asked yet." Sally shrugged, and Jason had to wonder if she was quarreling with Hope over something again. They stared at each other for a longer-than-comfortable span, the only sound the leisurely turning of pages between William's fingers.

"Whoever blinks first has to dust the bookshelves," William said. Sally and Jason both blinked, startled by the sudden sound. Jason glanced at William, but he wasn't actually looking, so he couldn't make good on his threat to make anyone dust all those shelves. As if William had the authority to enforce such a thing in his sister's house. Jason shook his head.

"I think I'm going to go before anyone saddles me with any housework. Hey, maybe you should talk to Hope about the transportation thing," Jason said. "Summer will be over before you know it."

You can take a vampire out of the night, but you can never quite take the night out of a vampire. Alex had been a day-walker—diurnal was Sally's word—for most of thirty years, but sometimes he still remained completely and hopelessly awake long after the sun went down. Fortunately, a little warm blood could cure his insomnia. Alex used to hunt for sleeping humans who could spare a pint on nights like this, but nowadays people locked their doors with keypads and had electronic security systems. Alex possessed a handful of modern burglary skills, but it was easier to just warm up whatever Sally had stocked the refrigerator with. It didn't have the same thrill, but it kept the townsfolk happy.

Emerging from the basement where he stereotypically made his bed, Alex was surprised to see a light on in the kitchen. As soon as he realized that part of the light he was seeing came from an aura, not a light bulb, he knew who else it was that couldn't sleep.

Richie was slumped over the kitchen table, clasping an empty glass between his hands and staring at it with foggy eyes. For the most part, Richie reported that he'd slept spectacularly since saving Jason from the Black Dog and thus putting his nightmare to rest. However, as Alex well knew from a few hundred years of prophetic dreams of his own, they never went away for long.

"Another nightmare, I take it?" Alex asked, coming around the corner. Richie jerked a little. Having spent his whole life among humans, it seemed that his cotu senses had never been honed to their fullest. He ought to have smelled Alex coming several minutes ago.

"Aye," Richie mumbled.

"The kind that'll come true, you think?"

"No, the kind that already did."

"Now, you're going to have to explain that one to me," Alex said. He took a gallon jug full of blood from the refrigerator and poured some into a mug.

"Just the fighting and all when I was traveling with Jack, I mean William, and your dad. I saw things I can't get out of my head."

Alex turned on the tap as hot as it would go. As he waited for the water to heat up, he wondered what the appropriate response would be. Violence had never really bothered him, coming from the family line that produced Vlad the Impaler. It confused him a bit when others got upset over a little bloodshed. Either Alex's confusion showed or Richie had just been waiting for a jumping-off point all along, because within seconds Richie was ranting.

"My God, what is it about this that you people don't get? *I killed someone.* And everyone here is just like, 'Oh, that's fine, don't even think about it.' Like I can *decide* not to think about it. Like I can forget what it felt like. I'll always be a murderer. *Always.* And I'm just supposed to live with that?" For the first time, Richie looked at Alex, and even though he was legally an adult he was still a lost, lonely kid begging the only grown-up in the room to tell him what to do. He could hardly have picked someone less prepared. Alex froze, completely terrified by the load of responsibility that had just clocked him in the head. The microwave beeped cheerfully. Alex took the opportunity to turn around and retrieve his blood, thinking madly about how to reply.

"Well, gee, Richie, what do you want us to say? Nobody blames you. It was entirely in self-defense. If you hadn't killed that vampire hunter, he would have had no problem killing you. Besides, if you hadn't gotten to him, William or Thomas would have done him in sooner or later."

"I know, but that doesn't make it okay. Even if you think I had the right...I didn't just kill him. I tore him up. I bit into his throat like an animal and tasted him in my mouth and it felt *so good,* I..." Richie's voice cracked, and he buried his face in his hands. "What is *wrong* with me?"

Alex sighed. *What have I done to deserve this?* He filled a bowl with the hot water and set his mug in it to heat up his breakfast.

"Look, Richie, you're in a different world now. I know you were raised as a human, but you have to try to get out of that mindset. Cotus are descended from carnivores, you know. They're made to be predators. If they hated to kill, the species wouldn't have survived. It's that natural selection thing."

"So I was born to be a homicidal freak? Thanks, that's really what I wanted to hear."

"No, that's not what I meant." Alex swirled the blood in his mug with his finger, staring into its crimson depths. "I can't understand where you're coming from, exactly. I've never been one to kill for fun, but I'm not ashamed of my God-given predatory instincts or of the exhilaration the hunt gives me. I know what I am. It's never bothered me. I'm not demonic. I'm not *rabid*. I keep my drive to hunt under control just like everyone else. You can control it too. Think about this. There are tens of millions of vampires in the world. We're all predators, obviously. But how many vampire attacks have you heard of lately?"

"I've only ever heard of one, back in Scotland," Richie answered after a moment's thought. "I assumed that there was some kind of big conspiracy to keep most of the public in doubt."

"Careful. You're starting to sound like Scarlet with her fairies and UFOs," Alex said, unable to help a small smirk at the gullible woman's expense. "We've figured out how to keep ourselves under control. There's a bit of a learning curve at first, but you get the hang of it soon. Even if there was a conspiracy to keep suspicious deaths quiet, if every vampire on Earth gleefully spent his nights killing humans left and right, don't you think somebody would notice?" Alex forged onward, not waiting for Richie to respond. "Most vampires kill rarely, if ever, and then often by accident. Even during the Middle Ages when vampires ran rampant, it just wasn't done. Violence is in our nature, but there's a conscience in there too. The predator inside doesn't own you." It was a fine speech. Alex was feeling rather proud of himself. Richie, however, seemed less impressed.

"Oh, so you think it's okay to look at other people as prey, as long as you keep the kill count low?" Richie sure knew how throw it back in a guy's face. Fortunately, years of living with Sally had inured Alex to acerbity, and he responded without pause.

"No, I'm *saying* that you have to accept your brain the way it is. You have a taste for blood, though not as much as I do, and that won't change. Trying to pretend it isn't there will just drive you crazy. You have to make peace with your predatory instincts and move on with your life. As I said, it's a different world outside the cushiony human sphere. Your life won't be the same."

"I don't *have* a life anymore!" Richie glared up at Alex.

"Well then I guess it's time to move on, isn't it? You know, you really ought to hang out with Jason more often; he's been working on this whole identity crisis, everything-I-know-is-gone sort of thing longer than you have. Maybe he could teach you something."

"But Jason's so *young*. And he doesn't know what it's like. He's never had a normal life." Richie shook his head. "I can't talk to him."

"People who've had normal lives are in short supply around here, kid. Besides, this is the new normal," Alex said. Still, Richie had a point. Jason was a lot younger than Richie, and much less worldly. They might as well be from different planets.

"What about Sally's brother, then? You know him better than anyone else right now. Isn't that a place to start?" Alex took an experimental sip from his mug. Still a little cool. He returned it to the water bath. Richie slid his glass around the table for a few seconds, not answering.

"Jack—er, William, and I, we sort of fell out after we got here. I kind of feel bad about it now, but I blamed him. I was mad at Sally, really, but she's kind of hard to fight with, since she just sort of deflects everything I throw at her. And, you know, she's probably right, so I can't really argue. Easier to stay angry with William."

Alex nodded. He understood perfectly. He gave Scarlet hell for two weeks after Sally broke up with him. Scarlet forgave him for it, though, as she forgave most everyone for most everything. Alex didn't know William very well, just what Sally had said about him, but there was a chance he was the forgiving type too.

"I'm not the best at touchy-feely conversations, but I've heard that those sort of things can be talked out," Alex said. "You should try it. In the morning. After you've gotten some sleep." Exhausted himself from all the counseling, Alex took his mug of blood and left the room as expediently as possible.

William woke with the sunrise as it shone through his window. He had spent a few nights in this room a long time ago, when the house was new, Sally wasn't even an egg yet, and Kitch Manor was just a seldom-used vacation home. It hadn't changed much.

A full-length mirror with ornate wooden edging faced him on the opposite wall. On the surface, purple whiteboard marker text in Sally's handwriting reminded him to brush his hair, wear a shirt, take a shower for goodness sakes, not lose his house key, etc. William argued with Sally the first time he saw that to-do list. Sure, he forgot things sometimes, or just lost motivation to do important stuff, but he'd made it this long, hadn't he? She said he needed structure. William told her that he refused to be treated like a child and erased the list. That afternoon he forgot to wear shoes and sliced the bottom of his foot open on his own knife, which he had neglected to pick up off the floor after he threw it across the room during one of his fits, which he tried not to think of as temper tantrums or "episodes," as others sometimes called them. He bandaged his foot himself and never told Sally, but she must've figured it out. The next morning, the purple list was back, and he hadn't complained about it since.

William reached under the bed, pulling out the first glass bottle that met his searching fingers. He laid back and sucked down greedy mouthfuls of the brown liquid inside. Thus fortified, he set about getting ready for the day, mentally checking off the points on the purple list. Once he was pretty sure he was presentable, William made a bee-line for the kitchen. He was often ravenous in the mornings. Actually, he was often ravenous, period. It was the curse of being a magical creature with a high metabolism and, until recently, little to eat.

Even before he stepped off the stairs, he could see Richie at the table. Cotus could see heat and ultraviolet rays as well as visible light, and few things gave off a stronger heat signature than a fire cotu. The brightness of Richie's body temperature shone through the wall separating them. Richie could surely have seen the cold, dark spot around William, too, if he were paying attention, but Richie knew so little about his senses that he probably wouldn't recognize what he was seeing.

William paused, unsure whether to brave Richie or not. Every time he'd tried to talk to Richie from the moment Sally told him he was a Guardian, Richie got mad and William ended up wishing he'd never started the conversation. Still, if Sally were right about what Richie was going through, maybe he should keep trying...

Finally, he let the empty ache in his stomach make the decision for him. Richie would just have to get over it. William sauntered into the kitchen and wished Richie a good morning like it was no big deal. Richie shook his head to get rid of the sleepiness and returned the greeting. He didn't sound furious, just kind of tired. William guessed that was a positive indication.

"You want any eggs?" William asked, retrieving the big skillet from a cabinet over the oven. "The only way I know how to do them is scrambled, so I hope that's okay."

"Uh, sure, that's fine. Could you throw three in for me?"

William cracked nine eggs in the skillet and took a whisk to them. Richie didn't say anything else, so William didn't try to make him talk. He asked Richie a few breakfast-related questions as he went along, and Richie answered them briefly. Even after all these years, William still struggled to grasp the complexities of tones of voice, so he wasn't sure how to read Richie's words or his silence.

He shoveled a third of the eggs and a piece of toast onto a plate for Richie and cut up a tomato into the half-dozen scrambled eggs remaining in the skillet. William slid Richie his plate and then sat diagonal from him at the table, eating straight out of the pan himself. Richie glanced at the skillet but didn't say anything. William had always liked that Richie didn't make a fuss about him eating like a horse or drinking like a fish. He usually felt awkward with people, but while they'd been on the road together, he'd rarely felt weird with Richie. Of course, their entire dynamic fell to pieces when they got to their destination. That was just his luck.

"I thought Europeans did that light breakfast with tea thing," William ventured, hoping to strike up the inane banter he and Richie used to have. Richie smiled just the tiniest bit.

"I thought Americans couldn't have a meal without bacon," Richie replied.

"Don't you know by now that I'm a vegetarian?"

"Hh—you're what? Why?" Richie's head snapped up, and his eyes widened with disbelief.

"It's a kind of a long story," William said, unwilling to explain. It was too exhausting for this early in the morning, and somewhat traumatizing. "I'll tell you some other time." William shoved a forkful of eggs in his mouth as a final hint, and Richie must have gotten the message, because he just shrugged and let it go. For a while they munched their eggs in comfortable silence, until Richie spoke again.

"Hey, Ja—William, um, I think I need to apologize."

"For what?"

"For being such a dick to you."

"Oh. Forget about it." William waved a hand dismissively. "I've done worse things to people when I was upset. I forgive you."

Richie was silent for a moment, looking stunned.

"I, okay. Thank you. I just don't know how to act now. Alex was down here a while ago guzzling blood out of a coffee mug, and apparently I'm a cat. It's all so *weird*. I don't feel like a cat. How does that even work? Oh, *and* I burned a hole in my pillow last night while I was asleep."

"I don't know about pillows, but I can teach you how to shapeshift some time, if you're ready. You'll feel more like a cotu when you look like one." William studied Richie and tried to picture what his natural form might be, but he couldn't quite conjure the image. Richie had probably been forced into a human shape as a tiny cub. Perhaps only his birth parents knew what he really looked like.

"I think I'll wait until I've learned not to set things on fire, first," Richie said. William tried not to look disappointed.

"All right, that's fine. I'm here to help however I can, you know," William said. "Sally is too," he added after a pause. "I know you aren't very fond of her—I guess most people aren't—but if you ask her to explain something to you she'll be your best friend, in her own odd way."

"I can't imagine Sally being best friends with anybody."

"You've got to understand, she's a lot like me. We don't *get* people. She can tell you everything about how the cardiac muscle works but she doesn't understand the workings of the heart any better than I do."

"Wow. That was very poetic of you," Richie said. "But I still don't think Sally and I are ever going to be friends, no offense. She's too, I don't know, *her*."

"You're a bit combative yourself." William could see it in his face as Richie started to argue, then realized he would just be proving William right. Richie's face warped into a sulk. William smirked.

"Well, whether you learn to like her or not, you might want to be a little less aggressive. Sally doesn't appreciate people who undermine her, especially men, and she's not someone you'd want to make an enemy of. Hey, are you busy later today? I was thinking about checking out that tiny movie theater downtown."

Things had changed more than Alex could comprehend since last year. He remembered how it used to be when he and the girls started a new school year of spying on children. The whole concept had always seemed a bit creepy to Alex, but it was Sally's idea. You didn't argue much with Sally once she got it in her head to do something. So every year they took on younger-looking forms in their own ways—except for Jenna, who was perpetually sixteen—and split up to search for new Guardians hiding in the school system. Last year, they finally found one. After Alex had stumbled upon Jason, everything had been different. Then Sally's erstwhile brother—Jack or William or whatever his name was—and Alex's father showed up with Richie, Guardian Number Two, which changed their plans even more. They weren't prepared for two Guardians to land in their laps at once.

"All right, let's make sure we all know what we're doing today," Sally called in her official-business voice. She leaned against the kitchen counter, a bagel in one hand and a schedule in the other. Behind her, William was scrambling himself some eggs and watching the proceedings curiously. Alex sat at the breakfast table with Scarlet, Jenna, and Hope. Hope was busy applying a mix of magic and make-up to make herself look like a fashionable teenage girl, but she paused to listen to Sally. The two of them hadn't argued seriously for a few weeks, so civility had returned to their relationship, at least for now. Richie was nowhere to be found. He rarely woke up before ten o'clock.

"Alex is in charge of Jason," Sally said. "I'm going to accompany them today. Classes won't start where I'm going for a few weeks. Hope is teleporting to that middle school in Georgia. Jenna is going back to Wimberley High School, since we haven't been there in a few years, and Scarlet will be teaching at that special arts school they just opened in Asheville. And, I have a job for you too, William." Sally looked over her shoulder at him. "You have to keep Richie safe, whether he wants you to or not. If you can do that, then the rest of us can be free to cover more ground."

"Oh, sure," William answered, turning to look at his sister with a smile. "Richie and I made nice. I think. I'm pretty confident that he'll put up with me."

It had been several months since William unexpectedly joined the Kitch Manor collective. Alex found him a very perplexing person. As with most people, Alex noticed William's aura immediately. It was a dark, almost murky aura, mostly gray. Healthy auras were colorful and exuded light. William's was a decidedly ill aura, but Alex had sparred with him a few times over the summer and discovered the hard way that William was quite strong in body, if a bit quick to fatigue. Alex wasn't sure why someone who seemed so vigorous would have an aura so faded. He hadn't asked Sally yet because she had been exceptionally busy, between the Guardians and Dracula, Sr. and that young werewolf, Tyler, who she had to reassemble. If she was going to make William primarily responsible for guarding Richie, however, they might need to talk about this.

Alex retrieved his breakfast while Sally continued to tell everybody what they already knew. No vodka in Alex's blood this time; Sally made him get rid of the hard liquor when their new guests moved in. Alex had pointed out that Richie was of legal drinking age in his own country. Sally had ignored him. She must have felt bad about it, though, because she was letting him drive her car to school today. Not the van—the Lamborghini.

"…and don't forget that her pedals are *really* sensitive, so you have to be gentle with them." Sally followed Alex into the garage under the other garage, continuing to give him instructions on how to drive her third favorite car.

"Sally, relax. This is not my first time driving a sports car," Alex said. He pressed the unlock button on the key fob and watched a pair of fierce headlights blink nearby.

"I remember the first time you drove a sports car," Sally said. Alex chose not to look at her, knowing she was glaring at him. Guess that wound still hadn't healed.

"Well, this isn't my *second* time driving a sports car, either. It'll be fine, and I'm sure you'll never let me do it again, anyway." Alex opened the trunk of Lamborghini and placed his backpack in it with all due respect.

"You got that right."

"You're still going to ride with me, aren't you?"

"Yep!" Sally climbed into the passenger side. Alex closed the trunk and got in behind the wheel. At least they would have a chance to talk. Alex started the car and steered it toward the exit.

"There's something I wanted to—"

"Ease up on the accelerator a bit."

"So help me God, I will leave you on the side of the road if you're going to do this all the way to school."

"Okay, okay. I'll just keep my eyes closed," Sally said, not even pretending to close her eyes. Alex managed to make it out of the garage without step-by-step instructions.

"I was trying to say, there's something I wanted to talk to you about. I'm not really sure how best to put it. Um, I'm not sure I'm comfortable leaving Richie and William by themselves at the Manor. It's not that I don't trust William, I'm just…well, I don't trust him."

"What?" Sally's forehead creased. "Why is that?"

"His aura looks, um," Alex paused to search for the right word, "sickly. I can't tell what it means, and it worries me."

"Oh." Sally looked down at her lap and examined her fingernails. "My brother's had a rough life, Alex. You don't endure the kind of things he has without scars. You can understand that. I don't really know what all's wrong with him, to tell you the truth, but we're working on it. Trying to, anyway." She sighed. "I'll be the first to admit that William's a train wreck, but we only need him to make sure that no one kills Richie. I'm confident he can manage that."

"How can you be so sure?"

It sounded like Sally didn't deem William capable of taking care of himself. Richie was more independent than Jason, certainly, but he was still in many ways a child. He needed supervision as well as protection.

"I spent a lot of time with William as a cub when our parents weren't around," Sally said, meeting Alex's gaze. "He wasn't very good at keeping up with day-to-day tasks, he drank too much, and sometimes he spoke to people no one else could see, but he was a good brother. Very affectionate, very protective, and I always felt safe with him. Safer than when our parents were home, that was for sure. Okay, yes, he does have some black marks on his record, like everyone in our family. Still, I would trust him with my life, and I trust him with Richie's. Besides, he's done a decent job of protecting Richie up to this point, has he not?"

Alex didn't say anything, just let the information sink in. Clearly, Sally had survived her childhood, and she attributed that, at least in part, to William. Alex had never met Sally's parents, but rumor had it that her mother, Lightning Strike, was not to be trifled with, and her father spent most of his time staying out of his mate's way or protecting others from her. If that were true, it was no surprise that she was more comfortable with William than with them. Did that make William trustworthy enough, though? There wasn't much competition from the rest of the family.

"It's like letting Scarlet watch Jason," Sally continued. "She's one of the most scatterbrained people I've ever met and has a tendency to turn into a wolf monster when the moon comes out, but we wouldn't think twice about putting Jason under her care because she has proven that, despite appearances, she is more than capable of handling it. And we need as many people in the field as possible. William has given us that freedom."

Alex remained unconvinced. He had a hard time finding it in himself to trust someone with an aura of smog. Richie spent months with William earlier in the year, though, and William was vital in bringing Richie to Brunswick safely.

"Okay," Alex said. "Just keep tabs on him, will you? For me?"

"Don't worry. I am."

2

Manitoba, Canada

Kylie sat in front of the computer, hands resting limply on the keyboard. Her two-page essay on *Romeo and Juliet* was due tomorrow, and so far she had two words written: Kylie Stiles. It didn't help that her cell phone was buzzing like an angry wasp a meter away on her bed. Kylie could imagine the texts. "OMG Kylie, can u believe Cara's shoes 2day?" "Hey K, party @ my place Fri. U comin?" It would be meaningless drivel for the most part, but Kylie would much rather be texting about footwear than writing a paper. She enjoyed the trivial distractions of middle school life. While not super-popular in her mind, Kylie had a lot of friends. So there was always someone to IM or hang out with when she wanted to avoid homework or her own thoughts. Ever since her parents died three years ago, being alone was the one thing Kylie could not stand. It was when there was no one else around that the morbid thoughts crept in.

Giving up on her own faculties, Kylie sighed and pulled up Spark-Notes for essay ideas. A slew of messages immediately cluttered the bottom of the screen. Kylie attempted to ignore them, but even as she finally found her inspiration and started typing, her eyes kept wandering. Finally she gave in and checked the inbox. As predicted, several of her girlfriends had commented on Cara's questionable choice in heels. Three invitations for the weekend, and—wait, what was that? An IM from Cara herself, and not about shoes. Cara lived across the street and had for as long as Kylie could remember. They had been best friends for a while when they were little but had grown apart over the years. Yet despite Cara's complete lack of fashion sense, they hadn't fallen entirely out of contact as adolescents. Still, they didn't IM often, their conversations mostly limited to the bus stop and the school. Even weirder was the message itself: *Hey K do u know there's some guy creeping around outside ur house?*

Kylie stiffened and glanced out the window behind her. There was no one standing beyond the glass staring at her, but that knowledge gave her little comfort. She looked reflexively over at her phone, a hot pink wafer with the letter K encrusted on the back in rhinestones. But she couldn't call Joon. Kylie was also hesitant to call the police, with her reputation. After being caught egging a house last Halloween and lifting a pair of shoes at the mall last month, she didn't want to draw any more attention from law enforcement. She should make sure there was really an emergency first.

What??? Kylie messaged Cara back on the computer and held her breath until Cara sent a response, accompanied by an inappropriately cheerful ding.

Idk there's just some guy @ ur side windows looking in. Should we call someone?

Kylie considered it. She could feel her pulse racing, but if she cried wolf again she would be grounded for a lifetime. *Is he breaking in?*

No just creeping, Cara replied. *I don't think he's armed or anything.* A moment later, another message from Cara: *Afraid joon won't believe u?*

That was precisely what Kylie feared. Joon, her twenty-two-year-old sister, was Kylie's legal guardian now that their parents were gone. That trauma had changed them both, making Joon a control freak and turning Kylie into a hoodlum. During the first few months Kylie had repeatedly called Joon at work, or called the police and had them call Joon, claiming that someone was trying to forcibly enter the house when she was there by herself. It didn't take long, of course, for the adults to figure out that Kylie was making it up, although whether out of mischief or paranoia they couldn't tell. Really, Kylie had done it because she couldn't stand to be alone anymore, but she would never admit that to Joon.

Just let me know if he does anything ok? Not two seconds after Kylie hit "Send," Cara informed her that *Doesnt matter now hes gone. Just walked into the woods. Ill keep an eye out.*

Kylie slowly released a lungful of air, trying to calm herself down. It was probably just some lamebrain from school trying to catch a glimpse of her shirtless. Wouldn't be the first time. Running a hand through her sleek, almond-brown hair, Kylie turned back to her homework. Her hands were shaky on the keyboard as she typed, oddly motivated by her non-encounter with the unseen prowler.

Joon came home from work with pizza, which was more than normal. She worked at Ronnie's Pizza Palace, and they let employees take home extra pizzas at the end of the day. She also had a box of cookies, though, balanced on top of the pizza box, and that *was* unusual. Joon didn't spend their limited resources on anything she didn't have to, unless she felt the need to apologize. Tonight, Kylie recognized the blue-iced sugar confections as Joon's way of saying she was sorry she'd called Kylie a lazy brat last night. They were arguing because Kylie hadn't spent so much as a minute working on that *Romeo and Juliet* essay she had been assigned a week ago. Kylie knew the insult was probably well-deserved, but Joon wasn't the kind of person who believed in fighting fire with fire, at least not anymore. The last few months there had been a lot of confections, and more than a few nights when neither sister was quite willing to break cookies together. Tonight, however, both were relieved that there could be dessert.

"I finished my essay today," Kylie said while following Joon into the kitchen. Joon paused from getting plates out of the dishwasher and favored Kylie with a smile. She didn't smile the way she used to, when she was a teenager and Kylie was her annoying-but-cute kid sister. Joon used to have the kind of radiant, Christmas-tree-with-a-million-lights grin that could lift the mood of a whole room. Now her smile was a sort of tired uptick at the corners of her mouth.

They took their dinner into the living room and watched the newest episode of a teen drama show that Kylie loved but suspected Joon hated. They hadn't eaten in the dining room in three years. The two empty places were too painful to look at, even when they removed the extra chairs.

The girls finished their cookies as the credits started to roll and moved to go their separate ways. Kylie would text until midnight while Joon did some sort of constructive adult task. The policy in the Stiles household had always been that kids didn't have to do chores on school nights, and Kylie had coerced Joon into keeping it that way. Sometimes Kylie felt bad about that. Other times she didn't.

Before she went to homeroom, Kylie slipped into the bathroom to check herself in front of a mirror for the tenth time that morning. Curls were the fashion now, so she had taken a curling iron to her uncooperative hair before catching the school bus. It wasn't curly, exactly, just a little wavy, but it would have to do. Kylie's eyes were a deep blue shade she shared with her sister and father. She touched up her mascara and added a little more silvery eyeshadow to bring out the color.

A denim miniskirt covered the top of Kylie's black leggings, since Joon wouldn't let her leave the house with the leggings alone. A black leather jacket over a fuchsia camisole and oversized feather earrings completed the ensemble. Kylie didn't understand the feather fad, but as long as they stayed in style, she would wear the silly things.

Reasonably content with her outfit and the mask of makeup, Kylie finally made her way to class. She had math at the beginning of the day this year. Kylie didn't mind, really, because she secretly enjoyed mathematics, but she had to pretend to hate it because, apparently, math was *never* in style.

As Kylie strutted into the classroom, faking a confidence she didn't have, she immediately noticed that Cara was there already, sitting with Lindsey, another girl in Kylie's social circle. Cara—she was wearing *those shoes* again—was talking at Lindsey while Lindsey nodded noncommittally and scrolled through messages on her phone. Kylie had planned to ask Cara about the odd events of the previous afternoon, but not with Lindsey there. It would be awkward. Unfortunately, Cara must have had the same idea, without the presence of mind not to bring it up in front of other people.

"Oh, hey, Kylie," Cara said loudly, motioning her over. Kylie sighed and sat down beside Cara, bracing for the inevitable. "That nut job didn't come back to your house yesterday, did he?"

"No, I don't think so," Kylie answered. Lindsey glanced up at them curiously. Kylie pretended not to notice.

"Well, I didn't recognize him, but I got a picture." Cara dug around in her purse and pulled out the dinosaur phone she'd had since third grade. Kylie and Lindsey both leaned over to look at the screen as Cara opened the photo gallery app and clicked on a thumbnail that showed the front of the Stiles's modest two-story. The photograph expanded to fill the screen. There was clearly a dark human figure hunched by one of the windows. Kylie shivered. Cara zoomed in on the man until the image started to pixelate. There wasn't much to see, as his face was obscured by a hunter-green hoodie. His right hand was pressed against the window frame, and Kylie noticed with a jolt that it was missing the first two fingers.

"Oh my God, who *is* that?" Lindsey gasped. She turned to Kylie. "What was he doing at your *house*?"

"I don't know. Cara just saw him creeping around. He walked off into the woods, and that was that." Kylie shrugged as if it didn't worry her. "It was probably just some loser playing Peeping Tom," she said, and she could almost believe that if the whole thing weren't so sketchy. After all, this was Canada. And Kylie lived in a low-crime town, at that. Cara and Lindsey shared a dubious look, but the bell rang before they could say something. The girls stopped everything to stow their phones lest the devices be confiscated. There was further commotion as the teacher walked in, and the class realized he was a substitute.

Kylie wasn't above a bit of shoplifting or property destruction in the interest of keeping up appearances, but teasing classmates and tormenting substitute teachers crossed the line. Fortunately, the crowd she had joined this year was more mellow than the self-styled "Bad Girls" she'd hung out with last year. Fashionistas had little interest in driving teachers up the wall. They were too classy for that. The same could not be said for the rest of the class, however, which immediately began showcasing their worst behavior for the poor defenseless math sub. Kylie just hoped that she would still get the chance to do some calculating to ease her mind.

Joon hated pizza. She hadn't always, though. A few years ago, when she was still a popular cheerleader gliding through high school, going out for pizza with her numerous friends was a weekly occurrence. She had nothing more to worry about than calories and keeping the sauce off her cute clothes. Looking back on those days, Joon scarcely believed that she and that careless teenager were the same person. Everything changed after her mother died.

Joon was nineteen, Kylie was nine. Joon was beginning to get over the rebellious, omnipotent, I-hate-my-parents stage of teenhood. She was going to start at college in the fall, major undecided, future bright. Then Mom went in for surgery. It wasn't major surgery. Mrs. Stiles routinely developed bone spurs. Removing this one would be no more dangerous than the half dozen or so procedures she had undergone before.

A nosocomial infection, they called it—a disease you got in the hospital. Their father told them Mom would be fine, and Joon and Kylie took him at his word. He may even have thought it was the truth.

Kylie was spared the worst of it. When their Mom started to get bad, really bad, they stopped letting Kylie come in to see her. Joon, however, was given the choice to talk to her mother on the phone, like her little sister, or to see her in person. Every time, Joon chose to visit their Mom in the hospital, even when her skin started to rot and Joon couldn't bear to look at her.

The strain was antibiotic resistant, the doctors told them. For the first week she did well, but the secondary infections were more than her immune system could handle. Fifteen days after surgery, the Stiles matriarch died. Technically, Dad's accident was unrelated, but everyone around him could see how he changed after his wife's death. He mimed his way through the daily routine, oblivious to the world spinning on around him. It was a miracle that he didn't crash the car sooner. The shock of his death didn't hit Kylie and Joon quite as hard because he had effectively died weeks ago, leaving a hollow shell wandering in his wake.

Joon still managed to take a few classes online, but college was mostly a dream she'd needed to sacrifice. Her parents possessed some savings, though not enough to keep up the house payments and support their daughters indefinitely, much less to keep up a college fund for Kylie. The moment her mother died Joon became someone else. She lost every trace of playfulness and optimism, all her youthfulness. Her friends claimed that she'd turned into her mother, but that wasn't it. Joon's mother had never been hopeless or lusterless, the way Joon became. Joon didn't know who she was now. Her entire life was devoted to shepherding Kylie and putting toppings on pizza. The work itself wasn't so bad. It was the associations between her job and her shattered life that made Joon hate pizza from the day she started at the Pizza Palace. It didn't help that she ate the damn stuff almost every day. They didn't have to subsist on leftover pizzas, but taking home free pizza from work cut down on grocery bills enough for them to afford a few luxuries, like extra savings and the occasional phone upgrade or pair of name-brand shoes for Kylie. Besides, Kylie loved pizza.

Joon meticulously arranged green peppers on a bed of tomato sauce and half-listened to the local news droning from the decrepit radio at the front of the kitchen. Theirs was a small town, about as rural as you could get without leaving civilization entirely, so this station, broadcast live from a studio above the music shop, was the only one that didn't sound like a study in static. The news was mostly a combination of weather, amateur economic analyses for the area, a few global news snatches, and political scandals involving members of Parliament. This particular report, however, mentioned something out of the ordinary.

"The biggest news bulletin of the day," said the announcer slowly, savoring the suspense, "is our town's first murder in seventeen years." The announcer's tone was more in line with reporting that he'd won a small fortune in the lottery, but there was no mistaking his words. The whole kitchen staff paused in their work, exchanging looks of mingled fear and disbelief. In the dining area, the customers nearest the kitchen window froze as well, overhearing, and promptly began murmuring to their neighbors and pulling out their cell phones. Joon's hand hovered over the pizza, a slice of bell pepper still pinched between her motionless thumb and forefinger.

"You heard me correctly," continued the man on the radio. "There has been a murder. Kevin Murphy's body was discovered this morning by a neighbor in his garage. The coroner in Winnipeg identified *cyanide poisoning* as the cause of death. So far there are no suspects. Murphy was a secondary school math teacher. We will continue to give you updates as they occur." The voice cut out and was replaced by the Top 40 countdown.

Within hours, the news on the radio had found its way into Kylie's school. It certainly explained why they had a substitute math teacher. The real teacher, Mr. Murphy, was dead. The students were left hanging somewhere on the spectrum between unbelieving and terrified. Kylie was a bit toward the doubtful end. This wasn't the craziest school rumor she had ever heard. On the other hand, the teachers seemed shell-shocked, too, so maybe it was real.

To most of the student body, who didn't know or didn't much care for Mr. Murphy, his absence would leave no ragged, bleeding hole in their hearts. It would probably hurt somebody like that, somebody who really loved him, but not anyone Kylie knew. It must have been the *idea* of his violent death that had everyone on edge. He was murdered in their tiny, completely unexciting town in the middle of nowhere. Kylie could accept this a little easier than most. She'd already learned that tragedy seeps into every corner. Her classmates, however, were shaken.

"Who could do something like that? *Here?*" Lindsey asked, leaning over the lunch table and whispering into the gathered knot of girls. It seemed that people felt the need to whisper when talking about things that scared them, as though fear itself might overhear.

"Jordan told me he was stabbed, like, twenty times," said someone to her left, in lieu of answering Lindsey's question. Several girls shivered and let out small exclamations, overdramatized but genuine.

"No, I think he was poisoned," Cara said. She preferred accuracy to a lurid story.

"Is there *nothing* else we could talk about?" Kylie said and groaned. The looks on her friends' faces plainly said that, no, there wasn't anything else. What could be more interesting than murder?

Kylie knew how to deflect the conversation. Sighing with exaggerated annoyance, she rolled her eyes and planted her gaze firmly on her carrot sticks. It worked like a charm. Instantly, the girls took the hint to heart. This was a gross, immature topic for the lunch table. They should have known. After a few awkward starts and stops, the talk turned to the usual matters. Discussing something as mundane as celebrities in rehab could almost make Kylie forget about Mr. Murphy. It wouldn't be so easy later, when she was at home alone, but the internet was always there to divert her. Kylie planned to drown thoughts of the homicide in a deluge of meaningless everyday drivel, just as she did with all the thoughts she didn't want to wrangle. In a week or two the incident would be scarcely a memory.

"Professor LaMont, the subject is waking!" Assistant Eighteen called from the operating room. The man had a title other than "number," of course, but Vincent LaMont never called his assistants by name. Their names were quite inconsequential and, besides, Vincent usually turned them into revenants after a few months of service. Since Vincent's revenants never remembered their names, why bother to learn them?

"Handle it, Eighteen! I'll be there in a minute," Vincent hollered. "Sixteen, go help him out." Obediently, the bulky form of Sixteen whizzed past Vincent at his lab bench and into the next room. Vincent continued his work, ignoring the grunts coming from the doorway behind him. He thought of his occupation as a science, although in truth he had no idea why his methods of reanimation worked. Magic ran in the family, but until his college days Vincent had stubbornly refused to take part in their nonsensical rituals. He intended to prove to his wayward relatives that their old-fashioned voodoo religion was bogus. Then he saw his first revenant, and he had an epiphany. What is magic other than science that no one understands yet? Unfortunately, his family didn't approve of the new direction in which he took his powers, but they were silenced easily enough.

Vincent took an earthworm from a tank full of the nematodes and dropped it in an electrified chemical bath, a new recipe, in which the worm would drown and—hopefully—return to a semblance of life soon thereafter. Both processes would take some time, so Vincent left his experiment and leisurely traveled into the adjacent chamber, where Sixteen and Eighteen were engaged in the work of examining a newly-rejuvenated corpse.

This particular revenant was not Vincent's best work. He was on a deadline, so he had to cut a few corners. Mass-producing revenants, however, has its drawbacks. If Vincent purchased cheaper ingredients and increased the intensity of the process, he could manufacture the roving dead at two-thirds the usual cost and in half the time. Doing so made them prone to flaws, however. Vincent wanted to be in attendance at every awakening to make sure none of his creations were too damaged.

Eighteen was one of Vincent's scientific assistants. At present, he was checking the creature's pupils, shining a light into them to watch for contraction. Sixteen was not one of the academic personnel. He was currently employed in bodily restraining the revenant's arms. The revenant itself appeared quite ordinary for its kind, with grayish flesh and wide, vacant eyes. A grotesque grimace marred its face as it struggled dumbly to free itself from its constraints.

"Reflexes normal," Eighteen said. "Heart rate sluggish but within parameters."

"He's a strong one, too," Sixteen said and grunted.

"Good, we need it to be." Vincent approached the human-sized tank and thumped the button that opened the drain. The fetid fluid surrounding the revenant rapidly swirled away, eddying around the corpse and the live tissue of Sixteen's forearms. The beast's mouth formed a few inarticulate sounds, but no speech issued forth, for Vincent had removed its tongue and voice box. Vincent discovered early on in his endeavors that revenants had a habit of moaning and mumbling and occasionally screeching, which made them most un-stealthy. They also had a nasty tendency to bite. After losing two of the fingers on his right hand to an unruly revenant, Vincent made a habit of pulling out their front teeth, too.

This revenant, however, still had all its teeth intact, save for the gold crown Vincent salvaged for resale. That was because the creature in the tank before him was his first designated attack-revenant. He had used revenants for violent purposes before, even for murder, but these newest projects were special. Vincent wanted them to have every possible advantage. Really, he suspected that killing a little girl hardly merited the offensive he was mustering. Still, one could never be too sure. His predecessor had failed, so Vincent was told, and his employers were anxious for results. There was more than a mere suggestion that to fail them again would mean death of a most unpleasant sort. Vincent normally stayed out of the high-stakes games, but the reward would be well worth it. If Vincent's plan worked, as he was confident it would, then the girl's power would be his at the moment of her death. The prospect was most enticing.

Vincent smiled down on his latest creation. He wondered what mundane existence the creature had possessed prior to its death. Whatever the case, its new fate would be much more glorious. Laying his mutilated hand on the revenant's forehead, Vincent began the solemn incantation that would make him master of the beast's broken, muddled mind.

When Joon came home from work, pizza box in hand, Kylie was sequestered in her room. The occasional giggle floated down the stairway, but otherwise Kylie declined to make her presence known. She was probably busy chatting electronically with one or more of her friends. Joon didn't see any reason to bother her yet. Joon was home early, after all, due to a calamitous pizza oven malfunction. Typically, Kylie would have free rein for another hour before her sister arrived to ask about the state of her homework. At least Kylie had managed not to do anything illegal since school started, so far as Joon was aware. If she wanted to relax for a while, that was all right. It might keep her off the streets.

Joon flopped onto the couch and turned on the television. She channel surfed, barely registering the images that raced by on the screen. Then a station caught her eye. It was playing one of the gory, dime-a-dozen slasher movies Joon used to love. Even in her carefree teen fantasy years, Joon understood that those films were violent, predictable, and mind-numbing, but they were popular among her peers, so she developed a taste for them.

She glanced up the stairs to make sure Kylie wasn't watching. No, the door to her room remained shut, obscured by a glittering, pink, beaded curtain. With a guilty quietness, Joon turned back to the TV screen and set the remote aside. *Hacksaw Slaughter 7* wasn't exactly after-work cool-down material, yet Joon found it oddly soothing. She had seen it in theaters a few years back with a bunch of friends. She had sat between Jeanette and Paul, who spent most of the movie trying his hardest to work his hand into Joon's shirt. The memory was not one of Joon's best, and she would sooner traverse Main Street in a chicken suit than relate the story about Paul to anyone in town, now that he was a convicted drug dealer in the big city who might or might not have run a dog-fighting operation on the side. Still, the recollection was not entirely unpleasant. Joon decided to leave *Hacksaw* on a few minutes longer.

Onscreen, a blonde with the figure of a corn stalk was hiding in a closet with a door just on the stronger side of common cardboard, whimpering. The saw-wielding murderer wandered the house with a casual but menacing gait, flinging open doors at random. After a minute or two of dramatic, discordant music, he came to the closet and immediately began chopping it down with his saw, not even bothering to try the knob. The blonde inside started screaming, no surprise there.

Almost immediately, an explosion of breaking glass and another scream accompanied her, but the sounds didn't emanate from the television. They were coming from upstairs. *Kylie!* Joon leapt to her feet and bolted towards Kylie's room. Joon flung the door open and flailed her way through the strands of sparkling, laughing plastic crystals to get into her little sister's room. Inside, a large, grimy man held Kylie aloft by one hand wrapped around her neck. Kylie was kicking and scratching wildly, trying to dislodge his asphyxiating hold.

Joon didn't stop to think or look for a weapon. She just ran, crashing into the intruder with as much momentum as she could muster. The man grunted with surprise, letting go of Kylie as Joon bowled him over onto the floor. Joon's advantage ended there, however, for he quickly refocused his attack onto her. Joon managed to get in one decent swing before the man retaliated in kind with one gray, filthy fist. She heard something crack in the bridge of her nose. Joon pushed her knee up into his groin, but he didn't even seem to notice. He pulled back his fist for another strike, then roared in indignation at the apex of the arc. Unaccountably, a cheery yellow pencil had sprouted from the side of his throat. A few languid drops of blackish blood dribbled from the wound.

The man whirled to face Kylie. She stood behind him, eyes so wide Joon could see the whites all the way around, another pencil gripped in her hand like she was going to stake a vampire with it. Looking at her sister, Joon saw a much better weapon within reach.

"Kylie, the bedpost!"

The man lunged toward Kylie at the same moment that Kylie dove for the iron bedpost, that irksome, loose post nobody ever bothered to fix. The post was knocked from her hand as she and the intruder collided. Joon caught it, grabbed it in both hands the way Dad had taught her to go to bat, and swung the bedpost into the back of the man's skull.

Joon didn't know what she expected, but at any rate she was not prepared to feel bone cave under the impact. The assailant paused, as though perplexed, and then crumpled. For a long time, neither sister moved. They stared at the figure bleeding on the pale pink carpet, waiting for it to resume the attack, or at least twitch. Finally the truth sank in—he wasn't going to stir.

Kylie and Joon ran to each other, nearly tripping over the body, and embraced. Kylie started sobbing into Joon's shoulder. With the adrenaline rush subsiding, Joon could feel the throb of her broken nose, but it didn't matter. Kylie was safe. That's what was important.

"Are you hurt?" Joon asked, pulling back to look Kylie over. Bruises covered her face and arms. She didn't appear to be bleeding, though.

"I think I'm okay, but, Joon, he can't be here! It can't be him!" She gestured spasmodically towards the corpse on the floor.

"You know him? Who is he?"

"It's Mr. Murphy, my math teacher," Kylie exclaimed, her high-pitched voice bordering on hysterical. *"That's my dead math teacher!"*

Joon, Kylie, and two local police officers sat in the living room, staring at each other dully and waiting for the coroner from Winnipeg to come downstairs with his report. The selfsame coroner had declared the body in Kylie's room very decidedly dead early that morning.

"Are you *sure* that's him?" asked one of the officers, a dark-skinned young man with a nervous habit of wringing his hands. Kylie nodded.

"Maybe he has a twin?" the other officer suggested, hopeful but none too confident.

"I don't think he was really dead in the first place," Joon said. The bandage the EMT had put over her nose tugged at her skin as she spoke. "That can happen, right? Death paralysis or something. Like in *Romeo and Juliet*. He was alive, but without a pulse."

"That can't be. Modern medicine can detect even the faintest pulses," the second officer said, shaking her head.

"And they found cyanide in his blood," the hand-wringing officer reminded them. "You don't just get up off the slab and walk out of the morgue after cyanide poisoning."

"You don't walk off the slab *at all*," Kylie said. Her voice still harbored a wavering, panicked note.

Footsteps sounded on the stairs, and all four heads swiveled to fixate on the coroner, waiting for him to end the speculation and give them some reason, any reason, to believe that their world hadn't been turned upside down. The coroner reached the bottom of the stairs and looked from one expectant face to another.

"I'll need to run some tests," he said, nodding sagely. Kylie and the police officers appeared to relax. Joon was not so easily mollified.

"Hold on. You have to tell us more than that. Did the dead man on my carpet die of cyanide poisoning yesterday?" Joon pointed up toward Kylie's room, as if there could be any doubt which corpse she was referring to.

"Of course not," the coroner scoffed.

"So he wasn't dead. You know, before I killed him again."

"No, my dear girl. Although, it is strange, the degree of decomposition, most unusual...but of course he wasn't dead. I will discover the meaning of all this. At any rate, the man is quite dead now, so he will not be bothering you again."

"Hmmm. Well, that's disappointing." Vincent clicked the little red square on the browser, and the article about the twice-murdered Kevin Murphy blipped off the screen. Over the top of the monitor, he spied Fifteen and Eighteen sharing a glance filled with mingled relief and surprise. They were expecting Professor Vincent to react more strongly to the news that his beloved Attack Revenant had been felled by a girl with a bedpost. Of course, they didn't know that Vincent had improved on the prototype. The earthworm hadn't given its life for naught.

"We need more muscle," Vincent said, staring at his assistants pointedly. They returned his gaze without comprehension. He sighed. "That means we need to go grave-robbing. Find Sixteen!"

It wasn't grave-robbing in the usual sense. By the time a body was in the ground, it was embalmed, and Vincent couldn't work with tissues full of preservatives. What they were doing instead was morgue-robbing.

Vincent pulled open another stainless steel drawer. The corpse inside looked promising, just a little decay around the orifices. He checked the tag. Less than 48 hours dead. This one might be viable. Vincent dared to allow himself a modicum of excitement. If the body in front of him was usable, it would be the first they had found all week, despite breaking into morgues the whole province over. Vincent walked around to the other side of the drawer. His eyes were well-trained from decades of raising the dead. Sometimes the tiniest details revealed a massive flaw in the material. Within seconds, Vincent noted that the angle of the neck was not quite right. He prodded the temple gently. The head lolled to the side, revealing a sharp misalignment between the head and shoulders. The neck was clearly broken. Vincent roared, slamming the drawer shut. Across the room, examining another corpse, Eighteen jumped, anticipating the worst from his volatile employer. Rather than throwing things at the nearest minion, Vincent stormed out of the building.

Outside, sitting on the cool concrete steps in front of the morgue, Vincent waited for his temper to subside. He cursed the Canadians for their sparse population distribution and long lifetimes. This was no place to raise an army of revenants. Vincent wanted dozens of bodies, not one or two. He couldn't risk that many murders. He could go south and fetch corpses from a more populous city, but transporting the dead, reanimated or not, was problematic on many accounts. They could rot, sustain physical damage, get caught in customs...

So musing, Vincent gazed into the distance, not really seeing anything. There were a couple of buildings, numerous trees, and a dark, empty stretch of road. The world was silent and still, as it often is at two in the morning. In that sleepy setting, the pair of headlights ap-pearing in the periphery came as a shock. It was an eighteen-wheeler, a slatted wooden construction mounted on its trailer. Between the planks of wood, scores of slaughter-bound snouts snuffled the out-side air.

The realization hit Vincent like a brick to the head. Of course that was the solution! It was so simple! Vincent laughed out loud, aston-ished that he'd never thought of it before. The anatomical differences would be negligible. He'd hardly have to change the process at all. It was perfect. Vincent ran back into the morgue to tell Eighteen that they needed to catch themselves some Canadian bacon.

Two-hundred and sixteen revenants. *Intelligent* revenants, too, at least in some measure; after Vincent's improvements to the formula, these new revenants possessed whatever faculties their piggy brains had known in life. For a moment, Vincent was disappointed that some had not survived the process. But then Vincent looked out upon the 100-kilogram pigs snuffling around inside the transport truck, an undulating sea of pink, white, and brown animals large enough to crush a man by simply sitting on him. A smile wormed its way up the side of Vincent's face. This was going to be a real good day.

Stepping backwards down the ramp, Vincent slammed shut the double doors with aplomb. He walked around to the side and climbed into the cab. Sixteen sat behind the wheel, awaiting instructions. Vin-cent gestured grandly towards the road ahead. Sixteen put his foot on the gas, and off they went to deliver their livestock.

3

Brunswick

Four minutes after school ended, Jason's cell phone rang. Jason opened his eyes and stared at his bedroom ceiling, trying to decide if he cared enough to answer. It would almost certainly be one of his friends checking to see why he hadn't been at school, and while it was nice of them to care, Jason really didn't feel like talking to any of them. *What's wrong? Well, it's a bit like having the stomach flu with barbed wire wrapped around my internal organs. Now leave me alone and quit asking questions.* Jason flung a hand on his side table to grab his phone and began to rehearse his "I'll be fine" speech in his head.

"Hello," he mumbled into the receiver.

"Hey, Jason, it's Cam." Cameron was almost shouting over the voices of other students and the thundering of his school bus over the asphalt. "Are you okay? Alex said you were sick, something about tangled wires, or crossed tubes. I don't know, but it didn't sound like much fun. I thought maybe I should make sure you were still, like, alive. I can tell you what the homework is, too, if you feel like trying—"

"Pause. Use words slower. Please. Quieter would also be good."

"Oh. Sorry." Cameron lowered the volume on his voice. "I was just saying that I wanted to know how you're doing, and I can give you our homework if you feel up to doing it."

"Sure. Homework. Great. I guess I could start on that," Jason said, rubbing at the headache that was developing behind his temples. "And I'm fine."

"You are a terrible liar."

"Thanks. You going to tell me the homework or not?"

"Yeah, gimme a second to fish out my planner." There was a zipping of zippers and shuffling of papers, then Cameron listed off the assignments for every class in minute detail. Jason took the barest of notes down on his phone to remind himself of it all later. As soon as Cameron hung up, Jason plonked the phone back onto the table and assumed the semblance of sleep in the hopes that it would bring on the real thing.

"Jason, may I talk to you for a moment?" Mrs. Adair motioned Jason over to her desk as the rest of the class left the room. Alex caught Jason's eye on his way out and nodded. They both remembered all too well what happened when a staff member wanted to talk to Jason alone last fall.

"Sure." Jason came and stood in front of her desk, confident that Alex was right outside the door, ready for action, in case a genie was impersonating the Latin teacher.

"It's about the homework you turned in Wednesday," Mrs. Adair began, her tone dusted with disappointment.

"Oh, yeah, I wrote that when I was sick, so it might not be my best work," Jason apologized.

"On the contrary," she said, "it's by far your best work yet. You wrote the longest, most complete story of anyone in the class, and you used vocabulary and constructions that we haven't even touched on. You have always been a great student, Jason, and I want to think well of you, but I'm forced to decide whether you're a genius or a plagiarist, and I don't know what to think."

Jason's eyes widened. *Plagiarist?* He'd never even cheated at Go Fish. No way would he cheat on schoolwork. And that thing was his "Best"? Cam said they were supposed to write a simple, summary story about the founding of Rome by Romulus and Remus, and Jason just scribbled something down without checking over it. He didn't even bother to consult his textbook or Latin dictionary. If that was the best he had ever done, he must not have been trying nearly as hard as he thought he had on his other assignments.

"I don't know what to say, ma'am," Jason said. "I don't think I'm a genius, but I swear to you I wrote that myself. I guess, I've been reading ahead in the textbook and studying on my own…I don't know, maybe I got ahead of myself…" Mrs. Adair studied him, searching for signs that he was lying.

"Are you available after school, Jason?"

"Yes, ma'am, I can be."

"Good. Meet me as soon as you can, and we will figure this out, all right?"

"Yes, ma'am. Thank you. I'll come right here after my last class."

"...and so she says I must either be 'a genius or a plagiarist,'" Jason said, jabbing a fork into his ravioli. "I mean, what am I supposed to say to that?" He spoke softly, since cafeterias have ears. It was bad enough that Mrs. Adair thought he was a cheater. He didn't want rumors flying everywhere.

"Well, *did* you plagiarize it?" Alex asked, sipping his "tomato soup" from a thermos.

"No! I would never," Jason said, raising his voice a few decibels and a whole octave in spite of himself.

"We believe you," Cameron said, shooting a glare at Alex. "Mrs. Adair will just have to accept that you're a genius."

"I'm not, though," Jason said. "At least, I don't think so."

"Sure, you are," Cameron assured him. "And this afternoon, you'll prove it."

"How?" Jason paused to swallow. "What does she want me to do?" Cameron half-frowned and shrugged.

"If you're innocent, it won't matter what she wants," Alex pointed out. "Unless she's going to try you for a witch, it should be easy to prove that you didn't do anything wrong, because you didn't, right?" Cameron gave Alex an incredulous look.

"You don't get out much, do you?"

"I do, too! But this is middle school. How corrupt can the system be?"

"In second grade I got a red card because the girl four seats down from me tried to throw a bagel at her friend in the cafeteria and it flew AAAALL the way across the room. The teacher just assumed it was me because I got in trouble more often than she did," Cameron said by way of example. "I had to sit in time-out while the other kids got to go to recess. Never underestimate the unfairness of school, Alex. In my experience, teachers don't trust you, kids are mean, and the world is out to get you."

"Oh. Gee." Alex looked truly surprised by Cameron's testimony and the passion with which he delivered it. "I was...homeschooled, before. My dad was tough, but he didn't punish me for anything I didn't deserve."

"Well, it's different out here," Cameron said. "I promise."

Jason nodded in agreement.

"You see now why I'm afraid to meet Mrs. Adair this afternoon? I don't think she's going to paddle me or anything, but my grades are really important to me. They're just about the only thing I have going for me."

"Hear, hear." Cameron waved a hand in the air.

"Tell you what: I'll stick around to make sure justice is served with your Latin teacher, how about that?" Alex said.

"Thanks," Jason said. Alex would have to wait for him anyway, and there was probably nothing he could do to see justice through, but Jason appreciated the empty gesture. It was comforting to know that Alex would be around, even though Alex was usually not very helpful with Jason's schoolwork. He was still a buttress of emotional support in his own odd way.

Mrs. Adair stared at the paper Jason had handed her. She glanced up at him over her reading glasses. She looked over at Jason's desk, confirming that nothing but his textbook was at his disposal when he translated the passage. Finally, she turned back to the paper and shook her head.

"All right," she said, handing the page back to Jason. "I can't argue with my own eyes. I don't know how you've learned so fast, but you're off the hook. You have to tell me your secret sometime."

"If I figure out what it is, you'll be the first to know, ma'am." Jason wadded up the paragraph he had spent a mere fifteen minutes composing and stuffed it in his pocket. This was beginning to feel a little too weird. The words had just flowed, and only after he finished writing and looked it over did he fully realize that he had been using a foreign language. Jason went back to the desk Mrs. Adair had put him at. As he packed up and swung his backpack over his shoulder, a suspicion poked at the back of his mind. Outside the classroom door, Alex was dutifully waiting for Jason and playing Tetris on his phone.

"Hey, how did it go?" Alex stashed his phone in a pocket of his leather jacket.

"I think it went okay," Jason said. "She believes me now. I guess I really am just that brilliant." He forced a laugh, but inside he couldn't shake the feeling that something out of the ordinary had happened.

Alex stared into the tree line, wondering exactly what it was he thought he was going to do here. When he was in the little meditation room in his tower, he was so sure that the strange, undulating energy patterns he could see at the forest margins would have an obvious source when he arrived on location. But the cool, dark energy emanating from the forest was no different than usual now, and nothing looked different, either. Furthermore, Alex was pretty sure he was standing in someone's backyard. A rusted swingset was close enough for a child to have swung into his back and knocked him on his face. Alex slipped into the woods before anyone called the police and one of the two officers from that closet of an office in the town hall came down to lecture him again.

The shadows welcomed him in, snuggling close around his body. The canopy was thick, and even on bright days it was dim underneath. The sounds of cars and barking dogs hushed the moment Alex crossed the invisible threshold into the forest, becoming much farther away than they really were. Alex scanned the area around him with inner and outer eyes. Nothing but trees and underbrush, misty wisps of magic floating on a breeze that couldn't be felt.

"I'm just here to make sure everything is okay, making sure there aren't any intruders or anything, you know?" Alex said out loud. What little insect and bird sounds there were quieted, listening. "I hope that's all right with you. Please let me find my way out when I'm done." With the formalities out of the way, Alex trudged deeper into the trees. The way seemed to open up before him. That was a good sign. The forest appreciated being shown respect. He hadn't believed that at first, but the forest was quick to teach a lesson to any who dare be rude or harmful. The vegetation would close in, paths would vanish, and a person could find himself hopelessly lost in a matter of minutes in the ever-changing woods when they were angry.

A mote of something weakly lavender caressed Alex's awareness. He stopped and spun in place, trying to pinpoint it. He looked up. He looked down. He even peeked between the leaves of several obliging ferns, but there was no trace of the energy to be found. Alex began to wonder if he was literally chasing ghosts. Or perhaps memories, strong enough to leave behind an imprint in the forest. But what he had seen from the tower was much bigger than that, blips appearing and disappearing throughout the forest as far as the third eye could see. Could the forest be collecting lost memories now? Surely if it did, it would have always done so. Maybe he had never noticed.

Alex kept searching for the mysterious energy blooms for over an hour before deciding that it was probably his imagination, and if it weren't, it was probably not important enough to keep tromping through the forest chasing incorporeal fireflies. Before he'd even spoke a word, Alex turned around and saw through the trees the same back-yard with the rusty swings he had been standing in earlier. He smiled.

"Thank you." Alex left the forest, and the trees settled behind him.

"Here goes…" Jason clicked the "translate" option and watched as the randomly-chosen wiki webpage ("Sigurd the Crusader") refreshed with Swahili text in place of English. He took a deep breath, fixed his eyes at the beginning of the first sentence, and started reading. When he reached the end, he clicked a link in the text and translated *that* page into Russian. He repeated the procedure four more times with four different languages before slumping back into his desk chair. Jason's experiment supported his hunch one-hundred percent. His stomach did a flip-flop. Sally had always said that he would develop a "gift" sooner or later, but Jason hadn't really believed it. What kind of ability could he possibly have? He who had to take sick days at least twice a month, he who would rather disappear into the wallpaper than talk to one of his peers. Jason closed his eyes and rested his head on the back of his chair, trying to process what this meant for him. Universal translation wasn't the superpower he would have asked for. It didn't seem very "super." How did it work? Was it just reading and writing, or could he speak other languages, too? Jason could only think of one person that might know how to answer his questions. She picked up on the first ring.

"Yes, Jason?" Sally's brusque voice crackled through the phone line. "Is something wrong?"

"Hi, um, no, I don't think anything is wrong. I wanted to ask you a question. Or questions. Is it possible to know a language that you've never heard before?"

"Certainly. There are a few people who can temporarily absorb someone else's native language through touch or telepathy. There's speaking in tongues or spontaneous writing in a foreign language, with or without demonic possession. And sometimes ancestral languages can spontaneously reappear down a bloodline. Although, that seems to be changing lately...why do you ask?"

"Well, something weird happened today that made me wonder," Jason said, trying to decide how best to explain. "Have you ever heard of someone being able to *read* languages he's never learned? Like, more than one? Maybe all of them?"

"It would explain a lot, actually," Sally said, dropping another book onto the growing stack in Jason's arms. "I'd noticed chatter in the research community about some groups gradually losing their powers, and I wondered what it meant. Do me a favor and put those in the sitting room." Jason nodded and wandered out of the library, too stunned to reply. He plonked the books down on the coffee table in the basement den and lowered himself onto one of the sofas. Sally arrived a moment later with yet more books and settled beside Jason.

"So, what does it mean?" he asked, watching Sally flip through pages.

"I think it means the first Guardians were more plugged in than I thought."

"I still don't understand."

"I don't either, really, but, see, there's a theory..." Sally paused until she found the page she wanted. "Here it is! See, H.H. Shaut put forth this hypothesis that each world has a finite amount of supernatural energy. It's the first law of thermodynamics. Energy cannot be created or destroyed. Somehow the original Guardians or someone more powerful who's friendly to the cause has found a way to re-channel existing energies into the new Guardians to prepare them for, well, war. Where's that line...ah, yes. 'Each time a spell is performed, the energy must necessarily come from somewhere, whether inside the caster or from outside sources.' If they want to make ordinary people stronger, that power must come from somewhere. I've wondered if the first generation of Guardians had to do something similar with themselves."

"So, I'm being, what, charged? Like a battery?" Jason skimmed over the passage Sally was referencing. He wasn't sure how he felt about someone he'd never met pouring magic into him...by taking it from other people, apparently, which made him even more uncomfortable.

"I suppose that's an appropriate analogy," Sally said, flipping closed the cover of the book. "Are you aware that the sentence I just read from that book was in German?"

"I—what?"

"You didn't even notice," Sally marveled. She shook her head. "This is amazing. Did you hear it as English?"

"I'm not sure." Jason tried to remember how it had sounded in his ears. "I don't think so. I just *knew* it." Jason picked up one of the books from the table and glanced at the title. *The Neurobiology of Xenoglossy*—but the words weren't in English. They just somehow made sense. Even "xenoglossy." He immediately recognized inside the jargon derivatives of the Greek words for "foreigner" and "tongue."

"I can see that these aren't words that I know, except, I can read them," Jason said with a shrug, trying to swallow the murmurs of fear inside him. "Does that mean something to you?"

"I don't know. Maybe," Sally said. "I'll have to do some research. Richie's ability seems pretty straightforward, but I've never heard of one quite like this. I have to ask, does it mean something to *you*? Richie's made me realize that not everyone sees a supernatural gift as a good thing. I guess this shouldn't be painful for you, but I've given up trying to understand how people think." Jason blinked at the xenoglossy book that he was xenoglossically reading and tried to find a way to put his confused thoughts into words.

"Well, I'm not upset," he said. "This probably isn't going to disrupt my life any more than it's already been disrupted. I'm just sort of disappointed. I was hoping for something a little more, I don't know, battle-worthy." Jason clasped his bony, spidery fingers on top of the book in his lap and stared at them. "I've always been weak. I thought maybe that would change if I had super Guardian powers," he murmured. "And what do I get? The ability to watch anime without subtitles? It's just not what I had in mind. But I'll deal." He could feel the weight of Sally's eyes on him. Jason opened the book and pretended to browse the pages. For far longer than Jason was comfortable with, neither of them said anything. He expected Sally to get up and leave, as she usually did when she was finished with a conversation. When she didn't, he quickly began to feel awkward.

"You might be surprised," Sally finally said. "Language is incredibly important, especially for your species. This might be a more powerful tool than you think. Just not physically powerful. Do you mind if I keep testing you? This is fascinating."

"Sure. Why not? Let's do it."

Richie sat cross-legged on the itchy grass by the shore of the lake. William had suggested that he practice his fire powers in places where water was readily available in case there had to be an emergency extinguishment. Where better than a lake? A private lake, at that, so there weren't any civilians nearby to burn. There was just William, currently swimming in the lake and keeping an eye on Richie, at least in theory.

Richie was working on lighting each of his fingertips with small flames one by one. It sounded easy when William told him to practice doing it, but it definitely was not. Richie was getting the hang of urging his fire out onto his skin, but he couldn't do so with any great degree of precision. Just focusing fire onto his hands was a challenge. Trying to contain it to the end of a single finger felt impossible. So far, the best he could do was three adjacent digits at a time.

"Am I interrupting anything?" Jason lowered himself on stilt-like limbs to the ground beside Richie, who abandoned the finger-flame exercise and twisted to face him. Jason had brought a plastic pail with him. Even though it was covered in foil, Richie could taste the fleshy, fishy smell it gave off. His human disgust battled his cotu proclivity for raw meat.

"Nothing important," Richie answered. "Why do you have a bucket of dead fish?"

"It's squid, actually. I brought them as a treat for my pet."

"Your *pet?*"

"Yep." Jason whistled. Richie expected a cat or maybe a fish-loving dog to come running, but instead a slippery gray head rose out of the water on several feet of neck like the damn Loch Ness Monster. Richie yelped and scooted away from the shore on his backside, but Jason didn't even flinch.

"Hey, Vanessa, baby," he cooed, pulling the aluminum foil back from the pail. He reached in and pulled out a chunk of tentacle, suckers and all, and tossed it at the creature. Vanessa's head darted out and snapped up the flying hunk of fish in jaws lined with reptilian teeth. She swallowed without chewing, the muscles in her neck rippling her food down her long throat. Then she settled down further into the water and watched Jason intently with dark eyes, waiting for the next treat.

"Y—you have a pet dinosaur," Richie said, gaping at the animal. Jason laughed and tossed another piece of squid over the lake.

"I don't think she's actually a dinosaur," he said. "She does look kind of like a plesiosaur, I suppose. I've been feeding her since I found her as a hatchling in a tiny pond in the park. But she's not the only reason I came out here. I need to talk to you. Do you want to feed her, too?" Jason held the bucket over to Richie. Richie grimaced but forced himself to take the offer. *When in Rome...* He reached in and picked out a slimy bit of cephalopod—*ew, ew, ew*—and flung it as hard as he could. Vanessa made a noise, something like a seal's bark, but higher in pitch, and jumped for the food.

"What do you need to talk about?" Richie wiped squid goop off into the grass. Their conversation was interrupted, however, by William's sudden appearance mere inches from Vanessa by the shoreline.

"Jason, is this Vanessa?" he crowed, startling both the boys and the beast.

"Um, yeah, that's her," Jason said. William grinned and held out a hand to rub Vanessa's slippery neck. The lake monster slowly lowered her head down towards the little swimming mammal, looking surprised and a bit cautious, but she allowed him to stroke her. Richie didn't think there was enough money in the world to make him get that close to that thing.

"Hey, can I feed her, too?" William beamed, apparently delighted to have met this behemoth. Jason nudged the treat pail near the shore with his foot. William crawled onto the muddy bank, aquatic plants plastered on his pale skin and swim trunks. He proceeded, to Richie's horror, to feed Vanessa by hand.

"She won't hurt him," Jason assured Richie. "Or she won't eat him, at least. She might nip. But to answer your question, I wanted to talk because I found out what my power is yesterday."

"Oh." Richie inhaled sharply. "Wow. I'm sorry. What is it?"

"Apparently, I can read, write, and talk in any language, when prompted. All the languages we've tried, at least. Sally and I worked it out." Jason huffed out a short breath. "How I'm supposed to save the world with *that*, I don't know."

"It doesn't sound that bad." Richie couldn't help thinking of his own "gift."

"Well, it doesn't hurt or anything. I'm glad about that, but I guess I traded in 'useful' for 'painless.' Your power saved my life. My power can't do anything but save my Latin grades."

"Jason, just be thankful it won't kill you." Richie was starting to feel a little angry with the world and a lot envious of Jason. It wasn't Jason's fault that he got the cushy gift, but it must be *somebody's* fault.

"I'm not sure I can be. I know what you're thinking, and you're right. It's not fair, I got the better deal, and I shouldn't complain. But I've lived within spitting distance of death since the day I was born, and probably been in pain longer than that. What's another thing to suffer through? It would have been worth it to me if my being in pain could help the cause. Do you get what I mean? I don't want to be the guy hiding behind the sofa when we're in danger. But I guess I always will."

"I would love to be hiding behind the sofa. I only ever wanted to be out of this—" Richie gestured aimlessly "—magic shit. All it's ever done is ruin my life. I thought you felt the same way."

"I did," Jason agreed. "Now I'm not so sure. I'm not sure what to think about anything." Jason lay back onto the grass, apparently immune to its scratchiness. His Pink Floyd *Dark Side of the Moon* t-shirt settled on top of his bony ribcage and sunken abdomen.

"Getting a power might have changed my perspective." He blinked at the wispy white clouds above him.

Richie nodded. He couldn't argue with that. Having one of these gifts changed everything. Most of all, it had changed how he thought of himself. He thought he was crazy. Then he predicted his brother plummeting from the roof and thought he was cursed. Now he simply thought he was a freak, albeit a freak with a destiny—not that he wanted one.

"I don't know, Jay," Richie said, watching Vanessa lick squid flavor off of William's hand. "We live in a weird world. Who's to say your power won't be the most important?"

"How?" Jason didn't bother to hide the unbelief in his voice. Richie didn't have an answer, so he didn't say anything, and Jason let it drop.

"Well, I've got to go. Cameron and I are supposed to meet Scarlet in the orchard for weapons training."

"Can I come?"

"Didn't you say you were training with William today?"

"It looks like he's found someone else to play with." Richie nodded toward the ice cotu and the lake monster. Jason smiled.

"I guess you're right. I'd hate to tear Vanessa away from her new toy. She doesn't get much interaction with people anymore. She's getting too big. I'll tell William where we're going, and we'll leave them to it."

4

Manitoba, Canada

The sun rose over the horizon, and it was officially delivery day. A few times a month the trucks drove to the small Canadian town with shipments of various goods, mostly industrial materials and perishables. Those days were always chaotic, with strange people and vehicles in and out from dawn to dusk or later. Even so, it was fairly routine, and no one would have considered that it was the perfect date for an act of undead bioterrorism.

The truck of porkers pulled into the distribution center. The workers redirected it to the slaughterhouse just out of town but didn't give it a thought when the driver stopped for a break before moving on. They didn't notice the passenger who emerged, undisguised, in the honest light of the sun, to casually unlatch the truck's loading doors and slide out the loading ramp. Both driver and passenger promptly vanished from the site, leaving the truck abandoned. For most of an hour, the truck sat silent.

A curious rosy-pink snout nuzzled open a door. A huge head followed behind, gazing with confusion out on the truck stop. Having been raised in a dank, smelly, windowless barn, the pig's eyes squinted into the sunshine. It stung, but he liked the way the light felt on his skin. Not sensing any obvious danger, the pig shoved the doors open and trotted out onto the ramp. His fellow swine filed out behind him. One imperative dominated every pig's mind. There was a very specific human that they had to kill. They didn't particularly want to hurt her or anyone else, but Vincent had done his work well, and they could not resist the impulse.

As pigs streamed out of the unmanned truck, the people around couldn't help but take notice. The workers stopped what they were doing and started to stare, muttering worriedly amongst themselves. Someone fetched the nearest managerial figure, who ordered several employees to try to close the doors and trap the remaining pigs in the truck. Everyone else was assigned to round up the dozens of animals that had already wandered out. It seemed the most logical way to handle the situation, but in fact the manager could hardly have made a worse mistake. The pigs were bigger than any man present and were driven by necromantic command to spread out and explore to find their target. No one was going to get in their way, at least not for long.

Two men pushed on the outside of each door, straining against the tide of pigs. At first, the pigs were surprised, and the workers succeeded in closing and locking the truck. Pleased with that effort, all the men set about surrounding the swine. They formed a human fence, and then just stood there, unsure what to do next. In order to guide the pigs back in the truck, they would have to open the doors, and then the rest of the pigs might escape. The men stared at the pigs; the pigs stared at the men. It was a pig that moved first, the same pig who had first nosed his way out into the sunlight. Already at the edge of the circle, the Alpha Pig plodded towards the nearest human and calmly made to walk under one of his outstretched arms. The man and the two to either side of him dove for the pig in an awkward rugby tackle. The pig squealed in anger and consternation. Then all the best laid plans of managers and workmen went awry.

The pigs rushed to the aid of their comrade, including the pigs still in the trailer. The doors burst open as a mass of undead pigs crashed into and through the men as though they were made of toothpicks. Most of the would-be pig wranglers broke formation and fled, willing to be a coward if it meant not being a corpse. The three who attempted to arrest the first escaping pig, however, were too close to the melee to get away even if they wanted to. They were trampled under the hooves of a swarm of furious swine, the life beaten out of them in moments. Holding onto their momentum, the pigs rushed over and past the bodies, making for the path of least resistance: the open road. A psychic nudge from Vincent told them that the town proper was to their left, and the pigs turned as one. The porkers ran in a pack along the highway, giving their high-pitched war cry. A car came around the corner and slammed on brakes as the terrified driver spotted the flood of porkers. The pigs ran overtop the car as easily as they tromped over the dock hands, unstoppable in their pursuit.

"What is all that noise?" asked the Pizza Palace cashier. Joon turned down the volume on the radio to hear what he meant. Outside, there was a great cacophony of moving feet, voices shouting, and some sort of squealing sound.

"Well, it is delivery day at the truck depot," said the busboy.

"They aren't normally quite that loud." Joon walked up to the front counter to peer out the windows. The cars were stopped in the street, many of the drivers stepping out to stare at something just out of view. Pedestrians, too, had quite forgotten their morning routines. Joon craned her neck to see what had captivated everyone.

Outside, the *crack* of a shotgun blast sang through the frosty air. The Pizza Palace employees rushed to the door and spilled onto the sidewalk. There was another shot, and somebody screamed. Shoving to the front of the knot of people, Joon finally saw the spectacle, and could not believe it. Stampeding down the avenue was a massive horde of mottled pigs. These weren't dog-sized and cuddly and bubblegum-pink like the ones Joon saw drawn in picture books as a child. No, these pigs were big enough to ride like a horse, and they looked angry. At the front of the bunch ran a pig who caught some of that buckshot square in the face. One ear was torn clean off, and the flesh at the temple was stripped down to the skull. The pig was unfazed, streaking along full-speed with tarry black blood flowing freely from his face and splattering onto the pigs behind him.

Black blood. Just like Kylie's math teacher, the one that was still trying to kill her long after he should have been dead. While some of the other onlookers laughed, thinking it all a joke, and most stood motionless with shock, Joon ran. Her flight inspired others to the same, but as they ran to the side streets out of the pigs' path, Joon sprinted straight down the pavement, headed the same direction as the zombies, in a desperate race to find her sister before they did.

Joon had no idea pigs could move so fast. The only reason they didn't run her over was that she turned off onto Saint George Street and they didn't. Her panic subsiding, Joon began to wonder what she planned to do when she got to Kylie's school. How would she convince the office to let Kylie out of class? If they didn't know about the pigs, there was no way Joon could explain it. And then where would they go? Somewhere out of town, she supposed, but they would have to walk home first to get the car. Joon never drove to work because it was so close to home. Maybe she shouldn't even bother. The practical side of Joon's brain pointed out that in all probability the pigs were *not* zombies. They probably just escaped from the truck depot and somebody would come to round them up shortly.

Joon's pace slowed as she began to convince herself that the peril wasn't real. She finally stopped walking altogether, but when she looked up she found herself standing in front of the school. *Should I go in?* They were probably waiting for her at the Pizza Palace, docking her paycheck by the minute. Kylie would be embarrassed if Joon came storming in and pulled her out for nothing. But, if there was a chance that Kylie might be in danger...

Another gunshot called out down the street. In less than ten seconds, Joon was in the school's front office making up a story to get Kylie out of class.

"Well, you see, Miss, there's, um, the police! Yeah, there's the police. You know we had that crazy incident a while ago? Yes, so they want to talk to us again," Joon rambled. The secretary at the desk appeared skeptical.

"Three weeks after it happened?"

"Ye—es," Joon said.

"They couldn't wait until after school hours?"

"I don't know. That's just what they said, okay?"

The secretary opened her mouth, probably to tell Joon, with all due politeness, to either get out or come up with a better lie. She was interrupted by the ringing phone.

"One moment, please," she said, putting the receiver to her ear. "Saint George's Junior High School, how may I help you?" The person on the other end said something rather loudly and with great animation. The receptionist's eyes widened. With a curt "Yes, Mr. Hughes," she clicked off the phone and picked up the mouthpiece for the public-address system.

"Students and staff, we are now on lockdown. I repeat, we are now on lockdown," she announced. *It must be the pigs,* Joon thought. *Now how will I get Kylie out?* There was no time to think it through. Already the secretary was pulling her into the mailroom to hide until the lockdown passed. Two stray teachers were in there before them. The receptionist closed and locked the door behind Joon and ushered everyone into the corner of the room farthest from the door.

"What's going on?" asked one teacher.

"I'm not sure," the receptionist whispered. "We just got a call from the provost saying to lock the schools down immediately, no questions asked."

"Maybe it's a terrorist threat," the other teacher theorized. The three continued to discuss it, although Joon was fairly certain that they weren't supposed to be talking during a lockdown. Joon didn't shush them. If they were inundated by a horde of pig-zombies, it would hardly matter whether they were being quiet or not. Instead, Joon pulled her cell phone out of her pocket. The school frowned upon phone use during class, but that had never stopped Joon, and she doubted her sister was any different.

Kylie r u there?

The teacher didn't notice the incredibly high-pitched tone that heralded the text message. Thus far it had proven beyond the range of most of her teacher's ears, as advertised, but several of her fellow students started at the piercing noise in the near-silence of the locked-down classroom. Kylie switched her phone to silent and texted back with the lighting speed of an experienced tweenage socialite.

Yes! What is going on?

Joon replied with a single word: *zombies*. Kylie's fingertips felt like frostbite.

Zombies like mr murphy?!

Yes, Joon answered. Kylie started to tremble. Before she could think of something to say, Joon sent another text. *If they show up, run home. I'll meet you there.* Then again, a moment later:

They're pigs not people. Be careful.

It took a while for the pigs to home in on their target. In their fury, they overshot many, many times. Only when they simmered down was it possible for them to use the little signal in their reanimated brains to navigate with any precision. "Getting warmer, getting colder, getting warmer again…red hot!" When they found her, they knew. Standing before the basic brick building, their need to find Kylie burned stronger than ever. The group split into four, one for each side of the floor plan. The pigs at the front entrance went in first, ramming the front doors with their bulk until the hinges echoed their squeals and finally broke.

The four groups surveyed the hallways and then reunited in the center of the ground floor, satisfied that they would not be interrupted. Now they discovered a peculiar thing. Their newly-acquired sixth sense told them that Kylie was near, but not laterally. She was floating above their heads.

The revenants looked upwards in unison. How would they get up there? A pig on the fringes of the group oinked, drawing his comrades' attention to the stairs. Perfect! Two by two the pigs proceeded to climb to the second floor. It was slow going, as pig hooves are not made for stairs, nor stairs for pig hooves, but with patience and persistence they succeeded.

Once upstairs, they began to sniff under the classroom doors. One of these wooden obstacles, surely, was concealing their target. Some of the rooms were silent but for heartbeats, while others almost buzzed with whispers. It was behind one of the quiet doors that they finally found the right scent. A ripple of excitement rolled through the assembled pigs.

In a now well-practiced maneuver, the nearest sow slammed the door with her bulk. Inside, the humans uttered various exclamations. On the fourth ramming, the wood splintered, and the pig forced her head through the crack. Many of the humans she saw inside screamed. A few laughed, which she thought odd. She pulled her head back, oblivious to the slivers that caught in her face, and with one good shove forced her upper body into the hole. More screams, fewer giggles. The pig laid eyes on the girl. She was one of the scared ones, no question. She didn't holler, but her eyes were huge and she was pressing herself into the back wall as if it might have the decency to disappear and let her out. The first pig wriggled through the door, and the second followed. They took their time. When the fourth pig arrived, they formed a semicircle opposite their target. Silence had fallen among the young humans.

Kylie glanced at each of the pigs, then up behind her towards the window. The pigs were surrounding her, fixing their eyes on her, appearing to ignore the other nervous students. There was no hope of breaking for the door. What was their problem? *Why are all the zom-*

bies in Canada after me? Kylie tried to breathe slowly, think clearly. How dangerous was a two-story jump? Not much time to think about it. On the cop shows, they rolled when they hit the ground and by so doing survived all kinds of daring leaps. She could do this. She had to. Quickly. Kylie snagged her science textbook—the first time she'd really used it so far that year—and heaved it at the window.

In her head, Kylie pictured the book sailing through the window in a spray of broken glass. The actual result was rather underwhelming. The corner of the textbook sprouted a spider web of cracks the width of a small coin and then fell dully on the floor. Kylie jumped to her feet as the pigs, alerted to her intentions, surged towards her. She turned to the window and jerked with both hands at the handle that would open it. It might have been far too late, had the flying textbook not triggered a panic. Every primate body in the classroom took Kylie's cue and ran for the door or windows at once, clogging the science lab with frantic children and frustrated pigs. Kids gathered up behind Kylie, pushing and shoving at her back but also shielding her from the undead menace. The pigs began to bite legs and push down the people in their way, but they succeeded only in intensifying the general bedlam. At last, Kylie managed to figure out the locking mechanism. She thrust open the lower half of the window, spared a single glance at the drop below, and propelled herself out into the air.

In the movies, a perilous fall is a slow-motion experience, filled with flashbacks and sometimes action or improbable stretches of dialogue. Kylie felt no such time warp. There was a moment of *whoosh*, as atmosphere streamed by like water rushing around a rock in the river. Before she could decide if she was right-side-up or upside-down, Kylie reached the lawn with a jarring hit below her left shoulder blade. Barely remembering to roll, she clumsily tumbled over the point of impact and spread the momentum over a meter or two. She stopped, panting in spasms, and opened her eyes. Little green ribbons of grass stood sideways across her field of vision. Kylie drew herself up, wincing at the pain in her side. She looked over her limbs, moved all her joints. Everything was bruised and sore, but she didn't think there were any broken bones. Good. Joon had told her to run home, and so she would. Kylie stood shakily, glancing up at the second-story windows. A wide piggy face stuck out, but there wasn't room for the whole body to squeeze through the opening. It wouldn't take long for them to find their way back downstairs, though.

A few of Kylie's classmates had followed her out the window—the teacher, too—and were sprawled around the turf. Not everyone had fared as well as Kylie. She was torn between helping her injured class-mates and running for her life. She compromised, calling the police as she jogged back to the house, hobbled a little from her tumble, but still keeping ahead of the pigs.

When large, unkillable pigs crash through the front doors, law and order tend to disband. Joon got her chance to find Kylie within mo-ments of the ruminant invasion. Pigs spilled into the office, smash-ing through doors hither and thither. The mailroom never stood a chance. Joon was ready this time, though. They barged in to find Joon standing in front of the three staff members holding a metal-legged chair like a lion-tamer. The zombies didn't look so very impressed, but they did leave. Whether out of respect for Joon's bravery or simple lack of interest, no more pigs came their way. As soon as the last pig cleared the front office, Joon was out the door.

Once outside, she turned to look back at the school, debating whether to go in and find Kylie or go home and wait for Kylie to find her. Waves of pigs were crashing through the side windows. There was little hope of wading through the mob to seek her sister. Fearing the worst, Joon sent Kylie an update—*going home now see u there*—and began to hurry down the street, glancing behind her every few steps for any sign of Kylie or an imminent pig attack.

Joon felt as though she'd been holding her breath the quarter hour until Kylie burst through the front door and hug-tackled her. Joon threw her arms around Kylie and squeezed like her sister might be ripped from her grasp at any moment. After a long time that would have been awkward under normal circumstances, they disengaged. Joon held Kylie at arm's length, examining her for injuries.

"What happened to you?" Joon asked. Kylie looked terrible. Her clothes were torn and dirtied. She was covered in scrapes, and her shoes were long gone. Little drips of blood welled on several small wounds on her feet.

"I jumped out a window to get away from the pigs. I'm fine, though. It was only the second floor. Forget about it. Right now, we've got to run. These damn pigs won't let me go." By force of habit, Joon almost scolded Kylie for swearing, as if that mattered right then.

"What do you mean, 'They won't let you go?' Are they *following* you?"

"I think so," Kylie said. "I lost them a while back by cutting through this skinny alley they couldn't fit in, but until then they've been behind me all the way from school. So come on, let's go!"

"Where?"

"I don't know! You're the oldest. You figure it out."

Joon didn't have time to think. Already she could hear a chorus of squeals outside. Where, where? *Well, pigs can't climb, so...*

"Kylie, go get Dad's shotgun and all the rounds you can find. Grab your coat, too, and put some shoes on. I'm going to pack a few things, and then we're going to hide out in the deer stand." Joon hoped their father's hunting buddies still used the stand and kept it in good repair. Joon grabbed Kylie's backpack off the kitchen floor—she wasn't supposed to leave it there but thank goodness she had—and flipped it over, shaking its contents out onto the linoleum. She stuffed a handful of granola bars, a couple water bottles, a flashlight, and two blankets inside. She checked her pocket. Yes, cell phone still there. Kylie came back with the shotgun held awkwardly under one arm and a drawstring bag of ammunition in the other hand. Dad had never gotten around to teaching Kylie how to shoot, but Joon had been hunting with him several times. She traded with Kylie, backpack for firearm, loaded the gun, and ushered Kylie out the back door.

Joon realized within minutes that heading into the forest had been the right decision. The pigs found their trail in no time, but they had yet to get closer than the edge of Joon's vision. Maybe their hooves weren't cut out for pine needles, or they were just too big to squeeze between the trees. Whatever the reason, they had lost the rolling momentum that made them so destructive in town. The girls didn't even have to run anymore.

That was the good news. Unfortunately, there was a hitch in Joon's plan. Neither of them had been to the deer stand since before their mother died. There was a trail to get there, sort of, but it was unlabeled, and they soon wandered off it. The forest was devoid of landmarks to their untrained eyes. They were ahead of the zombies, but they were decidedly lost. The more disoriented they felt, the slower their progress, and the greater the pigs' advantage. Then Joon heard the slithery, whispery sound of running water, and inspiration struck.

"Let's head for the river. There's a bridge there."

"What river?"

"Don't you hear it? I went fishing with one of my ex-boyfriends there a few times." Joon guided Kylie toward the sound of the water.

"*You* went fishing?"

"Well," Joon said, "that's what we *said* we were doing." Kylie gave her a scandalized look. "What? I was a teenager once, too, you know."

"Ew, gross," Kylie said and pretended to gag. Joon glared. Kylie ignored. "So, what's this about a bridge?"

"You'll see."

"That is the sketchiest bridge I have ever seen," Kylie said. And it was. The bridge was a hazardous tangle of ropes and rotting planks strung out above a steep ditch with a rock-strewn river below. The water near the banks was frozen over, but the middle still coursed at substantial speed. Gaps several centimeters wide separated the boards. "Can we even walk on it?"

"We can, but the pigs can't," Joon said. "At least I think so. Hopefully the river will stall the pigs for a while, and then maybe I can figure out where to go from here. You want to cross first?" Kylie shook her head emphatically. Joon nodded, gave Kylie's shoulder a squeeze, and stepped out onto the bridge. The plank groaned beneath the sole of her runners as she shifted her weight onto her front foot. She stepped on with her second foot. The boards warped, making the whole structure wiggle. Joon stood motionless, waiting for the wood to give, but it didn't. She took another quavering step, and another. The bridge complained and wobbled but didn't collapse. Quite to her surprise, a minute or two later Joon found herself standing on the other side. She glanced over her shoulder at Kylie, who was still standing across the way.

"See? You can do it," Joon urged. Kylie inhaled deeply and ventured out on the bridge, clutching the handrails to glean their illusory support. Joon kept one eye on Kylie and one on the woods behind her. A splash of pink appeared momentarily between two trees on the far shore.

"A little faster, Kylie. No, don't look back! Keep walking." Joon beckoned her sister onward. Kylie accelerated from the pace of a sloth to that of a slug.

"Oh, come on! You just jumped out of a window! This can't be that hard." The lower limbs of the pine trees rustled on the other side. A snuffling, oinking creature stuck its snout through a wall of deep green needles. Kylie jolted. She whipped her head around, saw the pig nose, and darted toward Joon. Her left foot broke through a plank and she didn't even pause, just ripped her foot out and kept running, rivulets of blood staining her sock. Kylie pounded onto the dirt bank and bowled Joon right over.

The girls turned back to the bridge, looking over as the pigs assembled on the bank, eyeing the water suspiciously. Kylie and Joon scrambled up and ran into the forest. As they turned their backs, the first pig strode onto the bridge, promptly breaking the rotten planks and splashing into the icy, azure water.

"How are we going to get back home?" Kylie asked.

"We'll find a way," Joon said, a promise she didn't know how to keep.

The two sisters walked for hours. In their fear and exhaustion, they didn't notice the forest changing—dark pines replaced by mottled hardwoods, peat melding into leaf litter—until the heat hit them.

"Does it feel like it's getting warm to you?" Joon asked, shrugging the coat off her shoulders. Before, she had been shivering, but now she was hot under her cardigan. Kylie nodded, shedding her coat as well. The girls stopped, really looking around for the first time since they left the pigs behind.

"Where *are* we?" Kylie wondered aloud. Joon had no answer, only another question.

"Is that...humming?"

They listened. Yes, something *did* sound like a woman humming. The girls started to walk toward the melody. As far as they were concerned, anyone who wasn't a zombie was their friend. It took a while, but they found the right direction. As they approached, the song became clear. They continued to follow the haunting strains of "Hey, Jude" until the humming abruptly stopped, mid-verse.

"Hello-ohhhh?" called a distant voice.

"We're over here!" Joon yelled, cupping her hands around her mouth. "We're lost! Can you help us?"

"Sure!" the voice replied brightly. For a while Kylie and Joon heard nothing else. Just as they were wondering if the person had decided to let them rot, the light thud of running footsteps on rich forest soil found their ears. Within seconds a human form materialized in the low tree-filtered moonlight in front of the two sisters. The woman skidded to a stop before them. Her short, blonde hair was tangled with twigs and leaves, dirt and scratches covered her tan skin, and her clothes—red plaid shorts and blue, turtle-patterned t-shirt—were patched and torn. Kylie took an involuntary step back from this wild apparition, but Joon held her ground in the interest of politeness.

"Where are you going?" the wild-woman asked, cocking her head to one side like a dog.

"You mind telling us where we are first, eh?" Joon asked. She was starting to feel a little silly, thinking about how to explain their situation. What could she say that wouldn't sound thoroughly insane?

"You're in Brunswick," the woman said. "North Carolina, USA. But sometimes you can get here from other places, too. Anywhere you can get lost, you can end up in Brunswick."

"North Carolina is, where?" Joon was trying to imagine any scenario in which they could have walked from Manitoba across the border without noticing.

"Kind of midway down the East Coast. You must be very lost, then. Where did you come from?"

Joon stared without comprehension. *How many thousands of miles?*

"We were in Canada," Kylie blurted, "running away from zombies."

"Oh no! What kind of zombies?" The wild-woman whipped her head to either side, looking for the alleged zombies. Joon began to wonder if she was dreaming, or maybe dead.

"Pigs," Kylie said simply.

"Huh. Never heard that one before. Let's get you somewhere safe. There's a werewolf Dawn Cabin a few minutes from here. I'll show you."

"Werewolf?" Joon exclaimed, but the woman had already turned and started running again. The sisters ran, too. Even if this person were an escaped lunatic, Joon would rather be in her company than left alone in the woods, whatever woods these were.

"Yeah, werewolves," their guide called over her shoulder. "Like me." *Maybe this is purgatory,* Joon thought. She wasn't Catholic, so she didn't know if this was what purgatory was supposed to look like, but it seemed like a reasonable supposition under the circumstances.

The wild-woman ran them hard, but, true to her word, she brought them right to the doorstep of a rustic log cabin. The windows were dark, yet the door was unlocked. She held it open for Kylie and Joon.

"Dawn Cabins are where werewolves can rest after transforming back into humans at sunrise. My pack has five, since there are so many of us. Most packs just have one or two, if they're lucky. I hear they even have them in cities, but I don't how that works. We don't have running water out here, but if you want to get a drink or wash up, help yourself to the water in the jugs in the cabinets under the sinks. There are snacks in the kitchen and an outhouse back yonder. Let me know if you need anything else. My name is Scarlet."

The space was small, one main room with a sofa, several chairs, and an old radio on a TV stand clustered by the fireplace. Some cabinets, a sink without a faucet, and a breakfast table were at the right-hand wall. On the left hung a bulletin board covered with papers and photos, and a door opened off to a small room with a washbasin and mirror. It wasn't a five-star hotel, but it was certainly better than the violent deaths the Stiles girls had been expecting. They both thanked Scarlet for the rescue.

"No problem," Scarlet said. "I needed to check up on the pantry anyway. We can hide out here until I make sure the woods are zombie-free, and then I'll take you to Sally's house. It's much nicer."

"Who's Sally?" Joon asked, flinging herself into the loving arms of a saggy, brown armchair. Looking across the room at Scarlet, she noticed that the self-proclaimed werewolf was barefoot.

"That's the woman I work for. I'm sort of like her private security. Anyone in need of help is welcome in her home. Well, unless they're genies. We're having a problem with them right now."

"Genies? Like the ones that come out of lamps?" Kylie said, taking a seat next to Joon. Joon's head was spinning. She didn't know how Kylie could act so calm.

On the inside, Kylie was *not* calm, not even remotely. Her heart flittered like a hummingbird at the thought of what she and Joon had just escaped, and a blind terror seized her when she tried to imagine what the future might hold. Only by mustering a mental haze to keep her in the present could Kylie stay sane. The present said there were zombies, werewolves, and genies. Okay, sure. That was believable enough, given what she'd been through lately. She could deal, as long as she didn't have to think too hard about the implications.

"I don't think genies live in bottles." Scarlet shook her head, and tangled, straw-blonde hair whipped around her ears. "They're more like witches, I suppose. They're nice folk, usually, but some of them seem to have gone kind of rogue. Sally's at war with them, so, you know, they can't come in the house. That's where I live. In Sally's mansion. I used to live in a little house with a bunch of other were-wolves, but that was just too crowded for me. I like my space." Scarlet wandered over to the kitchenette and started writing something on a notepad on the counter. "Make yourselves at home. What's ours is yours. Did y'all ever say what your names are?"

"I'm Kylie, and that's my big sister, Joon."

"Uh-huh. And you said you got lost in Canada, right? Is that where you're from?" The sisters nodded. "Are you going to go back?" Scarlet asked. Kylie looked over at Joon and found her sister facing her with the same clueless expression. Kylie wasn't sure they would even have a home to go back to or if they would be able to find out what became of their little town. She felt the sting of tears at the back of her eyes and blinked them back.

"I don't know," Joon admitted at last. Kylie's breath hitched in her throat. One quiet sob spluttered out before she could stop herself. She could feel Joon's eyes on her, waiting for the waterworks, but it wouldn't happen. Kylie was too old for that now. She took a deep breath.

"Scarlet, what's the best way to kill zombies?" she asked. She want-ed to sound cool and businesslike, but the quaking in her voice elim-inated that possibility. Scarlet glanced at Kylie before opening a cabi-net full of canned goods above the sink.

"It depends upon how the zombies were made," Scarlet replied, jotting something else down on the grocery list. "Beheading is kind of the standard, but even that doesn't always work. I don't know much about it, to be honest. Sally knows just about everything. We can ask her when we get there. How far ahead of the zombie pigs were you?" Joon estimated that they had achieved an hour or two by outmaneu-vering them.

"All right, then we'll wait four hours. If the zombies show up, I'll figure out how to deal with them. If they don't, we'll leave." Scarlet moved on to the next cabinet. The conversation, it seemed, was over. Without thinking, Kylie pulled her phone out of her pocket to fore-stall boredom. She clicked a few times and then stopped, staring.

"No cell service?"

"Nope. A lot of things don't work well in the forest. It has a mind of its own. We can get a few stations, though, if you want to try the radio," Scarlet said. Kylie let the phone fall to her lap, tears pooling in her eyes for real now. It wasn't so much that she needed the phone, although it was true that she was unaccustomed to life without it. The real loss was the idea of her phone, the promise of social life and escape from reality it held, that she wasn't sure she could live without.

Joon got to her feet and knelt by the radio. When she pressed the ON button, they were rewarded only with static. Most of the numbers on the dial returned empty noise or indecipherable gobbledegook. After a while Joon tuned in to a news station that was not entirely unintelligible. She sat back, and the sisters listened intently for news from Canada.

The Alpha Pig sniffed at the spot where their quarry had vanished. He looked back at his band of swine and snorted with frustration. The pigs spread out to search but found no sight or scent of the two human girls. Whither they had disappeared, no pig knew, but gone they certainly were. Now that they weren't nearby, though, Vincent's ruminant revenants discovered that the maddening urge for Kylie's blood had quite diminished. It was an odd but welcome development. The pigs began to drift off in ones, twos, and threes, munching on undergrowth and mushrooms. This wasn't such a bad place, really. Just a bit cold. The food was decent, the air smelled sweet, and there was plenty of space for everyone.

Vincent charged through the woods, following the trail of destruction left by the mass of undead pigs. He was sweating bullets despite the chill, panting, covered with leaves and dirt and scrapes—when he caught up with the revenants and found the young Guardian's mutilated body, it would all be worth it. Then he would claim his reward. Vincent wanted power, above all, and his employers had offered him dominion over *worlds*. Vincent saw a pink curly tail in the shadows in front of him. He might have shouted for joy if he wasn't so winded. Vincent picked up his pace and ran into the thick of the pigs.

For a while, he continued to believe that the gory remains of the girl and perhaps her sister would turn up sooner or later. However, as he rushed to and fro among the now-docile pigs, hope faded. There were no bones on the ground, no freshly-bloodied snouts to be seen.

"Where are they?" Vincent roared. The pigs, startled, looked up at their master. Vincent fixed the pigs nearest him with an accusing eye, one by one. "Have you *lost them*?" The pigs looked at Vincent and looked at one another. They didn't understand a word this human was yelling, but they knew that he was angry.

Vincent ranted and raged and cursed, stomping about like a lunatic. A couple of the pigs tried to gently direct his attention toward the spot where Kylie and Joon vanished, but he took no heed. The pigs decided he would just have to figure it out for himself. They began to disperse. Vincent kicked one as it walked past, but the revenant didn't feel it and continued undeterred. The ire began to seep out of the necromancer as he watched his now-independent creations wander off into the forest. They were good revenants, he had to give himself that. After everything they'd been through, they were still standing. Walking, even, and walking away from him heedless of his wishes. How could they be so calm? Maybe it wasn't their fault they had lost their prey. The Guardian might have been better prepared than he'd given her credit for. The only way to know now would be to find her again, and find her he would, whatever it took. Vincent turned away from the swine and began to follow his own trail of destruction out of the woods.

Months would pass before anyone dared go into those woods again, whether to track down the pigs or anything else. When at last a few brave Animal Control officers did venture forth, they discovered scores of pigs, including a sow with a litter of waxy-skinned undead piglets. Many of them were walking around quite happily with seemingly fatal, unhealed wounds from their invasion of the town that past year.

The animals were too large to capture by hand and proved immune to tranquilizer darts. After meeting a pig whose face was mostly grinning skull, the officers decided that somebody else could control these animals if they wanted to, and they high-tailed it out of there. In the wake of the officers came a few brash huntsmen, intending to exterminate the pigs. They never returned. No one was willing to take on the pigs after that. Since the pigs didn't care to chase after the people, either, the townsfolk let them alone. No humans in the forest, no zombie swine in the streets—everybody was satisfied, and the pigs lived out the rest of their afterlives in peace.

5

Brunswick

Sally was halfway out of bed before she processed the fact that she had been awoken by someone screaming upstairs. She didn't pause to think about it, just kept running, even after the cries stopped. She was vaguely aware of Alex coming up behind her, but she easily outpaced him. When Sally reached the second floor, she saw that Richie's door was open. She skidded to a stop inside the entrance and was relieved to see that it was only because William had gotten there first. Still on maximum alert, Sally scanned the room with every sense to make sure there wasn't murder afoot. There wasn't—only Richie shaking inside a cocoon made of his comforter and William sitting on the bed stroking Richie's hair. An odor of fear and burnt cotton hung in the air.

"I take it this wasn't a pleasant prophecy," Sally said. Richie shook his head. The sound of Alex's slapping feet echoed up the stairs, and Sally waved a hand outside the room to let him know there was no emergency. Momentarily, the footsteps slowed and softened.

"What was it?" Sally asked.

"Give him a minute," William said in protest. Sally hesitated, doubtful William would care that time to recover could mean time to forget important details.

"It's fine," Richie said. "What good is a warning if I don't share?"

William looked skeptical but held his tongue. Alex arrived at last, and Sally stepped into the bedroom to give him space to do the same. More frantic footsteps on the stairs suggested that Jenna and Hope were catching up.

"It's okay, guys," Alex hollered down the hall. "Go ahead, Richie."

"All right." Richie swallowed. "The way it started, it was like I'd been abducted by honest-to-God aliens. I was strapped to a table on my back, naked, with a really bright light overhead. There were a couple people moving around the table, but I couldn't see their faces, just the silhouettes of their heads and sometimes their hands. Then one of them picked up a scalpel or something and put it on my stomach, and that's when I realized this wasn't just a crazy dream where I don't have any clothes on. They cut me open and one of them...They put their hands *inside*. I can't even describe the pain. I couldn't move, I couldn't scream, there was *nothing* I could do. And then I saw one of the hands with a pair of scissors, and they went in and I couldn't feel what they were cutting, but suddenly I was *freezing*. Then I woke up, and I'm still cold."

The other women must have entered while Richie was talking. Sally hadn't noticed. Now they all looked at each other in stunned silence. William's hand had fallen from Richie's head and lay motionless on the sheets. Sally forced the shock of the grisly picture down and was the first to speak.

"You have no idea what this means?"

"No. I'm sorry," Richie answered.

"There's no need to apologize. Just let us know if you learn anything else, okay? You're doing great." Sally eyed the other responsible adults. "Why don't we let him get some rest. Hope, William, would you mind sticking around for a bit to make sure he settles in all right?"

"Yeah, of course," William said. Hope nodded.

"Great. We can talk about this more in the—" Sally was interrupted by the telephone ringing. "Oh, what now?"

"Kitch Manor, Sally speaking."

"Hi, Sally! It's Scarlet. Something weird happened while I was supervising last night's hunt. I found these two girls out in the woods, a bit banged up, and I've got them in the southeast Dawn Cabin. They said they escaped from zombies. I don't see any zombies, but I promised I would bring them to you. Jason's not at the Manor, is he?"

"No, he's probably still asleep."

"Oh gosh, I didn't wake you up, did I?"

"No, Scarlet, you didn't wake me up. Richie had a nightmare, and *he* woke everybody up. It seems like it was pretty gruesome, though, so I can't very well blame him. So, yes, I'm most certainly up. Come on over. I'll just lock Richie somewhere safe, and we'll see about these girls."

Upstairs, Hope and William were tending Richie. Downstairs, Alex, Sally, and Jenna waited in the basement sitting room for Scarlet to bring the mystery girls to the Manor.

"They can't be from Brunswick," Jenna said. "Scarlet would know them. They must be lost." Of course they were *lost*. Jenna meant something more specific. Brunswick was an uncanny place that existed in many locations at once. Sometimes, people and objects that disappeared in one spot would spontaneously appear in the woods. That was how Brunswick was established to begin with. A bunch of missing persons in the forest met up in a meadow a few hundred years ago and decided to call it home. So the story went, anyway. None of the original inhabitants remained to verify the legend.

"I wonder what kind of zombies they were," Sally said. "Assuming that they're telling the truth, which Scarlet seems to think they are. We might have to hunt the zombies down if they're the dangerous kind."

"There are zombies in those woods all the time. Why bother?" Alex picked at the hem of his sweatpants, trying not to fall asleep. Early mornings—not his thing. He rearranged his wings against the back of the sofa. He probably should have put a shirt on, but when he heard Richie screaming Alex didn't really think about stopping to get pretty. Come to think of it, they all looked kind of rough to be meeting guests, with Sally in plum, polka-dot pajamas and Jenna in a flannel nightgown, and everyone's hair in a tragic bedhead style. But then, what could you expect at four in the morning on a weekday?

The outside door to the basement opened and Scarlet came in, followed by a girl around Jason's age and a young, blonde woman who looked similar enough to be the child's sister. The lost girls walked with the stumbling gait of complete exhaustion. Scarlet was characteristically bouncy and energetic.

"Good morning, guys! This is Joon and Kylie! They might need to stay in Brunswick for a while until we figure out what to do about the zombies. Their hometown was overrun."

Alex stared at Kylie, and then stared some more. She wasn't astonishing to look at by herself—long, tawny hair, dark blue eyes, a little skinny preteen girl dressed like every other Alex saw at Jason's middle school. But her *aura* was like only two others Alex had ever seen. Joon's aura was similarly bright, but not the same color, more of an aquamarine, with a few sharp edges within that spoke of chronic stress.

Scarlet was narrating a bizarre tale of how undead pigs invaded the sisters' small Canadian town and tried to kill them. Huh. Weird. But then, not so weird, if Alex was right about Kylie. Alex had never heard of genies making zombies, but there was a first time for everything.

Alex sent Sally a telepathic picture of how Kylie appeared to him for confirmation. *Do you see what I see?* his brain asked hers. He wanted to be sure he wasn't projecting his own wishful thinking. Most humans would have a hard time interpreting an image sent to them mentally, but cotus excel at it. Instantly, Sally absorbed what Alex showed her, even though she never took her eyes off Scarlet.

I believe I do, Sally replied. *That is quite a find, isn't it? You never know what might be out in the Brunswick woods. I knew there was a reason I set up shop here. Aaaand now I get to tell another child that they can't go home again. Lovely.*

"No, that can't be right. That can't be *real.*" Joon shook her head. Shattered light shone through the crystal-glass window in the upstairs storage room where Sally had taken her aside to talk.

"Joon, you were lately chased by zombie swine from Canada to North Carolina overnight. Do you really find it so hard to believe she was targeted because she's of high magical value?" Sally was right, and Joon knew it. After everything that had happened, Joon couldn't very well pretend that the paranormal was just a myth. But Kylie, a guardian of the universe? How? Why? She was only a kid.

"I know it's a shock. That's why I wanted to tell you first," Sally said. "See, the average grizzly bear has better conversational finesse than I do. I was hoping you could help me break the news to your sister."

"And, we can't go home? Ever?"

"Someday, maybe, but not anytime soon. Not if you want her to be safe."

Though Joon was taken aback by Sally's bluntness, she appreciated the honesty. Of course, Joon wanted nothing more in the world than for Kylie to be safe. So, there was no other way.

"I'll tell her," Joon said. "You don't have to come. I think it should just be me."

The pain from Richie's nightmare—it hurt worse than the Black Dog vision, worse than anything he'd ever felt—evaporated not long after he woke up, but a chill had settled in his core. Even burrowing into every sheet and blanket in the room hadn't warmed him up.

"Have you ever tried writing these dreams down? It might help you remember more," Hope suggested, her voice soft and soothing. She sat with William at the foot of Richie's bed.

"No. I guess I never thought about that." Truth be told, Richie had never wanted to dwell on the nightmares that much, but he knew now that they were important. It was a good idea, if he could muster the courage. He went over the dream in his mind again, trying to pick out any detail that might be useful, but he mostly remembered the sensations and emotions, not the sights and sounds. Richie trembled at the memory of those hands moving inside his abdomen. William leaned over and put his hand on the pile of blankets approximately where Richie's shoulder was underneath all the fabric.

"I'm sorry, Richie. I didn't mean to cause anymore distress," Hope said.

"It's okay. We have to figure it out somehow." Richie sat up straighter and tried to put on a brave face.

"That's very altruistic of you. I wish I had picked up on something actionable. Such a horrible thing to do to someone…and it seemed to me like whoever it was didn't survive."

"Do you think that's why I'm so cold?" Richie's eyes widened. *Is this what dying feels like?* He wasn't sure he wanted to know.

"It's just a guess. What about you, William? Any ideas?"

"What? Oh, uh, no, nothing." William took his hand back and leaned against the footboard.

"Sally wanted to talk about it later. Maybe she got something out of it," Richie said. Hope nodded.

"Perhaps she did." She sighed. "At least, I hope so. There's not much we can do about it as long as our only suspects are little green men in flying saucers."

"I believe they're supposed to be gray, not green," Alex said from the doorway, making all three people in the room jump.

"Don't sneak up on me like that!" Richie said and pulled the blankets even tighter around himself.

"Sorry, I didn't mean to sneak," Alex said, raising an eyebrow. "I just thought you guys would want to know what Scarlet called about."

"Not really," Richie said, at the same time that Hope said, "I'd appreciate it." Alex apparently took that as near enough to an affirmative and went on with his story.

"She found these two girls lost in the forest and brought them to Sally. There was something about zombies, and anyway, the younger sister has the same aura as Richie and Jason. So now they're staying here with us." For a few moments there was silence as everyone sorted out what Alex had just rambled, but once Richie worked it out, the cold in his belly was almost forgotten.

"There's another Guardian? And it's a *girl*?"

"I think she's a little young for you," Alex warned. Richie was unfazed.

"What about her sister?"

"Well, maybe. Jenna's getting them settled in down the hall. Why don't you go see for yourself?" Alex said. That sounded like a fantastic idea to Richie.

"All right! Let's go!" Richie threw off his blankets and ran a hand through his hair to smooth out the rioting tangles. He was still in bright red pajamas with singed sleeves, but it would do. "You wanna come, Will?"

"I think I'll sit this out," William mumbled, crossing his arms over his chest. "You have fun."

"What, you're going to miss such a golden opportunity? Oh, wait, that's right, you're not into chicks, are you? Well, that's fine, you can still be my wingman. Come on!" Richie grabbed William's wrist and dragged him, stammering, out into the hall.

"Glad I could be of assistance," Alex called after them. Richie could practically hear him rolling his eyes.

Kylie floated into the bedroom like a ghost, not quite sure she was really there. Only the soreness in her side and stinging cuts on her leg, now bandaged, proved to her that all this madness was really happening. Cell service was back, and her phone was buzzing every few seconds. She'd have to check all those messages, in a minute. In a minute. When her brain stopped whirring.

"The sheets are in the wash as we speak. Scarlet is buying everything you should need, and if there is nothing else, I will leave you alone," said the ginger girl, Jenna, as she set a stack of pillows on the bed. "Don't forget the time zone is different. Be prepared for some jet lag."

"Thanks," Joon said. Her smile was drawn into a thin line. Jenna nodded and bowed out. Kylie sat down on the mattress, thinking maybe she was ready to check her phone. Sometime in the near future she might actually get to see those people, so she'd have to catch up with them sooner or later. She took the phone out of her pocket and turned on the screen.

"Kylie, there's something I have to talk to you about," Joon said, sitting down beside her. Kylie nodded, expecting Joon to reveal that they would be in this insane place for a couple weeks or something. Whatever. It was fine. Kylie didn't want to go home a moment before the pigs were gone.

"Sally pulled me aside earlier this morning—" Joon was cut off when a short, chestnut-haired guy slid into the doorway on his socks. Sally's brother, William, who the sisters had met downstairs a little while ago, trudged into view behind him.

"Hello, ladies. The name's Richie. I'm in a room a few doors over. Now, tell me, which one of you lovely girls is which?"

"I'm Joon, and this is Kylie."

"You're just in time. This place was starting to turn into a bit of a bachelor pad," Richie said. He plopped down on the bed on the other side of Joon.

"I think the four women who lived here already would beg to differ," William said, rolling his eyes.

"Are you going to work with me or not, mate?"

Joon giggled. Kylie leaned forward to see the exotic stranger past her sister's inconveniently placed body. In doing so she caught Richie's eye.

"Hello, little sis. You certainly are the prettiest of us yet," Richie said.

"Us…?" Kylie asked, although on the inside she was more interested in having been called the prettiest. There was a beat of silence, and Richie's smile waned.

"Has nobody told you yet?" Richie looked back at William. William looked over at Joon. Kylie followed their lead and stared at her sister as well, distantly aware that some significant exchange had occurred but clueless as to what it might mean.

"I was about to tell her," Joon said, "before you came in. I've been trying to find the right words."

"There aren't any right words," Richie said, a deep gravity replacing the flirtatiousness in his voice. "Might as well tell her now, while we're all talking about it."

"Tell me *what?*" Kylie met Joon's eyes. Joon sighed and put a hand on Kylie's back. And then she told her. Kylie lost her grip on her cell phone. It slipped out of her hand onto the floor as Joon struggled to break the unfathomable news as gently as possible. The phone clacked onto the hardwood, top corner first. The screen shattered and it slid underneath the bed, disregarded.

Jason walked up to the porch of Kitch Manor, his long and ever-growing legs taking the stairs two at a time. He adjusted the gargoyle's knitted winter toboggan on his way in the front door. His mother followed behind him, fidgeting with her scarf. They were both a little nervous, he supposed. Jason and Richie had just crashed into each other without a formal introduction. They hadn't needed to worry about bonding much, either. Richie saved Jason's life, so they were kind of friends by default, but distantly so. Meeting the newest Guardian would be more of a social endeavor, and Jason did not like those.

There was no one in the front room, which has clearly been designed as a foyer, but was now more of a den. They found Jenna in the adjacent sunroom, reading, and she told them that Kylie and Joon were out back.

"In this weather?" Pansy exclaimed.

"They *are* from Canada," Jenna replied.

Jason and Pansy wound their way to the west wall of the ground floor and outside into the screened-in patio. Kylie and Joon were sitting with their backs to the door, watching a movie on somebody's tablet computer. They both had headphones in, so they didn't hear the Drakes come up behind them.

"Um, hello?" Jason said, just a little louder than normal volume. Both girls jumped and whipped their heads around, then relaxed when they saw only two nonthreatening human beings. Sally had said they were chased into Brunswick by a hostile horde. It was natural for them to be on edge. Jason knew the feeling, although not with zombies.

"Hi." The older, blonder girl smiled and took out her earpieces. Her sister removed her headphones, too, but didn't quite manage the smile.

"Hey. I'm Jason, and this is my mom, um, Ms. Drake." He held out his hand, and each of the sisters shook it and gave their name. The older girl, Joon, had a firm, brisk handshake. The younger one had an arm like limp spaghetti. She was Kylie, the Guardian Jason had come to meet. Her handshake didn't inspire much confidence, but Jason wouldn't hold it against her. It had been over a year since Jason's first brush with Guardianship, and he still felt like overdone noodles. Kylie's world had been upturned only a few days ago.

"So, how are you girls settling in?" Pansy asked after a long quiet moment.

"We're getting there." Again, it was Joon who answered. "Sally says that Kylie can start homeschool in a week or two, and that will probably help. A little structure, you know." Joon and Pansy continued to converse like parents do, while neither Jason nor Kylie said a word. They just looked at each other. Kylie could have been one of hundreds of girls at Jason's middle school, wearing brightly-colored, tight-fitting clothes and more make-up than face. Kylie was just a normal, human girl, totally out of place. Jason tiptoed around his mother and came to sit beside Kylie, cross-legged on the floor. Thanks to his latest growth spurt, Jason was just a couple inches short of her eye level.

"What're you watching?"

"Some stupid documentary about aliens and pyramids." Kylie sighed. "I don't even know. We usually watch horror movies, but that's just a little too real for me right now."

"Yeah, I feel you. That's why most of my favorite horror flicks are B-movies, because they're too lame to be real."

"I don't know what to believe is real anymore. I know there are zombies, and werewolves, and *cat people*, and that one guy is a vampire...there's just so much. What else is out there, too?"

"I can probably answer most of your questions," Jason said, "and Sally's library can tell you just about anything else. It's really fantastic. That's where I learned most of what I know about the Guardians. We can check it out anytime you're ready."

"Uh, okay, but, not today, please. That's more than I can deal with. But maybe you can tell me about zombies? I don't want to be surprised again."

"Well, I don't know a *whole* lot about zombies, but I'll try. Where do you want me to start?"

"Where do they come from? Do they ever rot away? How many ways can you kill them? What—"

"Whoa, slow down! One at a time! Okay, so they come from dead bodies, obviously. Someone has to reanimate them, and there's more than one way to do that. There are even living zombies made using certain plant cocktails, but the undead kind require magic. Whether or not they rot, and how you have to kill them, depends on what kind of ritual was used to bring them back."

"Do they remember who they were?" Kylie's voice wavered at the end, and Jason had to wonder how many zombies she had met who'd been people she'd known.

"I don't think so," Jason said. "I guess there could be some memories firing off in their brains, but they aren't meant to be people, exactly. Zombies are made to do their master's bidding. They aren't meant to think, only to do what they're told. But, then again…"

"It depends upon how they were made," Kylie finished. "I guess it's more complicated than I'd thought. Did you learn all this from Sally?"

"No. Some of it I picked up just because I grew up here. We accept the magical side of the world. Well, except zombies. It's illegal to make those here. You know, the whole slavery thing. There are some wandering around out in the woods, though. We don't really know how they get there. I know this is a lot to take in, but I promise, it isn't too hard to wrap your head around once you get used to it."

Sitting in her bed in the basement of the Manor, Sally pulled up Tyler's file on her laptop and opened the email containing the latest x-rays she'd ordered. He was healing quickly, faster than a human would from such grievous wounds as he had sustained, but that made it difficult to stay ahead of any problems in the progress of the complex injury. Sally wanted to keep a close eye on it, but she also preferred not to subject a twelve-year-old child to any more radiation than necessary. She nestled into the pile of pillows at her back and then began scrutinizing the white shadows of the numerous pieces of metal hardware in Tyler's hip and leg to make sure they had all remained in their proper places. Lost in the high-contrast image in front of her, Sally had no idea how much time had passed when she was startled by someone pounding on the outside door to the basement. Locals knew that was the door to her practice, such as it were. Assuming anyone making like a battering ram against that door must be experiencing an emergency, Sally slapped the laptop shut, threw on a bathrobe, and sprinted down the small maze of corridors toward the door.

Two werewolves met Sally at the door holding most of a body on a sheet of plywood between them. Sally recognized both of them, but not the corpse. The trunk of the body had been ripped open from collarbone to groin and the contents most indelicately handled, but the face, though smeared with blood and gore, was unblemished.

"Miss Sally, our afternoon patrol found a body," the female werewolf said.

"I can see that."

"Our alpha said that the Codes demand we bring it to you for investigation," the other messenger added.

Sally nodded. She had stipulated that any murder victims be brought to her for autopsy, given that Brunswick didn't have any proper law enforcement, and the poor, mangled creature in front of her most certainly appeared murdered.

"I don't recognize her. Do either of you?" Sally glanced from one werewolf to the other.

"No," the female said, "we've never seen 'em before." She shook bouncy curls of flaxen hair out of her face. Her eyes darted without pause to look at anything but their dripping cargo, and her rapid, shallow breaths puffed the bitter scent of her anxiety past the barrier of air conditioning. The more Sally looked at it, the more this kill jangled her own nerves, but she doubted it was for the same reasons.

"Right then, come with me." Sally whirled around, robe fluttering behind her. "I've got a room we can use down here." She barreled down the hall and stopped at a door just before the junction with the living room. She fished out the chain around her neck and unlocked the door with the key that had the pink skull on it. Inside the long-neglected Dissection Room 1, papers littered the gurney and a tank of bright orange frogs took up most of one counter along with their heat lamp. It would have to do. She had things going on in Dissection Room 2. Sally gathered up the papers and shoved them in a drawer of paper gowns where they would be right at home.

"Okay, slide it onto the table. *Carefully!*" Sally watched the werewolves maneuver the corpse onto the gurney and winced as something, or part of something, fell out of the open body cavity and onto the floor. Not a great start to an investigation.

"Leave the board against the back wall and get out of here. I've got work to do," Sally said. The delivery crew was quick to do as they were told, not even bothering to shut the door behind them. Sally took an audio recorder off the frog-free counter and set it by the body's head.

She took a small remote the size of a heavy-duty laser pointer and pressed the big "on" button at the top. She listened for the tiny electronic whirring that told her the six hi-def video cameras around the room had turned on. Focused on the table from various angles and two distances, they somewhat addressed the need to photograph an autopsy or dissection while also wrist-deep in one. Sally started the audio recording as well, then put on the first of many sets of gloves and started narrating even as she dug around in drawers for supplies.

"Today's date is September seventh, 20—. The time is, ah, I don't know, I don't have my phone on me. I will record the time at the end. Let me just scoop this off the floor real quick." *Way to sound like a* real *doctor, Sally.* She rolled her eyes at herself and grabbed a tray out of an upper cabinet. She carefully scraped what turned out to be a deliberately excised kidney off the tile and onto the tray. She remembered another kidney removal and tried not to think about it.

"Gather evidence first, speculate never," she said aloud, standing and setting the tray of kidney on the table beside its owner. "So, external examination, sort of. Appears human, Caucasian female, about five foot four, brown hair." Sally peeled back an eyelid. A second, thinner lid underneath covered the eye from the other direction. "Brown eyes. Presence of nictitating membrane rules out 'human.' No clothes left and no identifying scars or tattoos that I can see right off the bat. Clear signs of trauma, though."

Sally began to describe the damage she could see from the outside in as much detail as possible. Even without breaking out the tools, on closer examination Sally could see enough organs to realize that the human shape of the corpse belied its true identity. The absence of certain organs could have been explained by a variety of things, most likely the injuries. The twin uteri were so badly damaged it was hard to say for sure if there was actually supposed to be one or two, but the small, iridescent spheres and silvery, wire-like veins that connected them could only belong to a cotu. Another step in identifying her, but not in explaining what the hell happened.

"There are traces of bleeding around all the wounds, so she must have been alive or very, very recently so when they were inflicted. These are very clean cuts. They must have been made by a smooth blade. It looks like scalpel incisions to me, but obviously I'm most familiar with those. I'm going to take up-close photos before I continue on to the internal examination."

An exhaustive photography session later, Sally took out her gleaming instruments one by one and began incising, though it proved to be almost unnecessary. The abdomen was already cut open down the center and under the rib cylinder. Sally set the audio recorder down on the table and continued to give an inventory of her observations. Hardly an organ in the abdominal cavity was left in place. Attachments had been cut and everything shoved to the sides. Some organs were removed entirely, including the most important one of all. Sally stopped narrating mid-sentence. She ran her gloved finger over the empty niche in the spine where the Stone was supposed to rest. There was a cold, slimy feeling in her stomach. Sally pulled her hand out and leaned against the table. She took a deep breath, her scent glands soaking with the smells of aging blood, disinfectant, and frog water. She started talking again.

"Extracirculatory veins severed and protective sac torn around Stone. Stone removed. I maintain blood loss during mutilation as the most likely cause of death, but removal of the Stone is also a possible cause. It would be difficult to determine which resulted in death first. Just when you think you've seen everything." Sally remembered Richie's dream of several days before. Was this what he had predicted? But this poor girl had died only hours before. Why had Richie's nightmare given so little warning this time? Unless this was going to happen again.

When Sally emerged at last from her basement lair, Alex and the girls were waiting in the living room for her. At the sound of the door, every face turned to Sally. She closed the door, came over, and flopped down on the sofa between Jenna and Scarlet. Sally never slumped, but Alex read defeat in the slight sag to her shoulders.

"Scarlet told us what happened. So what do you think?" Hope barely waited for Sally to get seated. She wasn't the only one who was impatient, though. They all were. The last time they had faced a murder like this was before the Brunswick Codes, and the town was bound to grow ever more anxious the longer it took to find answers. The Codes were accepted by almost everyone in Brunswick now—some residents couldn't even remember a time before them—but peace is always fragile, and Alex's skin prickled at the thought of old conflicts erupting.

"I don't know what to think," Sally said, rubbing her temples. "There's not much to work with. I can tell you plenty of gory details about how she died, more than you would ever want to know, but I can't find anything to tell us who killed her. How're y'all faring?"

"I think I know who she is," Scarlet said. She forced a smile to lighten the atmosphere.

"That's a good start," Sally said, a little more brightly. Everyone leaned towards Scarlet, anxious for word of some progress. Scarlet shrank back into the cushions, intimidated by the attention.

"I just, you know, worked my way through the werewolf grapevine, and it seems like a she-cotu in Black Mountain disappeared a couple days before we found the body. Here, I found a picture." Scarlet reached into one of the many pockets on her cargo shorts and pulled out her cracked and bruised cell phone. She flipped it open and pressed a few buttons, then held out the phone for the others to see. It was an image Scarlet had taken of a Missing Person poster. Alex squinted at the phone. The picture was hard to see on the small, pixelated, much-abused screen, but Sally was willing to venture that it *could* be the face of the body downstairs.

"Any indications why someone might have killed her?" Sally asked. Scarlet shook her head.

"I'm still working on it," Scarlet apologized, averting her eyes like it was a personal failure on her part that finding information was a time-consuming process.

"I have a theory," Jenna spoke up. "We can't pin everything on my in-laws, but sometimes the perpetrator really is one of the usual suspects. John Knightwood certainly wasn't happy when his son got community service for vandalizing the Nocturnal Peoples Community Center. Perhaps he took out his anger on a randomly chosen cotu—an out-of-towner, so the Brunswick Codes couldn't touch him. Then ripping out her Stone would be symbolic." Jenna referenced her past so rarely, sometimes Alex forgot that she had at one time been married off to a Knightwood, a family of human supremacists which had been causing trouble since the early days of Brunswick, but who refused to leave. Apparently, that would mean giving ground to the subhumans. As theories go, it wasn't bad.

"I could maybe believe that John is capable of murder, but a murder like *that*?" Scarlet said. "I'm not sure even someone as hateful as him could manage it."

"Hate can make people capable of incredible things," Hope said. The other girls continued to discuss the possibility of John as the murderer, but Sally was chewing her tongue in that peculiar way of hers, deep in thought. Alex kept his eyes on Sally, sure that one of her insights was imminent. After a few minutes, Sally finished her musing and interrupted the conversation.

"What sort of job does John have again?"

"He's a lawyer," Alex replied. "Remember when he did that case a few years ago, defending that human guy who tried to kill his sister with a silver penknife, because she turned out to be a werewolf?"

"Why does it matter?" Hope asked.

"I'm just trying to decide if he would have the skill. He wouldn't need much—this wasn't professional surgery—but he would have to know a little cotu anatomy."

"Isn't it possible he could have just looked it up and winged it?" Hope asked.

"I suppose anything's possible," Sally said. "But I want more than a hunch to go on before we investigate John, or any of them. Imagine the backlash from that community if we blame a Knightwood and then find out we're wrong."

"Do we have any other suspects?" Alex asked. No one said anything for a long moment.

"Maybe a cotu serial killer," Jenna suggested. "Someone with a fetish for Stones."

"Jesus, I hope not," Sally said.

"Probably not. That was a little out in left field."

"Aliens?" They all turned to stare at Scarlet once again.

"Are you serious?" Alex asked, trying not to be sarcastic. Scarlet once told him that you could set bowls of honey inside circles of mushrooms to get on the good side of the fairies, and everyone knew that fairies were pure myth. She might believe aliens abduct and eviscerate cotus, too.

"Sure. It could happen," Scarlet replied. Hope and Jenna exchanged a long-suffering look.

"I suppose it could," Sally said. Alex couldn't tell if she was just humoring Scarlet or actually taking Marvin the Martian into consideration as a suspect. "But let's watch John Knightwood for a while before we start looking into extraterrestrial criminals. From a moral standpoint, I certainly wouldn't put it past him." Alex nodded. He remembered the trouble John caused when he was a younger man. Nothing so great as murder, but perhaps only by serendipity. He and a few of his buddies hid in the trees during a full moon and shot at the werewolves below with homemade silver birdshot several times before they were caught. Later he escalated to playing Van Helsing and tried to put a stake in somebody. Fortunately for John, that someone happened to be Alex, who decided not to kill the brat, mostly for political reasons. Maybe that had been the wrong decision.

Sally hadn't updated the writing on the mirror since the day before yesterday, and it was making William nervous. He understood that she was a little busy, what with the murder and all, but, still, how he was he supposed to know what to do? William looked himself up and down in the glass. Shirt, jeans, hair brushed, was that everything?

"You're forgetting something, you know," William's reflection chided him. It crossed its arms and shook its head, tsk-ing.

"That's not very helpful." William glared at the surly thing in the mirror.

"What fun would that be?"

William growled and looked down at the floor, hoping his reflection would give up and leave him alone. He stared at his sock-covered toes for a solid ten seconds before realizing what he was missing.

"Shoes!" Triumphant, William ran to his closet and dug his shoes out of the pile of junk that littered the floor. His reflection stayed put and rolled its eyes.

"Finally! You're so *stupid*, Jack. I can't understand how you've survived this long."

"My *name* is *William*." He fought the urge to throw a shoe at the mirror and shatter his doppelgänger into countless minuscule shards. The damned thing would just show up somewhere else.

"Whatever you say, Jack," the reflection said, smirking. "Hey, while we're getting reacquainted, why don't we have a little fun? That slut down the hall's probably still asleep. What was her name? Julie? Jane?"

"Joon," William said, gritting his teeth and trying hard to focus on tying his shoelaces. "And she's not a slut, okay? She's just some girl."

"Aren't they all the same?"

William couldn't stand it anymore. He jumped to his feet and whirled on the mirror, fists clenched so tight his fingernails drew blood.

"I *told you* we're, I mean I'm, not going to do that anymore, okay? It's just...wrong!"

"You didn't used to think so."

"Well, I've changed my mind."

"Apparently not much, because I'm still in here." The reflection tapped a finger against its temple. Then it reached behind its back with the same hand. William knew what he would see before it brought its hand back around. Sure enough, his reflection pulled a knife out of its pocket—*the* knife, abandoned in a gutter over a hundred years ago but somehow always there to remind him. It thrilled William to see his old friend, the blade, but it terrified him too. With a knife in his hand, he was never quite sure who was wielding whom.

"So, what do you say?"

William had no idea what he would say, but as it turned out he didn't get the chance. A knock came at the door, and William took the opportunity to avoid giving an answer. Thankfully, Mirror William was startled by the sound, and promptly turned back into a normal reflection. William got up and opened his door to Richie, standing there shivering in his pajamas with his arms crossed protectively over his chest. It was just barely after sunrise; Richie was never up this early unless one of his first-person prophesying episodes woke him up. William ushered him into the room. Richie closed the door behind himself. He flopped down on top of William's pillows, staring vacantly at the ceiling. William sat on the other end of the bed and waited for him to speak.

"You know about that body someone found, right?" Richie's voice, normally a big, boisterous sound, was small and wavering.

"I'm pretty sure everyone in town has heard."

"Her belly was cut open and her Stone was taken out," Richie said, an octave above his usual pitch. William swallowed.

"Yeah."

"Well, that's just like the dream I had, and I thought it must have been about her. I felt terrible that I didn't know enough to save her, but now I'm not sure the dream was even about her because I just had the same nightmare again tonight. God, why is it so cold in here?" Richie hugged his knees to his chest, shivering more than ever. William grabbed the comforter from where it lay abandoned in a heap on the floor and handed it to him. "What if it's me this time?"

"No, no it can't be you," William argued. "I mean, that's never happened before, right? None of your dreams have been about you. The last one was about Jason." Richie shook his head and burrowed further into the blanket.

"The first time it was me. The first nightmare I had that came true, it was only a little thing, I dreamed that I failed a test at school and it happened the next day. I only remember it because the questions on the test in my dream were the exact same as the ones on the real test, but of course I thought it was a coincidence at the time. So, yeah, it was me then, why couldn't it be me again?"

"Well, it won't. They'll have to kill me before I'd let that happen to you," William promised.

"I know. Thanks." Richie tried to smile. "But…you can't always be there, you know?"

"Why not?"

"Things just don't work that way. What if you're asleep? You can't watch me forever."

"Well, well, we've been working on your fire powers, you'll be fine. Between the two of us, you'll be fine." William nodded, trying to work up confidence in his own logic. It made sense, didn't it? He could keep Richie safe. And Richie wasn't totally helpless himself, so, it would be okay. It had to be.

He looked back up at Richie. Richie nodded too, but the set of his face and the slouch in his posture didn't reflect William's hopefulness.

"Maybe. I'll stay close to home, I guess. Maybe it'll be all right. Dammit, I shouldn't have to worry about this. No one should. Just… why? Who would do that to somebody else?"

Jack would. William stiffened, terrified for a moment that Richie had heard the voice, too. Richie was still staring into space, looking disgusted as he thought about the kind of person that would cut up other people. Of course he hadn't heard it.

You would, though. You know I'm right.

Not to Richie. I'd never hurt him.

Whatever you say…

"Shut up," William grumbled under his breath.

"Did you say something?"

"Um, no, nothing. Nothing."

Kylie r u ok?

Where r u?

No one can find u what the hell is going on?

Kylie talk to me

Plz txt back

Kylie sat on the patio, her new favorite place to be alone, and scrolled through yet more text messages from her friends. Many of them had given up trying to contact her by now—they probably thought she had either forsaken them or was dead—but a few of her besties were still holding out hope. Her fingers itched to text back, to say she was alive, to ask what the damage was back home, but just like the past hundred times she'd checked her phone, she didn't respond. She wasn't sure why she kept torturing herself this way. She just couldn't let go.

Through the glass door, Kylie could see Joon at the kitchen table with Sally. They were finalizing Kylie's registration for homeschooling in North Carolina, a place she couldn't even point out on a map. How they could do that when Sally was also trying to get the two sisters declared dead in Canada was a mystery, but Kylie didn't care. They'd figure it out. Alex wandered in the room, saying something to Sally. He looked up and met Kylie's eyes. She turned away, but a minute later she heard the patio door slide, and Alex flopped onto the couch diagonal to where Kylie was sitting.

"What's up, kid?" He tilted his head and waited for Kylie to say something. Her first thought was to get up and leave. Jason assured her that Alex intended her no harm, but Kylie remained suspicious of anyone that wasn't strictly among the living. He seemed like he meant well, though, and Jason seemed comfortable with him.

"I'm just, I don't know, moping I guess. Checking my phone. Everybody wants to know if I'm all right, and I can't tell them anything." Kylie clicked the screen off but continued to stare at it.

"Uh-huh." Alex, too, fixed his gaze on the blank phone screen. "Have you thought maybe you should get rid of that thing? I mean, you can't really use it, except to torment yourself. And, I don't know much about technology, but don't those things have GPS trackers? You should probably go ahead and drop it in the most convenient swimming pool or something."

"I suppose you're right." Kylie curled her fingers around the phone. "I guess I'll just go find a swimming pool then, eh? In the fall." She gave Alex a good-naturedly exasperated look.

"Okaaay, what about the lake?"

"That's polluting! How you could you even suggest such a thing?"

In half an hour, Kylie stood by the muddy shore of the lake, Kitch

Manor looming in the distance behind her. The walk had been shorter than she expected, which was good, because she hadn't talked herself out of it yet. Now that she was here, though, it was hard to follow through. Kylie pulled back her arm, tried not to think about what she was doing, and threw her cell phone as far out into the lake as she could. It wasn't a fantastic throw, but it was enough. The phone plopped into the murky water several feet out and instantly sank from sight. Kylie turned to go back to the Manor, not sure whether she was predominantly relieved or heartbroken.

A few minutes later, a round, gray head like a slippery football with eyes rose up from the water and bobbed to the shore. She spit out the dead cell phone in the mud and duckweed by the bank, watching Kylie's figure retreat into the distance. Well, that was just no fun at all. Who taught *that* girl how to play fetch?

6

Brunswick

"What *are* you watching?" William stumbled down the last few stairs, blinking drowsily at the bloody massacre on the television screen.

"Oh!" Joon looked over the back of the couch, surprised to find someone else awake at three AM. "I'm sorry. I didn't wake you up, did I?"

"Uh, no. No, you didn't," William answered, rubbing the back of his neck. "I wasn't asleep. Mind if I join you?"

"Not at all." Joon curled up her pink-slippered feet to give him the option of sitting beside her. William stared suspiciously at the vacant seat for a moment before taking it.

"It's just some silly, gory monster movie," Joon explained. "I can't watch them with Kylie anymore, since, you know, what happened. They scare her too much. I still love them, though. I know, I'm weird, but they're kind of my weakness." Onscreen, a giant creature that looked as much like a pile of scrap rubber as anything else tromped through a farm amongst a few flustered but otherwise unimpressed chickens.

"You're not weird. Does this have a plot I should know about?"

"I came in during the middle, so I wouldn't know. From what I've seen so far, I think it has something to do with college students and a cursed mud puddle." Joon shrugged. She didn't really watch horror movies for the quality of their story. Bloody films with gaping plotholes were much more fun. William nodded and fixed his eyes on the screen. Joon settled down into the cushions and watched the supernatural histrionics, wondering how she could still enjoy this sort of thing after living out her own horror movie.

"I really need to find a job," she said with a sigh. William glanced her way, tilting his head in puzzlement.

"Where did that come from?"

"All I've done since Kylie started classes is sit around and watch these movies. It's helped keep me sane, I guess, in a way, but I need to be useful again, you know?"

"I wouldn't know what that's like. I've never exactly been a contributing member of society."

"I'm sure that isn't true," Joon said. He looked down at the floor and didn't say anything. Joon decided to change the subject. She surveyed the room for inspiration.

"Whose portrait is that over the fireplace?" Joon had never paid much mind to the three framed figures on the wall, but she needed something to talk about.

"Oh, that's my parents and my aunt," William told her, brightening. "The house was built after I'd moved away, so I'm not in it. It's a great painting of them. Photography was still a little too newfangled. The rich folk still preferred old-fashioned canvas. Momma is the brunette and the platinum-blonde in a man's suit is my aunt. She's a little…eccentric."

"She's still around?" Joon squinted at the portrait, but in the dim light of the television all she could see was vague shapes, and she didn't remember what it looked like. She made a mental note to take a look later, when there was daylight.

"Well, she's still alive, if that's what you mean," William answered. "They all are. I haven't seen any of them in a long time, though. They moved to Australia after the youngest left the nest."

"Wow. That's quite a move."

"They kind of had to. People around here were wanting them to leave. No one wants my family around. We seem to be genetically unlikeable."

"Aw, don't say that," Joon protested. She nudged William's leg with her foot. "I think you're likable."

"You *do*?"

"Of course." Emboldened by his meekness, Joon stretched her feet out into William's lap. It had been a long time since Joon had felt free to be a little irresponsible, and she had missed it. "If I didn't like you, I wouldn't have let you sit with me, would I?"

William shifted, looking at her feet with some bafflement. He lifted his hand, and Joon hoped to goodness he wouldn't push her off, because then there would be no end to the awkward.

"Well, I guess that's true…" His hand landed on her foot, caressed her ankle. "Thank you."

It was nearly sunrise. Joon had long since fallen asleep, but William remained awake, still watching the television and stroking Joon's feet. He'd been nervous at first. He wasn't sure he trusted himself this close to a woman, yet it seemed to be going well enough.

Sure, sure, it's all fine and dandy now, isn't it? Rachel sashayed into view from behind the sofa, blood dripping from the tattered hem of her once-white chemise, now stained a rusty orange. William closed his eyes to the specter, a knot tightening in his chest. Not her again.

You know, we were like this once, Rachel whispered. Her steps came closer, and William couldn't fight the urge to open his eyelids. She knelt at his feet, strips of slithering muscle visible where swatches of her skin had been torn away. She reached out an arm, bone peeking through a gaping hole in her wrist, and William pressed himself back into the couch to avoid the dead woman's touch. To his horror, she put her twisted, bleeding fingers not on him, but on Joon. Rachel's fingers danced up Joon's shin, leaving red spots on the fresh skin.

Will you love her like you loved me?

William swatted Rachel's hand away from Joon, who murmured in her sleep and curled her legs up into her body. Rachel's blood rubbed off onto her pajama shorts.

"I didn't love you," William said, trying to keep his voice low. The last thing he wanted was for Joon to wake up while this thing was in the room.

But you wanted me, Rachel taunted, fluttering her lashes above glassy, pearl-colored eyes. *And you want Goldilocks here, too, don't you, you filthy son-of-a-bitch? It's just a matter of time before she joins me and my sisters.* Rachel licked her lips and smirked.

"See, this is why I think you aren't a real ghost," William said, "because why would you want other girls to die like you?"

Is it so strange to think I want company? Rachel's eyes flashed, and her smile turned into a sneer. *What if I want someone else to understand? Someone who has suffered the way I did?* She stood, hands fisted at her sides. The blood from her wounds flowed more freely, an impossible amount of red liquid seeping into the carpet beneath her. *Someone else who knows what it's like to be torn apart by your claws and your teeth and your—*

"Shut up!" William leapt to his feet and stared down at the dripping crimson succubus standing before him, nearly touching her. "You deserved it. Joon doesn't."

Are you so sure? You once thought I was flawless, too.

"I don't have to put up with this," William growled, shoving past Rachel, trying to ignore the red smear the touch left on his palm. He darted for the stairs, leaving the ghost in the living room to stare at Joon's clueless, sleeping form.

The purple laptop mocked her from the top of the breakfast table. *Come on, Kylie,* she imagined it taunting. *It's just an eight-line poem.* Yes, and it was eight lines more than Kylie knew what to do with. Of all the things she'd had to do in school, interpreting poetry was the most loathsome. She could escape an undead porcine horde, but throw Emily Dickinson at her and she was paralyzed.

"Jason, can you help me with this?" Kylie begged, not bothering to hide a pathetic moan of disgust. She slouched back in her chair. Jason got up from the seat across from her and knelt at her side. He was tall enough to reach the keyboard even from his knees.

"What's up?"

"Does your thing with languages mean you can do English homework?"

"We'll see. Is this Emily? Yes, it is. What's the problem?"

"I don't know what she's talking about, and her punctuation is weird," Kylie whined, her eyes pleading with the master of all tongues. Jason laughed warmly, nodding.

"She does like her dashes. She uses 'em like commas, colons, periods. You can use the sentence structure to infer what they're supposed to be. But let's just start with the first line. 'Much Madness is divinest Sense.' You get what she's saying?"

"No," Kylie pouted.

"She's saying that what is called 'madness' actually makes total sense, 'to a discerning eye.' Then the third line is basically the antithesis of the first."

"The ant-what?"

"Antithesis. The opposite. 'Much sense' is 'the starkest madness.' So the first three lines are kind of one broken sentence. See if you can figure out the rest yourself." Jason got up and went back to his own assignment, leaving Kylie to struggle alone.

"So your gift really does cover English homework," Kylie said, procrastinating with conversation.

"Maybe," Jason replied, head still firmly planted above his math book. "I don't think so. That seems like kind of a stretch from universal translation to universal poetry interpretation."

"Well, maybe I'll get the gift of literary...something that'll make this easier." Kylie threw her hands up in despair.

"Is that really the coolest thing you can think of?" Jason challenged good-naturedly, eyeing her with a glint of mischief.

"Well, I've thought of other things," Kylie said. "There's always invisibility."

"Cliché, my friend. Far too cliché. Also, it kind of requires you to, you know, be naked. That's, uh, not a can of worms I want to open." Jason sat back, math problems abandoned. He looped an arm over the back of his chair to twist toward Kylie.

"Okay, how about mind-control?"

"That's more interesting. I feel like that ability might be a little dangerous to have, though. It's a slippery slope from an extra cookie at lunch to world domination."

"All right, then, mister," Kylie said, enjoying their game. "What would you have wanted?"

"Selective permeability."

Kylie blinked. "Come again?"

"My biology teacher said that cell membranes are selectively permeable," he explained, leaning forward in his excitement. "They only let through what they want to. I thought that would be awesome. Like, sometimes I'm bulletproof, but sometimes I walk through walls. Maybe that's more like selective density..." Kylie stared at him, trying to decide if his show of nerdiness was more impressive or weird. Jason eyed her face for a moment and then shrugged, relaxing against the back of the chair again.

"Doesn't matter what I wanted, though, does it? I got what I got."

"I wouldn't exactly have asked for *any* of it," Kylie said. "I don't think any of us would."

"Not for all the money in the world." The steamy Scottish accent made Kylie's heart flutter. Richie walked into the room from behind her, bound for the pantry. "At least you two get to see your families."

"What, does yours not know?" Kylie asked.

"No, they don't," Richie replied, retrieving a bag of potato crisps. "They don't even know where I am or if I'm alive. I thought my so-called 'gift' was hurting them, so I ran away over a year ago. Then I found out the truth and that was worse, so I never went back." He joined them at the table and shoved a handful of crisps in his mouth.

"I'm not sure I wouldn't rather have my mom be somewhere else," Jason said. "I'd miss her, but at least she might be safe. Emphasis on the *might*, I guess." He reached over and stole a bite of Richie's snack.

"I couldn't," Kylie said, shaking her head. "I couldn't live without Joon. She's like my sister *and* my mother now. The only family I've got left. Can I have some of those?" Richie tilted the bag her way.

"Well, we're kind of like a family," Jason said. The other two Guardians stared at him blankly for a moment.

"You know...like, brothers and sister? Anybody?" Jason looked at them, slumping down in his seat when no one said anything. Richie and Kylie glanced at each other.

"I guess...I'd never really thought of it that way," Richie replied at last. "I was thinking more like 'fellow bitches of fate' or something." Kylie gave a little gasp, quite by accident.

"I like Jason's idea better," she said. "It's a lot more comforting." Jason regarded Kylie with silent gratitude.

"I'm not usually one to see the silver lining," Richie said with a shrug. "It's probably a good thing one of us does."

"How do you feel about Halloween?" William looked up at Joon from his sketchpad. She sat against the foot board of his bed, applying for jobs on Jenna's tablet, but paused when he spoke.

"I'm not sure it'll be the same after being attacked by a zombie horde. I used to think it was a lot of fun, though. Why?" She brushed her hair out of her face and turned her cerulean eyes on William.

"I was just, thinking," he said, adding a few strokes to his sketch, "my sister's birthday is on Halloween, and she likes any excuse to throw a party. I've never really understood the birthday party thing, obviously we didn't do anything for mine—"

"What? When was yours?" Joon let the tablet drop to her lap.

"Hmm? Oh, last week. But Sally is—"

"Seriously? And you didn't say anything? Well, we are going out for dinner for your birthday *tonight*, mister!"

"We are?"

"We are!"

"Oh-kay. Thank you." He stared at his sketchpad for a couple seconds. Did that qualify as a date? "This is not how I planned this conversation."

"I'm sorry. Please continue. About your sister's birthday Halloween party," Joon said, smiling.

"Right! So, Scarlet was telling me that Sally used to do that very thing: Halloween birthday parties. But she hasn't done one in ten years, give or take. I was thinking about throwing one for her. Except I have no social graces or planning skills. You seem like you do."

"Ooh, that sounds like fun! God, I haven't thrown a party since high school, though. But, like, how hard could it be?" Joon narrowed her eyes and smiled wider. "I bet we could do it." Her face fell into a more thoughtful repose. "Still, we'd probably need help. Is there anyone other than us who isn't incredibly busy right now?"

William shrugged. "Jenna doesn't look that busy?"

"She doesn't look like much of a party person to me, either." Joon tapped a fingernail against the edge of the tablet. "But I'm being judgy. I shouldn't be judgy. She might be a crazy party animal."

"I don't know about that." William raised an eyebrow. "It won't hurt to ask for her help, at least. And you have to give her tablet back some day." He pointed with his pencil.

"Right." Joon looked down at the screen in her lap, and her face crumpled. "Trying to find a job is depressing." William nodded, hoping she couldn't tell that he had no idea what looking for honest work was like. Joon stared at the listings for a few seconds before setting the device aside.

"Hey, what are you drawing?" she asked. William clutched the sketchpad to his chest.

"Nothing."

"Oh, now I *have* to see!" Joon's eyes glittered mischievously. She lunged for the sketchpad. William yelped and leaned back to dodge her. Now that she was practically in his lap, though, he found it a little hard to concentrate on the game of keep-away, and Joon won the battle in short order. With a cry of triumph, she wrested his artwork away and sat back on her calves to examine it.

"Is this me?"

"Yeah. It's not done yet," William said.

"It's amazing. A little creepy, but amazing," Joon said. She glanced up at William and smiled. "You don't think you could have found a more glamorous moment to capture me in, though?"

"Why? Who wants to remember anyone the way they were posed and made-up? I'd rather capture you the way you really are."

Joon ran her fingers along the edge of the paper. It made William uncomfortable for her to be looking at his handiwork. He didn't like to show his drawings to anyone, but he especially did not like Joon scrutinizing his portrait of her. That's what he got for drawing her from life, but the temptation had been too strong. He was almost ready to rip the sketchpad out of her hands when Joon spoke again.

"Can I keep it?"

"Wh—I told you, it's not finished yet," William protested.

"Really? Sure looks finished to me." Joon squinted at the sketch, obviously trying to find what was missing. William felt the tightness in his chest easing.

"Trust me. It's not quite ready. Let me finish it, and then you can have it." William held his hand out, and after a moment of hesitation Joon returned his work.

"Okay. I'm going to hold you to that."

"I'm sure you will. If you're done with the tablet, should we go talk to Jenna now?"

Joon was surprised to find Jenna's room so colorful. Jenna had seemed drab to her, but the woman's room was all springtime pastels and cute flowers. Almost every inch of wall was lined with bookshelves, but those too were painted with small flowers and insects. The youthful decor did exaggerate Jenna's teenage appearance. In the middle of her fluffy, blue paisley comforter, she seemed suddenly childlike. Perhaps that was why her dress was usually so, well, old. At least then she looked grown up.

"We were hoping you could help us out," William was explaining, lounging in a swivel chair at Jenna's desk. "You've spent more time with Sally than I have in a long time, and we think a spectacle befitting Sally will require at least three people to pull off."

"You two are asking me to help you plan a birthday party?" Jenna said slowly, looking between them.

"A birthday Halloween party," Joon said.

"That's a new one. I would love to help, but I really don't think I'm qualified." Jenna shook her head.

"Why not?" Joon asked, at the same time as William said, "And you think I am?"

"It'll be fun," Joon said, not waiting for an answer. She had noticed that Jenna was the quiet one, but Jenna shouldn't let that stop her from joining their conspiracy. "You were our first choice, you know."

"Well, I guess, if you really want me to. But you've been warned—the last time I organized a party, we were fighting the Second World War."

"And I've never organized one in my life." William shrugged. "Just blame anything that goes wrong on me. I'm sure Sally will anyway. What else are brothers for?"

Joon ran through everything Sally had told her about William and the sports car as she did her make-up. It was Kylie's make-up, actually. Joon hadn't bothered to replace her own since they came here. The foundation wasn't quite the right shade. Joon didn't have any especially nice clothes, and her only jewelry was the simple daisy earrings she had been wearing when they ran into the woods. At least those were special.

Joon studied herself in the bathroom mirror, dissatisfied with her efforts. She knew she shouldn't be trying so hard. It was just a birthday dinner for a friend, and a new friend at that. But there was no denying that she wanted to impress him. Joon adjusted her magenta blouse and sighed. It would have to do. She grabbed her purse on the way through the bedroom she shared with Kylie and made her way down the hall to William's room.

He was on a bean bag in the corner with his bookshelves. He had dressed up too, sort of. His usual plain, black t-shirt had been replaced with a black button-up. His hair was still wet from a recent shower.

"Ready?" Joon asked. "If we get there soon, we might still beat the worst of the rush." William looked up with a start at the sound of her voice.

"Oh! Yes! Where's there?"

"You'll see." Joon was confident he'd like the restaurant she'd picked, as Sally had strongly suggested it. Joon wasn't as sure about herself, but hey, as long as it wasn't pizza. She motioned William to come hither and led the way to the car.

Joon knew some about the insides of cars, but not much at all about makes and models. What she could say for sure about this one was that it was sleek, shiny, painted glittering gold, and very expensive. Joon loved it and doubted she should be touching it.

"Sally's letting us take one of her good cars?" William spoke quietly. Maybe he was afraid Sally would hear and reconsider. Joon's mind tried not to boggle at the phrase "one of." What were the not-good ones like?

"Well, how did you think we were going to get there? Can't just call a taxi. Sally said I have to drive, though. I don't know what that's about, but, sorry?" Joon gave him an awkward, apologetic smile. William shrugged and climbed into the passenger side. Joon noticed for the first time that he had brought his sketchbook with him. What did he think he was going to need that for? It must be an artist thing.

"So how old are you this year?" Joon asked when they got on the road, trying to make conversation.

"A hundred and, uh," William paused, looking out the window, "seventy-five." Joon could think of no response. He didn't look much older than her. She couldn't begin to guess what that age meant to his own kind.

"Your earrings are nice," William said after a while.

"Oh, thank you. They were my mother's," Joon said, glad for the change in subject.

"They were," William said, echoing her. Joon felt the weight of his gaze on her for a long moment. She kept her eyes on the road. He hadn't said it like a question. More like an invitation. Joon readjusted her grip on the steering wheel.

"Both of my parents," she said at last. "How did you know?"

"Something in your voice. I don't know. So have you been taking care of Kylie by yourself?"

Joon nodded. The exit from town was coming up in front of them, so she needed to focus. The road appeared to dead-end abruptly in a wall of trees, but a friendly "You Are Now Leaving Brunswick" sign assured Joon this was indeed the way out. That didn't stop her heart from racing as she sped toward the columns of wood in front of her. William was gracious enough to forestall further conversation. Joon thought her heart might burst when the front bumper hit the trees, but it sailed straight through like Sally promised it would. A second later they were on a forested mountain road, and Joon began to breathe again. The GPS app on her phone, in which she had already input their destination, came to life, blurted a flurry of confused instructions, and finally told Joon to continue for six miles on the road she was already on. She hoped nobody in Brunswick was directionally challenged.

"That's tough. I had to take care of my little siblings on my own a lot of the time." William picked up right where they left off. "I always felt like I was doing the wrong thing."

"Oh my God, I know what you mean!" Joon paused to navigate a switchback. "Kylie keeps doing all this preteen angst, plea-for-attention stuff, and like, I hear you, but I have no idea what you need me to do."

"Right? You should have seen my brother at that age," William said. "I was so far out of my depth."

"You have a brother?"

"Yeah, but he's not on speaking terms with the family anymore."

"Yikes." Joon sucked a breath in through her teeth. "Not with anyone?"

"No one. You can put that in the 'could be worse' category." William made a tally mark in the air with his finger. Joon shuddered to think of becoming so estranged from her sister.

"You're obviously still close with Sally. You did something right," Joon said. A smile like a match flame flickered across William's face.

"Thanks. She wasn't an easy child, either, but disarmingly adorable. I knew all her tricks, though, so the cuteness only fooled me about fifty percent of the time."

They were still talking parenting when Joon pulled into a parking space at The Smiling Sprout Café. They either hadn't gotten there early enough, or everyone else had had the same idea, but the wait wasn't going to be too long. It was a charming little restaurant, all wood and natural decor. There were plants everywhere, even suspended from the ceiling in gravity-defying planters.

"How'd you find this place?" William asked, dropping onto a bench beside Joon.

"Sally told me," Joon said, a bit sheepishly. She grabbed a menu from the hostess stand and handed it to William, certain he would realize why here pretty quickly. She was right. His face lit up almost immediately.

"I have never seen a menu with so many things I can eat on it."

"If I'm not mistaken, you should be able to eat everything on it." Joon leaned against his shoulder so she could see, too. "Oh, that all looks really good." She didn't mean to sound quite as surprised as she was. William gave her an amused side-eye.

"What do you think vegetarians eat? Grass?" he said. A woman waiting across from them chuckled and tried to hide it by coughing. Joon supposed she deserved that.

"Okay, touché."

"Joon, party of two?" a pink-haired waitress called. Joon and William followed her to a table with a few stems of golden pathos trailing onto it from a low wall.

"Sally offered to pay, and since I still don't have a job yet, order gold leaf on everything if you like because we have the card of a woman with multiple sports cars," Joon said. William laughed.

"I don't think this is a gold leaf kind of place. But I'll take a good look at that drink menu. Still no luck with the job search?"

"Actually, I do have an interview Thursday for a waitressing job." Joon was glad that a little independence might be within reach, but she didn't feel too proud admitting that her best career prospect was as a waitress. At least, not to someone who probably didn't have a waitress anywhere in his family.

"That's great!" William said. "It is, right? Are you excited about it?"

"I think so. I just hope they don't ask for references," Joon said. "What's my last manager going to say? 'Well, she was a great employee right up until she ran off in the middle of a shift and never came back.'"

"I see how that could present a problem. I don't suppose there's any way of selling a good story to your old manager now, is there?"

"I doubt it." Joon shook her head and then brightened. "But enough about me! I have a present for you."

"Oh Lord, you didn't," William moaned theatrically.

"I did!" Joon reached into her purse and pulled out a small, rectangular package neatly enshrouded in Christmas tree wrapping paper. "Sally and I couldn't find any birthday wrapping paper, so, uh, merry birthday." Joon held it out across the table. William took it and tore the paper off in strips, unveiling a pack of twenty-four colored pencils. Joon didn't know thing one about what made a quality colored pencil, but these came from an art store and cost way more than she thought they had a right to, so they must be decent. William's admiring look indicated she had chosen well. She relaxed.

"Wow. Thanks. I actually brought something for you, too." William sat down the pencils and began to flip through the pages of his sketchbook. Joon started to protest, but then William found what he was looking for and flipped the book around to show her. She completely forgot what she was going to say.

It was the sketch of her he'd been doing that morning. True to his word, he had finished it, in exquisite detail. Every eyelash, every fold of her clothing, even a lifelike shine to her eyes—Joon wasn't sure she looked that real in the mirror. William had included the tablet she had been holding and the scene of the bedroom around her in equal quality, but he had only imparted color to Joon. Splashes of watercolor graced her clothes and body. Except her eyes. Those he had carefully rendered in intense shades of blue acrylic.

"That's beautiful!" A little inner voice pointed out that it was also a bit unnerving how well acquainted William was with her body, but Joon pushed the thought aside. He'd been nothing but a gentleman.

"So you like it?" he said, sounding like a nervous schoolboy.

"I love it! You're incredibly talented," Joon said. William grinned and carefully tore the page from the sketchbook. He handed it to Joon. She took it with only the tips of her fingers. It had been worth the wait for William to finish this. Joon would never have thought she could look so amazing sitting on the floor with messy hair.

"Sir?" Fifteen's timid voice was followed by a couple soft knocks at the door. "I think I found something." Vincent looked up from the pile of desiccated ingredients on his bed and gave her a withering look through the wood.

"I'm in the middle of a very important spell, Fifteen. Come back in a couple hours."

"I think you'll want to see this, sir," she insisted. "It could lead us right to the girl."

"Fine, fine, I'll put everything on hold *just for you*." Vincent didn't think Fifteen, using a computer, had a snowball's chance in New Orleans of finding someone who simply vanished, but she seemed certain. Vincent thought it wouldn't be so bad to let her keep herself busy, but now she kept bothering him while he was trying to do real work. Why couldn't she just go play video games with Sixteen and Eighteen?

Fifteen led him downstairs into the former living room of the rented house they had converted into a lab and living quarters. By the time the landlord figured out what they'd done to the place, they hoped to be long gone, although they had already stayed longer than Vincent would have liked.

"It took a while to get my hands on decent facial recognition software, and then to train it to track their faces, but we have a few hits from within a few square miles of each other, and I think I'm on the right track," she explained. Vincent nodded along, almost listening to the techno-babble. Fifteen's laptop, shiny silver with a slew of Southeastern Louisiana University stickers on the back, sat half-open on the coffee table amongst a trash heap of papers and takeout coffee cups.

"Please get to the point. I'm a very busy necromancer." Vincent swiped a few water bottles off the couch and sat down.

"Right." She opened the laptop and quickly logged in with about thirty keystrokes. She turned the screen to face him. A series of images of a young blonde woman filled the space. She was on security footage at the post office and the bank, having dinner with some guy in the background of another person's selfie. Incredibly, there was one beautiful, crisp picture of her and some green-eyed brunette on a sofa in their pajamas, watching TV, with white text in a gray bar across the middle reading "My leading ladies <3". Vincent could feel Fifteen watching him and glowing with self-satisfaction.

"That's the sister, isn't it?" she said.

"You're damn right, that's the sister." Vincent couldn't stop the grin that spread across his face. "I'll be a son of a gun. You did it. Where are these? You said it's all the same place."

"Almost the same place. They cluster around a location in western North Carolina. If we can find a flight, it shouldn't take too long to get there."

"Then start looking for one! I'll go tell the boys to pack it up. We're moving house."

Chantrelle sang along to the song in her headphones as she whisked the clothes out of her suitcase and flung them in the dresser drawers of their new digs. It certainly wasn't home, nothing ever was, but it was nicer than the last place. No roaches ran in terror when she turned on the lights. She could actually see herself in the mirror on the wall, not that she wanted to see her tight curls right now. She had let her hair go unattended during the last two days of travel, and now it was turning into some kind of wild beast. Well, there'd be time to deal with that tonight. Unless Professor LaMont was in one of his moods and they just had to get started *right away*. Chantrelle rolled her eyes at the thought. This thing he was working on now had made him worse than ever.

"Fifteen! Get in here!" The professor's voice boomed through the mostly empty building. *And here we go,* Chantrelle thought. But she dared not disappoint him.

"Just a second, sir, I'll be right there." She shut the drawer with her hip and made her way down the hall to the front room, a sad little kitchen piled with all the stuff they had yet to set up and hook up and science up. Professor LaMont had her laptop sitting open on the kitchen table on top of Quan's duffel bag. Nik leaned over the professor's shoulder on one side and Quan loomed over them both on the other.

"I need you to tell me your password," Professor LaMont said, sounding much like Chantrelle's petulant little brother.

"I'm sorry, my password is my face. Here." Chantrelle lifted the computer up to face level. Quan discreetly slid his duffel off the table and onto his shoulder while the software worked to recognize its mistress. Once it did, Chantrelle typed in the twenty-character random password she had memorized, hit enter, and handed the laptop back to the professor, wondering for a moment why she bothered with all the security when she was just going to give the thing to the boys anyway.

"So, what do you need, sir?" Chantrelle asked, doubting Professor LaMont would be able to use most of her programming. When it came to biology, the man was a genius, far outstripping anything Chantrelle could hope to accomplish. She might never catch up to his sorcery, either. But when it came to tech, she had him thoroughly beat.

"You said on the ride over that we could triangulate where the most promising image originated from once we got close enough to the cell towers," Nik said.

"But despite his enchanting use of long words, Seventeen can't begin to tell me how to do such a thing," Professor LaMont added. Nik shuffled his feet. Chantrelle closed her eyes for a moment before answering.

"I said it was possible to do that, in theory, and that I *might*, just might, be able to work out how to do it." Chantrelle glared at Nik who shrank even further into his sweater under her simmering gaze. She thought he would know not to tell the professor about that when she made it clear that she hadn't even tried it yet, but maybe she was the fool for expecting Nik to have a lick of common sense. Professor Vincent continued to stare at her expectantly. Over his head, there was sympathy in Quan's soft eyes. He must know there would be no rest for Chantrelle until she figured out how to find the source of the best signal. If she could do it. There would be no kind of rest ever if she couldn't.

"All right, I'll need to find some more equipment first." Chantrelle's shoulders sagged, just a smidge.

"Oh, while you're out, can you get some things for me?" Professor LaMont jumped up from the kitchen table and snagged a piece of paper out of the top of a box of paper and plastic dinnerware sitting on the counter. He handed it to Chantrelle. It was covered in his familiar chicken scratch, a variety of the scrawling, slanted cuneiform every professor seemed to adopt after a few years in academia. The list included things such as rice, chicken, live chickens, thirty pounds of lab-grade salt, and snake skin powder—"NOT powdered snake skin," he had told her time and again, though she couldn't see a difference. Chantrelle deemed it unlikely that finding all twenty-odd items he wanted, several of which she had never seen before, would take any less than several days. She didn't know what he would want her to get first and was afraid to ask. He would change his mind by the time she returned anyway.

"Yes, sir," Chantrelle agreed. She went back to her room for her purse and the communal credit card, then sailed out the front door, remembering dully when shopping used to be fun.

Rescued and Refurbished was something a little more than a junk store. Set in an old warehouse just at the edge of what passed for Brunswick's main thoroughfare, it sold everything from odd knobs and nails to beautiful restored furniture. Jenna supposed it was a bit like a one-man flea market. It was one of her favorite places in town. She usually gravitated toward the ample selection of used books, but not today. The owner rotated the stock seasonally to keep things interesting. It worked to his advantage, as there were few places to shop in or near Brunswick, so this time of year Rescued and Refurbished was the only "Halloween store" around. Give it a month or so and it would be the only available Christmas shop. But it was Halloween on Jenna's mind. Halloween and Sally's concurrent birthday. Birthdays received little fanfare in the Manor, in part because Alex had no idea when his was and it seemed cruel to make a fuss over something he couldn't have. There had been years when Sally had thrown Halloween parties, but she always insisted that they weren't for her birthday, and Jenna could believe that Sally honestly just enjoyed the excuse to stage another holiday celebration. Mostly they just watched marathons of Hammer films and ate Scarlet's spooky cupcakes on Halloween these days, while Hope did whatever witches do in the basement somewhere.

But not this year. Jenna powered through the smudged glass door of Rescued and Refurbished with a rare smile on her face. She surveyed the black-and-orange explosion before her, calculating her method of attack. The idea of organizing a party on Sally's behalf, not under her direction, was so joyously backwards. Jenna hadn't planned a social occasion in decades and was never very good at it, or so her mother said. She doubted William knew what he was doing, either, even though it was his idea. None of that would stop her. She could put up tacky Halloween decorations like the best of them, if she put her mind to it. Jenna concluded that the aisle with the glut of plastic skeletons showed promise. Sally liked skeletons. Jenna ensnared a squeaky-wheeled cart with one spindly arm and dragged it behind her into the stacks of bones.

With no regard for theme or style, Jenna tossed anything that struck her as particularly interesting or Sally-like into the cart as she weaved her way through the shelves and the scattered piles of seasonal wares. The more macabre the better, she supposed. That would be to Sally's taste. She avoided the books, as that was not her purpose and she would be tempted, as always, the leave with every last one of them. Jenna was in the process of examining a couple packs of white candles that claimed to bleed once lit when the scream of tortured hinges caused her to jump. She glanced around, but to her relief the smattering of other patrons hadn't seen her get spooked by a door. It was the side door, open and lazily drifting wider ajar in the wind. Just inside, John Knightwood stood and scanned the rest of the store with narrowed eyes while his only daughter grabbed a shopping basket. Jenna was unpleasantly surprised to see them. She didn't think any of their clan shopped local. There were too many people they didn't like to associate with. It was, however, quite characteristic of the whole family to walk off and leave the door gaping open. Jenna rolled her eyes. Her heart quickened as John and his progeny proceeded to walk right past the aisle in which she stood, but they were too busy whispering between themselves to notice her. Once she was sure they were past, Jenna dropped the candles onto the mountain of Halloween bric-a-brac in her cart and wandered over to the door, thinking to stop all the bought air from getting out.

Jenna had never come through this door, and when she reached it she immediately realized that it wasn't really meant to be a customer entrance. A few bits of trash escaping from the half-open dumpster were blowing about the alleyway. The bloodied rubber arm of some discarded decoration lolled out of the open side of the dumpster. The Knightwoods must have meant to avoid attention by eschewing the main entrance, only to be foiled by squeaky hinges. That brought a little smile to Jenna's face. She closed the door and went back inside. And turned around. And peered out the door again. There was something not quite cheesy enough about that rubber arm. The cracked crust of dried blood wasn't like the bright paints splattering everything in the store. After a moment of reluctance, Jenna plowed forward and leaned over the dumpster. It was as she had feared. No silly mannequin but the mangled body of a young woman lay buried in the garbage. Jenna's first thought was to call Sally, and then for a moment she panicked, remembering that Sally wasn't supposed to know where Jenna was. She was immediately embarrassed at herself. Her, a grown woman, paralyzed by the fear that reporting a murder might spoil her friend's surprise party. She ran back inside to fish her cell phone out of her purse and call Hope instead.

Up to his elbows in reanimation sluice, Vincent glanced at the watch sitting on the counter beside him and wondered for the millionth time where the hell Fifteen had got to. He knew it was a long list of errands—that was the point, in fact—but certainly she would come back at dark whether she was done or not. No one was *that* committed. Well, maybe Fifteen was. He'd never had a student quite like her. She had better come back soon, though, because he needed her to do that triangulation thing with the computer. It wouldn't hurt to have another pair of hands to deal with Sixteen and Eighteen, either, although Vincent had to admit that he wasn't looking forward to that conversation. Vincent grabbed the pliers off the counter with one grimy hand and splashed back into the fluid to start to work on Eighteen's incisors, avoiding the young man's glassy brown eyes.

Could something have happened to Fifteen? Vincent pulled Eighteen's tooth free with a small sucking sound and let it drop to the bottom of the coffin-sized metal tub. That seemed unlikely. She had always seemed perfectly capable of handling herself, and this tiny town didn't seem like a particularly dangerous place. The entrance to the town was cloaked, though. Vincent hadn't considered that they might be trying to hide something aside from the population of witches or sorcerers that must have done the cloaking. Vincent fumbled on the second incisor and it dropped down the late Eighteen's throat. Vincent cursed. Oh well, it was probably fine. Should he call Fifteen? Did he even have her cell number? Doubtful. Vincent shook the gunk off his arms and walked around to the other tank where Sixteen was marinating. Fifteen was a grown woman. She ought to be able to handle a few errands. She was just late, that was all. Very late, given that it was after midnight, but just late and nothing more. It was probably fine.

7

Kauai

"Ah, there you are, sweetheart. Kelly, right?"

"Just Kell." Kell flopped her suitcase down on the sofa in their egregiously tropical hotel room, relieved to see that there were, in fact, two bedrooms. She most regretted failing in her mission to kill the young Scottish Guardian during these appointments with Daemonicus. But then, it wasn't like she had a choice. If she hadn't found this bizarre businessman, Jasmine probably would have killed her. She would have deserved it, of course, but she wanted to live all the same.

Today was the first time Kell had seen Daemonicus when he wasn't sitting behind a desk, and it was a bit unnerving. It was also the first time she'd seen him in anything but his spotless white suit. He was wearing a floral Hawaiian shirt and khaki shorts, and that just seemed absurd.

"Yes, quite a change from my usual outfit, isn't it?" Daemonicus said, his tone friendly as ever. "But then, that is the point. I will be here for a few days while I get everything in order, so I might as well try to blend in. Are you going to stay the duration?"

Kell nodded. She had to see this through to the end. Besides, the Queen was demanding daily reports.

"Good. Your magic might be of use in this operation. There seems to be a shortage of witches lately, and getting onto the 'Forbidden Island' without magic would be quite the chore."

"What Forbidden Island?" Kell asked, not liking the sound of that. Daemonicus had only told her that he'd found a Guardian in Hawaii. He hadn't said anything about forbidden islands.

"Well, that is the romantic name for it." Daemonicus sat down on the room's only couch, a lumpy blue travesty, and gestured for Kell to sit beside him. She did, albeit a little stiffly. Daemonicus pulled a smartphone from his pocket and clicked it on, extending his hand toward Kell to show her the map on the screen.

"The island's actual name is Ni'ihau, and it's off the coast of the one we're on now." He pointed at a small, unassuming swath of land on the map. "Ni'ihau is a private island, and unfortunately I cannot persuade the owners to grant me a visit for any price. My reconnaissance team has found the island well-guarded, therefore I think we will need some magic to get ashore unnoticed." Daemonicus turned his sharp gaze on Kell and raised an eyebrow. "I assume you can make that happen?"

"W-well, one genie can't do a lot by herself, but I'm pretty good at teleporting, or I might be able to make you kind of invisible," Kell offered, knowing that invisibility would be pushing her limits. Genies lived in groups for a reason. They almost always worked spells together. Trying to do too much alone might kill her, but if it got a Guardian for Jasmine, then it would be well worth it.

"Wonderful." Daemonicus smiled darkly. "Perhaps we can finish our hunt by the end of the week after all. I am still in the process of recruiting, since no one knows what this creature can do, but we should be ready to breach the island in thirty or forty hours."

Kaimana sprinted as fast as possible up the side of Kawaihoa. The sun had set and the Unulau wind blew from the northeast. It would be the perfect time to see Unulani. The dark, dry soil mushed in surrender under his pounding feet. Far behind him, his two brothers did their best to keep pace.

"Kai! Wait for us!" Anakoni tried to run as fast as his older brother, but he was neither tall nor fit enough to match Kai's powerful, long-legged strides. Even farther down the mountain, the eldest, Kapena, meticulously picked his way up the incline. Kai stopped, jumping from one foot to the other while he waited, impatiently, for his siblings to get there.

"You know Unulani won't be there until almost sunrise, right?" Anakoni panted, skidding to a halt beside Kai. "There's no hurry."

"Good; we'll be sixty before Kap gets up here."

"It never hurts to be careful," Kapena said. It was one of his many mottos. Anakoni rolled his eyes. Kap never so much as put his clothes on in the morning without weighing alternatives and considering every consequence. It might be wise, but it was most frustrating.

Eventually Kap navigated his way to his brothers. Koni fell into step with him and Kai, yet again, ran ahead. After several repetitions of this ritual, the three young men reached the top of Kawaihoa. It had once been a volcano, but its fires had been quieted long ago, and now it was just a hill. But it was not just *any* hill. It was the only place on the entire island of Ni'ihau, possibly the only place in the world, where a person could glimpse the mysterious "floating island" of Unulani.

It wasn't as though Kai had *never* seen a floating island before. They appeared around Ni'ihau at least a few times a year, in various places. Unulani was the only one that was always in the same place, at the same time, and Kai had never managed to be patient long enough to spot it. Patience, however, was a valued trait, and something he was trying to cultivate. Tomorrow was his sixteenth birthday, and Kai had decided that waiting up all night for Unulani was a fitting way to start this new season in his life. Kap and Koni had both done it before, and Kai had to make sure his parents knew that their "spirit son," as they called him, was just as good as their own children. He wasn't restless, or pitiable, or cursed, or whatever else they might think. He could be as hard-working as Kap, as clever as Koni, and as patient as anyone else on the island, they'd see.

At last, the three young men reached the crest of Kawaihoa. There was a marker to tell them where to position themselves, and they gravitated toward it without speaking. This was the third time Kai and his brothers had tried to see Unulani together, so they knew what to do. The first time, Kap had been a teenager trying to show the world to his younger brothers, who were just a little too young at the time and couldn't manage to stay awake. The second time Kai got bored and went exploring around Kawaihoa, and of course missed the island's appearance entirely. This time, though, Kap had come prepared, with a plan to keep them all alert and awake until dawn. He refused to tell his brothers what it was, though, until they were all settled on the dusty ground.

"So what is this secret scheme of yours?" Koni asked, leaning back on his hands.

"Since we have nothing to do, and we are a talented bunch, I thought we might spend a few hours composing a song for my wedding."

"You mean you *finally* asked her?" Kai cried. Kap nodded. Though usually a stoic man, Kap beamed. Everyone on Ni'ihau had known for years that Kap and Abigail Kaohelaulii were interested in each other, but neither was willing to admit it. They had sort of started courting a few months ago, and now at last they were getting around to it.

"And she said yes? Miracle of miracles," Koni teased, smacking Kap on the back. "Congratulations. When are you getting married?"

"Next month. I know it's a little soon, but, I think we're ready." Of course they were ready. They'd been ready since they were kids.

"We better get to work on that song, then, shouldn't we?" Already, the tune was forming in Kai's head. The love of music was one of the handful of things that the three brothers all had in common. If they couldn't come up with the perfect song together, no one could. It was a great plan. They were all too excited to fall asleep now, and they certainly weren't going to wander off with such an important task at hand.

Thomas Drake stared at the world map on the floor of his trailer, trying to decide what to do about it. He wasn't expecting the spell to work, but it had. The years under Hope and Sally's tutelage were finally paying off, it seemed. He wondered if the enemy had a similar spell and felt cold dread settle into his bones. He shook it off and examined the little glowing embers on the map once more. What he had created was essentially an energy map, showing these bright white dots everywhere that there was a concentration of magical energy. He recognized the centimeter-wide spot over North Carolina as Brunswick. It could hardly be anything else. Thomas had thought maybe he could use the other points of light to figure out where the other Guardians might be, but there were more dots than he knew what to do with. Big glowing spots, little glowing specks, and everything in between, at least a hundred of them, scattered around the globe, even a couple in Antarctica. This was going to be harder than he'd anticipated.

There had to be a pattern here somewhere. Which ones were places, and which ones were people? Thomas knew that ley lines, the energy highways in the earth, usually converged at energetic places, Brunswick included, so...

After a lengthy fight with his decrepit printer and spotty Internet connection, Thomas took a pile of papers and meticulously lined them up, overlaying his energy map until the continents matched. Sure enough, most of the places where several ley lines converged, there was an energy nexus glowing through the paper. Thomas grabbed a pen and circled the places where there were lights, but no ley intersections. There were fewer than ten.

Thomas could eliminate a few of the dots right off the bat. There was one in the middle of the Australian outback, but since that was the location of the largest cotu commune in the world, of course it would be magically energetic. Another was one of those Antarctic spots, and he wasn't even going to try to go there, so why consider it? Some of the other coordinates, when put through a search engine, proved to be overtop natural formations that were known to be powerful. Soon there were only two mystery dots left: one off the coast of Ireland, and one out in the middle of the Pacific Ocean on the Hawaiian chain, though it was hard to tell which island.

So, which one to try first? It was probably going to be equally difficult either way. This was a terrible idea, really, almost certain to put Thomas back on the radar, but he'd spent a little time examining Sally's journal on his unplanned visit to Brunswick—she ought to have better locks on the basement door if she was so smart. He knew he should've just left, but he had to know why his son had been out in the woods facing down that black beast, and why Jason and Sally even knew each other. His companions probably thought he'd skipped town after Richie ran off into the forest, but he had been around a lot longer than that, seen and heard things around Kitch Manor that he wasn't equipped to understand. Fortunately, he knew from the old days that Sally was a meticulous journaler, and sure enough while she and her posse were upstairs, Thomas learned all he needed to know. The sooner all twelve new Guardians were in one place, the sooner Jason would be safe.

Hawaii or Ireland, Hawaii or Ireland…well, at least he would know how to drive in Hawaii. Besides, what were the chances of two Guardians from the British Isles? Hawaii might be part of the U.S., but the map made it clear that the islands were way out in the middle of the ocean. Thomas folded up his layered map and shoved it in the outside pocket of a beat-up backpack. He was never much for suitcases. Too cumbersome for someone on the run. Thomas shouldered the bag and held out his other hand, drawing circles in the air with his palm. Shimmering, alternating pink and hyacinthine spirals curled into the air. The ability to form portals was the one cotu power Thomas inherited from his parents, whoever they were. Once the portal reached Thomas's abnormally tall height, he stepped through just like stepping over a threshold, and in an instant he was swamped by the warm tropical air and fruity fragrance of Hawaii.

Kell watched with astonishment as her hand slowly grew translucent, and then disappeared from view entirely. She looked around her. Daemonicus and the three other vampires he had brought to help them were also invisible. Kell hadn't thought she could do it, but she had, and she was hardly even tired. With the other hand, she rubbed her fingers over the cool, unyielding surface of the quartz crystal Daemonicus had lent her to amplify her powers. Suddenly the weight of it in her palm seemed a great comfort.

"Are we ready?" Daemonicus's smooth, deep voice emanated from somewhere in front of Kell. She nodded, then remembered that he couldn't see her, either.

"Yes. Do you have somewhere specific in mind for me to take you?"

"Somewhere inland, not too close to the town. Do you need coordinates?"

"No, I'm good." Kell closed her eyes out of habit, although since her eyelids were now transparent she needn't have bothered. She focused her mind on where she wanted to go, and the four men she intended to drag with her. With a snap she felt in her chest, Kell popped out of place and almost immediately arrived at her destination.

"Okay, did everybody make it?" Four disembodied affirmatives answered her. Good. Nobody teleported inside a tree or anything. Kell took in her surroundings. Not that many trees to speak of, actually. It was mostly lower-lying vegetation, not like the thick palm forests on Kauai, their jumping-off point. A few trees dotted a wide strip of pasture until a row of mountains intervened. There were a few sheep visible grazing in the fields, but it was late at night, and most livestock would be holed up somewhere safe until morning. In the other direction, more pasture, until the island curled up in a hill and then fell into the sea.

"So now what do we do?" asked one of Daemonicus's hired hands.

"We have a guide coming to meet us," Daemonicus answered. "You might be tempted to call it something else, but it'll find the Guardian for us, I guarantee you." Kell didn't know what to make of this strange speech, but she pretended to understand and waited, fidgeting, for Daemonicus's guide to make an appearance. After a few minutes, Kell felt static bristling the hair on her arms and a sudden increase in air pressure assaulted her eardrums. Kell started to really consider just what type of person could lead them straight to a Guardian. Something that could sense power, certainly, maybe a spirit entity? She gasped as the ache in her ears increased almost unbearably, but the pain receded as quickly as it had come on, and the charge in the atmosphere abated. The unmistakable feeling of being watched burned at the back of Kell's head. She turned to see the culprit and was dumbfounded. The thing's shape was common enough: a simple floating orb. It wasn't made of light, though, as one would expect if it were a spirit guide. It looked sort of like a crystal ball, a floating glass sphere with *something* moving around inside. The outside, the "glass," was so clear that it was defined only by the way it refracted the sunlight and the clumps of black wriggling on its inner surface.

"Ah, here it is," Daemonicus said, "or it seems I should say 'here *they* are.'" Before the words finished leaving his mouth, the glassy ball melted, clumps of liquid dripping to the ground, and the little animals inside swarmed out. Kell couldn't tell quite what they were—big insects, small bats, tiny dragons? They were dark, winged, a couple inches long, and they whizzed through the air in a single coordinated mass, first this way, then that, up, then down. They were trying to find something, it seemed, maybe searching for a scent. Kell thought they might be the creepiest thing she had ever seen, even more so than the Black Dogs in Jasmine's dungeon.

All at once, the guides found their direction, and zoomed away off to Kell's right. Daemonicus called for everyone to follow them. The critters were much too fast for Kell, although probably not for the vampires, but she tried her best to keep up. Not only were they speedy, they took turns in crazy angles and sometimes changed their minds and doubled back to go another way. It didn't take more than a few minutes to exhaust Kell. She lagged farther and farther behind until, quite unexpectedly, she felt a pair of arms scoop her up.

"Sorry about this, Miss," Daemonicus said. "I was hoping for a Crawler, not a Swarm, but one can't be too sure what you'll get when summoning demons."

"We'll have to continue this later, I think. The sky is beginning to lighten," Kap said. Koni and Kai stopped arguing over lyrics and whipped their heads around to look east. The dawn sky was striped purple and magenta. The three brothers got to their feet and clustered around the marker, watching intently for Unulani. For several long minutes, nothing happened, and Kai could feel the boredom seeping through, but then Koni yelled and pointed at a dark spot in the waves. Within a heartbeat, the patch became an island. Kai whooped for joy. *Finally*, he had done it. And it was worth the wait. Unulani was beautiful, even though there was little light to see it by. The beaches glittered with clean white sand, and even at this great distance large cream-colored shells could be seen scattered on the shore. Beyond the beach there was a wall of lush, green trees, branches sagging with the weight of mangoes, breadfruit, and other bizarre, colorful fruits Kai had never seen the like of before. Kaleidoscopic birds flew over the forest. Kai wondered what strange, marvelous songs they must sing. No man knew. It was impossible to reach the floating islands, any of them. By the time you approached, they were gone. Perhaps they were spirit worlds. It was anyone's guess.

"It's beautiful," Kai whispered. Koni murmured in agreement. From then on, they watched the sun peek over Unulani in silence, transfixed. At any moment, the light would hit the island, and it would vanish. They didn't want to waste a second. An insect buzzed around Kai's ear. He swatted at it absently.

"Ow!" Koni smacked at his neck. "I think something bit me." He pulled his hand away and all three men stared, confused, at the dazed creature in Koni's palm. Its body was round with eight joint-ed legs, like a spider, but it was much bigger than any spider known on Ni'ihau, and its head more closely resembled that of a lizard. Nei-ther scales nor fur covered the black, leathery skin. Two pairs of red-tinged, clear wings like a fly's protruded from the top of its back. One wing was torn from the collision with Koni's palm. Momentarily, the broken wing fell off into Koni's hand, and the bud of a new one poked through the thing's flesh.

"What is that?" Koni gasped, looking to Kap for an answer. Kap shrugged his shoulders.

"I don't know. It gave you a nasty bite, though." Kap was right. Kai pushed Koni's hair out of the way to see better. A single tiny punc-ture in the side of his neck was already beginning to swell and turn a deep crimson. Koni tilted his hand, dropping the spider-bug on the ground, and rubbed the bite. He winced.

"Christ, that hurts." Koni pulled his hand away, a smear of blood on his fingers. For once, Kap didn't remind Koni not to take the Lord's name in vain.

"I think we need to get you back to town," Kap decided. "We should take that animal and see if anyone recognizes it. Where is it?" Kap squatted on the ground, searching for the thing.

"Forget the bug," Koni snapped. He had curled his arms around his torso and was starting to shake as though with cold, though the winds were warm. "C-can we just go? I don't...feel right." His knees buckled and Kai reached out to steady him. Despite his shivers, Koni's skin was as hot as sunbaked sand.

Kap gave up on his search and went to his brother. Together, he and Kai guided Koni down the slopes of Kawaihoa. At first, Koni walked mostly under his own power, needing his brothers just to help him keep his balance. By the time they had reached the base of the hill, Kap and Kai were carrying him. The top of Kawaihoa obscured the sun entirely, so the men were left in its shadow. The family's two Arabian horses, one black and one ruddy brown, dozed there, waiting for them. The black mare snorted awake as Kap and Kai hoisted Koni into the saddle. Koni slumped over the horse's neck, and she turned to nuzzle him worriedly. Kai sat down to yank on his riding boots while Kap hooked a foot in the stirrup to pull himself up behind Koni.

Kai heard a dull *smack* and saw Kap hit the ground sidelong. He leaped to his feet, one boot on, one abandoned in the dirt, but before he could go to Kap's aid something grabbed him by the shoulders from behind and threw him down on his back. All he could see above him was the sky, but something hidden from his eyes had to be there. Two hands pinned Kai's arms down, an elbow pressed into his chest, and sharp thorny points sank into the soft flesh of his throat.

Kai bent his legs and thrust his knees into what felt like his assailant's abdomen. The creature, ghost or demon or whatever it might be, was struck off balance momentarily. Kai heard a grunt, whether of hurt or just surprise he couldn't tell, and the weight rolled off his chest. The thing wasn't totally invisible; Kai could see a hint of its movement in the predawn light, now that he knew where it was. Still, how could he fight something that was not of this world? He couldn't run, either. Koni needed him. Kai crouched, watching for the thing to pounce again. He could faintly hear one of the horses screaming behind the sound of his pounding heart.

When it sprang at him, Kai thought he was ready, but the creature was faster and stronger than any man. It slammed into Kai's body with the force of a massive ocean wave, knocking the air out of his chest. It latched onto his neck again. This time, it held Kai's legs down, too, holding him fast against all his struggles. Its tongue flickered against his skin. He heard it swallow. Only as he began to weaken and the purple-pink sky above began to fade to gray in his sight, did Kai absorb the realization that this demon was drinking his blood.

"Don't kill the horse," Daemonicus bellowed. Kell's spell was deteriorating as her energy drained, and she could see a faint, holographic Daemonicus rushing over to tear one of his translucent vampires away from the sleek red stallion a moment before his teeth would have pierced the horse's throat.

"Do you have any idea how much a strong, healthy Arabian like this would be worth?" Daemonicus stroked the horse's long nose, wrapping an arm around its neck to prevent the frightened animal from bolting. Its round brown eyes were rolling in panic, but as Daemonicus murmured soothingly it began to calm down and stopped trying to pull away.

The battle seemed to be over, so with a word Kell ended the spell, and everyone slowly phased back into the visible realm. The vampire that had nearly bitten the horse was now helping Daemonicus hold onto it. The other horse, and the boy laid across its back, were nowhere to be seen. The other two vampires, faces and chests streaked with blood, knelt with one of the Hawaiian men draped over their arms. The one holding the younger man pressed a wad of his own shirt against the Guardian's neck wound to stifle the blood. No one seemed interested in preserving the life of the boy's brother. The vampire grasping him was busy licking the last drops of blood from his throat. Kell gagged and turned away.

"You want us to chase down the third one, too? Get rid of all the witnesses?" asked the vampire with the Guardian in his lap.

"No. The sun is about to overtake us," Daemonicus said, glancing skyward. A thin sliver of bright orange was appearing above the horizon. "Besides, I doubt that boy is long for this world. Get us out of here, Kell."

Thomas sipped a cup of Hawaiian-grown coffee and wondered what he was going to do now. He was close to the Guardian, if indeed that was what his map had found. The hard part would be tracking it down. To his surprise, Thomas found himself wondering, *what would Sally do?* It was a weird thought, but one he did have occasionally. Sally was quite adept at certain things, including finding obscure people and objects, if she put her mind to it. The first thing Sally did when she was looking for something was to read up on it. Thomas found reading a bit boring himself, but if that was what it took then he would buckle down and do it. He asked the barista where he could find a library, figuring they would surely have either newspapers or computers he could use to find some clues. The barista pointed him in the right direction and off Thomas went, coffee in hand.

The librarian was a squat, cheerful woman who was more than happy to help. They did have a newspaper archive, as it turned out, and some of the papers were quite recent. Thomas thanked her, grabbed everything printed in the last three months, and sat down to examine them. He felt a little strange skimming newspapers for phrases like "rain of toads" or "miracle healing," maybe even "chicken eggs hatch snakes," whatever struck him as weird. There was only one other patron nearby, though, and he seemed fully engrossed in whatever he was doing on one of the library's computers, so he probably wasn't judging Thomas's weirdness.

Thomas scanned every headline. A few things jumped out at him, but they were all small articles tucked in the back pages, lacking the depth of information Thomas would need to determine which of the oddities were mere freak occurrences and which might be more supernatural. He set the newspapers on a side table and switched to a computer to see what he could dig up about these suspicious events.

The kittens with cloven hooves were a hoax—no surprise there. The UFOs spotted over Waimea Canyon at night turned out to be exceptionally well-lighted drones. Still no progress in the case of the four kids who went missing but left their shoes behind, the socks still inside them. Thomas had no idea what that meant, but it might be worth a look. He typed "missing child AND shoes and socks" into the search bar and pressed enter.

Without warning, the heretofore silent man at the computer beside Thomas exploded—not literally, just angrily. He jumped up, swearing, and punched the computer screen. The computer was a tough old dinosaur with a glass face, so he did more damage to his knuckles than he did to it. Thomas pushed back his chair, not sure what, if anything, he ought to do. The librarian scurried over and put a hand on the man's arm. He jerked away, fist lifted like he meant to hit her, too, and Thomas darted in between them.

"Whoa! Calm down! What's the problem?" Thomas took the man's fist and guided it back down to his side. He gritted his teeth and shrugged Thomas off, then stomped away and out the front door, letting it slam shut behind him.

"Should I call the police?" the librarian whispered. Thomas shook his head.

"Not unless he comes back." Just to be safe, though, he followed the guy out. Thomas found him beside the door sitting on the pavement with his back against the wall, legs curled into his chest, head resting on his knees.

"Sir? Are you okay?" Thomas sat down beside him, not afraid for his own safety. He was a sorcerer with three blades on him. One human, no matter how volatile, was not going to faze him.

"I'm sorry," the man said, lifting his head. He kept his gaze straight ahead, not looking at Thomas. "I don't usually lose my temper like that." He was a tall man with thick, ropey muscles on a lean frame. His skin was a rich bronze, his jawline chiseled and square.

"What happened, if you don't mind me asking? I know computers can be frustrating, but most people don't, you know, attack them."

"I can't stand computers, but that's not the problem. I've been trying for two days to find help for my son, Anakoni. He's ill, and we have had several Hawaiian healers and Western doctors come to the island to see him, but they haven't been able to do anything. The Internet was my last resort, and as you may have guessed, I wasn't getting anywhere." He closed his eyes and massaged them with a thumb and forefinger.

"God, I'm sorry. I know how that feels." Thomas laid his hand on the guy's shoulder. "Hey, would you mind telling me what's wrong with him? I'm no M.D., but I know a thing or two about medicine."

"I doubt that will help. I'm starting to think it's a spiritual disease."

"Then you're in luck, because I know even more about that," Thomas replied. "Come on. Talk to me. What's your name again?"

"Roland," the man answered, and looked right at Thomas for the first time. "Koni and our two other sons didn't come home a few nights ago. When we were just beginning to get really worried, one of the horses they'd taken found its way home, with Koni strapped into the saddle, barely conscious. He hasn't fully woken up since, but he thrashes and sometimes tries to speak, although I can't understand him. His fever is so high it hurts you to touch him. Nothing they've given him has brought the fever down. One of the doctors did a blood test yesterday and couldn't find an infection. No one knows what to do, but he can't go on like this…" *Fever without infection.* That was a tell-tale sign of possession, but Thomas didn't want to leap to that conclusion.

"Have the other two boys gotten sick?" Thomas asked.

"They never came home," Roland said, voice breaking. "They found Kap's body, but Kai is still missing." Thomas stared at the ground, thinking. This would distract him from his mission, but if he *could* help, well, he would have to. If Roland's son was possessed, he might not find anyone else nearby that could be of any use.

"Would you take me to see him?" Thomas asked. "I'm not sure, but there might be something I can do. I think you're right about it being spiritual. I think—maybe—that a demon is trying to invade your son's body." Roland's eyes widened, and for a second Thomas couldn't tell if he was horrified that Thomas was right or just afraid to be sitting next to someone so crazy. Then Roland stood up and reached out a hand to pull Thomas to his feet.

"Yes, please come with me. Our house is on Ni'ihau. Outsiders aren't normally allowed, but I think they will make an exception."

Inside the simple abode, Koni was stretched out on a low bed in the main room, almost naked with sweat streaming off his dark, flushed skin. The muscles in his lean limbs were stretched taut and twitching. Arteries pulsed and strained in his arms. A grimace split his face, and tears leaked from the corners of his rolling, bloodshot eyes. He muttered low, unintelligible syllables, spittle foaming on his lips. Thomas knelt beside the sickbed. Ropes entwined the stricken man's wrists and bound them to the sides of the bedframe.

"Why is he tied up?" Thomas suspected he already knew the answer.

"He wouldn't stop scratching," Roland said, joining Thomas at his son's side. "He tore at us, at himself. We had to make him stop." Behind them, Thomas heard Roland's wife, Mele, quietly sobbing.

"I understand," Thomas said soothingly. "We do what we have to. Now, remind me: How long has he been this way?"

"Almost two days. We have tried all our medicines, and nothing helps," Roland said. "A haole doctor came, too, and couldn't tell us what was wrong. The whole island is praying for him, but…"

"Keep them praying," Thomas said. "It helps more than you may think." He pressed a hand to Koni's wrist, feeling his racing pulse. His flesh was so hot it nearly burned Thomas's fingers. This was more serious than Thomas had been expecting.

"Is there a priest on this island?"

"I'll go get him," Roland said. He sprinted out the door, leaving Thomas with Koni and Mele. Thomas imagined Roland was eager to have something, anything useful to do.

Mele came and stood at the head of Koni's bed. She and Thomas watched Koni, neither speaking to the other. Thomas knew how she felt. Once he'd had to keep vigil over a dying son as well. Words would be no comfort to her now.

"It is a demon, isn't it?" Mele asked after a long time. Thomas nodded.

"Did Koni…do something? To invite it in?" Her voice broke on the last syllable, and Mele covered her face with her hands. Thomas touched her arm gently.

"Only he knows that for sure, but some demons don't have to be invited. Someone has to bring them into our world. After that they can attack anyone. It may not have been his fault."

"But now? Will…" Mele swallowed, pushing back another wave of tears. "Will it take his soul?"

"Not if I can help it." Thomas looked her in the face, his eyes soft and sympathetic. "You should talk to him. Call him by name. He won't respond—although the demon might—but he's in there, and he can hear you. He needs to know that you're counting on him to keep fighting. Now, I've got work to do, but if anything changes, come tell me."

The clergyman on Ni'ihau was named Iakopa, though Thomas doubted he was pronouncing it correctly. The priest, or whatever his title was, didn't seem to care at the moment what Thomas called him. They were busy trying to organize an exorcism, without much success.

Finding a cross was simple. There were five in Roland's house alone. After the crosses, though, Thomas and Iakopa started to disagree. Thomas had attended three exorcisms, and his protocol called for white sage, holy water, the Lord's Prayer, and a little Latin. Unbeknownst to him, however, the Hawaiians had their own traditional approaches to possession, and Iakopa was inclined to stick to them. After much back and forth, they reached an amenable compromise, and before sundown the two seat-of-their-pants exorcists and Koni's parents were gathered at the bedside.

"This is going to be long and ugly," Thomas reminded Roland and Mele, handing a wooden cross to each of them. "Dangerous, too, for everybody. Keep calm, keep praying, and do exactly as we tell you." Iakopa added something in a language Thomas didn't understand. Koni's parents nodded. Thomas didn't ask. He was probably just telling them not to listen *too* closely to this crazy white guy. Whatever. As long as it didn't get in the way of the task at hand, Thomas didn't care what they thought of him.

"Are we ready?" Thomas asked.

"Almost." Iakopa set fire to a pile of leaves in a clay bowl on the floor. Thomas didn't know any of the sacred plants Iakopa had chosen, but Iakopa was sure that they would work well in the place of sage, if not better. With white sage increasingly scarce, Thomas was prepared to believe him. The vegetation was only partially dried, so it would burn slowly and with a lot of smoke. In a short while, the fragrant vapors began to fill the room with an herbal perfume. It was a strong smell, not unpleasant, unless you're a demon. Thomas heard Koni cough behind him.

"Now we are ready." Iakopa picked the smoking bowl up and set it down again near the headboard. Koni moaned and twisted as far away from the plume of smoke as he could while bound by both wrists and ankles. He coughed again, a violent, convulsive motion that wracked his entire body. Koni's mother glanced at him nervously.

"I told you it would be ugly." Thomas wrapped his long, skeletal hands around Koni's wrists, just in case, and waited for Iakopa to take the lead.

"Would all those gathered here in the name of the Lord—" Koni spasmed "—please join me in prayer."

Roland and Mele bowed their heads and closed their eyes, clutching their crosses like lifelines. Thomas and the priest kept their eyes wide open and trained on Koni. The three Hawaiians began a prayer chant in their native tongue. Thomas didn't even try to follow along. He figured the Lord's Prayer would suffice. As long as they were all praying something, it ought to work.

Koni hissed, like red-hot iron plunged into cold water. His parents stopped, startled, but Thomas and Iakopa didn't pause for a moment. Underneath his hands, Thomas felt Koni's skin getting even hotter, and the force of Koni's straining arteries thumped against his palms. First Roland, then his wife, haltingly resumed the chant. Koni started to growl something in Hawaiian but was interrupted by a coughing fit. Without breaking stride, Iakopa took advantage of the moment of vulnerability to dip a finger in the dish of blessed seawater by his feet and draw the sign of the cross on Koni's forehead. Koni howled; the water instantly turned to steam. A bright crimson "†" was left behind on his skin.

On television, Thomas had only ever seen exorcists scream at demons, as if the force of their audio waves might knock the foul things loose. Thomas preferred a subtler approach. He leaned over, casting his long sliver of a shadow on Koni's chest, and murmured in his ear:

"Tell us your name."

Koni sneered and spit bloody saliva at Thomas's face. Unshaken, Thomas wiped the slime off on his sleeve. Iakopa flicked a few drops of their improvised holy water on Koni as a rebuke. Koni cursed and pulled back, fighting his restraints. His nails dug into Thomas's hands. Thomas tightened his grip and repeated the command.

"You have no authority over us, Thomas Michael Drake," Koni snapped. "You *belong* with us." Koni's parents eyed Thomas curiously. He ignored them. That was none of their concern.

"I am no longer another tool of your master's," Thomas said, meeting Koni's fevered gaze steadily. "I speak for the powers of Heaven, and I demand that you tell us your name."

"We have no name," Koni roared. "We are the Swarm. Legio sumus. And there are more of us than there are of you. Nos numquam superabitis." Thomas and the priest glanced at each other, on the same wavelength perhaps for the first time. This was going to be difficult. Driving out one demon would be plenty hard, but a multitude of them was quite another matter.

"One at a time, then?" Thomas suggested. Iakopa nodded.

"You can't do that," Koni said. His tongue flicked out, snake-like, and ran over his lip. Iakopa grabbed the bowl of smoking plants off the floor and held it near Koni's head, gesturing for his parents to keep praying. Thomas started repeating a passage of Latin he had learned from a priest in Tennessee. He didn't understand many of the words, but it had worked at his first exorcism.

Koni was trying his best to writhe away from Iakopa and his sacred burning leaves. He cursed God. He cursed Iakopa. He cursed his parents and his church and the Bible and promised Thomas that he would pay for this treachery. Thomas and Iakopa didn't relent. Mele, too, proved ironclad in her determination to win the battle for her son's soul. Roland faltered more than once, however, even asking Iakopa to stop, he was hurting Koni—which, of course, was true, but unavoidable. Koni spotted his weakness and wasted no time in attacking it. He interspersed his vitriol with pleas for Roland to save him.

"Poppa, please, help me—get your filthy paws off me, priest! Te uremus! Father, the smoke, it burns, please, help—" Koni broke off into another fit of coughing. He gagged, then choked, eyes bulging. Thomas's mind raced. Was it a trick? What if it wasn't? Thomas released Koni's right wrist and bit through the rope.

"What are you doing?" Iakopa protested, backing away from the partially-liberated demon.

"Don't worry, I've got it." Thomas pinned Koni's free arm behind his back, grabbed his shoulder, and rolled him onto his side. His parents had abandoned their chant and were watching intently. Koni's spine arched and his abdominal muscles tightened. He heaved twice, and then a gooey, black thing the size of a golf ball dropped out of his mouth and onto the sheets. Koni fell back onto the mattress, limp and panting.

The black ball, dripping digestive fluids, unwound, shaking out its wings. The little spider-dragon blinked its obsidian eyes a few times, perplexed, then it caught sight of Iakopa. It took flight, aiming straight for Iakopa's neck. Thomas froze, caught between helping Iakopa and holding down Koni, who could reanimate any moment. Mele was not so encumbered. She snatched the tiny monster out of midair and stuck her fist into the holy seawater. With a screech and a sizzle, it fell apart in her hand, pieces of it sinking to the bottom of the dish. She washed it off of her and sat back on her heels, staring at the obliterated demon.

"Well, that's one, then," Thomas said.

"How many more are there?" Roland asked.

"I don't know. We'll just have to keep going and find out. Um, I think we might need more of that water, though."

8

Brunswick

Sally could hear Jenna leading a debate about the nature of serial killers with Hope and Alex in the den beyond the Dissecting Room door. That Jenna had turned up a murder victim by herself sent a current of pride through Sally's nerves, but Jenna's growing interest in comparing the details of these murders to famous killing sprees of the past put Sally on edge. Although, given the nature of the crimes, she supposed she couldn't blame her.

Sally tore scraps of clothing off the corpse, talking at the recorder sitting unmanned on the gurney. Only portions of the poor creature's black leggings and her ankle boots and socks remained. All the other victims had been stripped completely, so Sally wondered if there had been some reason to rush with this one.

"Female, African descent, dark brown hair, brown eyes. Apparent cause of death, blood loss or Stone loss, same as the last," Sally droned on, tugging off the left boot with a steadying hand on the woman's cool leg. The sock underneath was covered in smiling pandas. "Rigor mortis would suggest—oh hello, what are you?" Sally dropped the sock on the floor, forensic protocol forgotten. On the outside of the ankle, overlapping the joint, was a black tattoo about an inch and a half across. It showed the snarling face of a cotu in silhouette, with a six-digit number inked between its flattened ears: 070682. Sally laughed out loud at her good fortune. She whirled about the room until she found pen and paper and jotted down the number.

Sally burst through the door into the basement den waving the piece of paper triumphantly above her head. Her housemates ceased their discussion and turned to stare at her.

"I take it you've found something?" Alex said.

"I have indeed! I know who this one is! Or I will very soon. Anyone seen my laptop? It's around here somewhere."

"Right here." Hope pulled a sleek purple laptop out of the magazine rack beside the sofa where she sat and held it out. Sally took it and sat down between her and Alex.

"Thanks. I found an ICCA tattoo on her ankle, so I'm going to look up the serial number, and that will tell us who she is. Well, was."

"Really? I don't think I've ever seen one before." Hope left her seat and made for the dissection room. Sally rolled her eyes.

"It's really not that exciting," Sally called after her. "Almost had one myself, you know." Jenna switched from the armchair to the sofa beside Sally to watch as she worked.

"You can just look these people up?" Jenna asked. Sally nodded, typing the number she found on the woman's skin into the search bar of a non-descript online database. The title "International Council of Cotu Affairs Database of Dangerous Individuals" was at the top of the screen in a large, dark blue serif font.

"That is the idea," Sally continued. "You couldn't always do it this easily, of course, but it was always part of the plan to make it possible for other cotus to keep track of those supposedly too dangerous for society."

"Like you." Jenna's smile was full of irony. Sally laughed, but with less mirth than Jenna displayed.

"Yes. Like me. Ah, here she is! Chantrelle Montagne, from Hammond, Louisiana. Now the real detective work begins. Oh, joy of joys."

"What did she do?" Alex asked, leaning over Sally's shoulder to see the page himself.

"Looks like she couldn't control her powers. Downright criminal." Sally said and snorted.

"That's a bit harsh," Alex said. Jenna was silent. Hope returned from the dissection room, shutting the door behind her.

"We were talking earlier about what we should make of John's special guest appearance right before Jenna found the body," she said, taking Jenna's recently vacated chair.

"It's certainly suspicious, no question about that," Sally said. She continued to scan the brief synopsis of Chantrelle's life on the ICCA database. "I think we should start watching that family pretty closely. They still haven't done anything we can prove, at least not yet, but they've done enough to draw our attention. What do you think?"

"That's a lot of people to follow. Do we know enough people to keep an eye on them at all times?" Alex said.

"Well all we can do is try. John would be the priority, I think," Sally replied. "Nothing in this woman's history jumps out at me. I'm going to go finish the autopsy and keep digging into Chantrelle's life later. Although any of y'all are welcome to do some of that work yourself while I take care of the body."

"I can probably handle that," Jenna said, reaching for Sally's computer. Sally handed it off. If the other corpse was any indication, further dissection was unlikely to yield more clues, but Sally hated to leave any job unfinished.

This meditation thing had never been Vincent's strong suit, but he'd read and been told that these kind of spells—second sight, third eye, sixth sense, whatever—required extended periods of focus and all that. Vincent was almost completely certain it wasn't working. Cross-legged in the dark, on a pillow on the floor of an empty hall closet in the rental house, Vincent was very aware, that was for sure. Aware of all the aches in his knees and back, the rotting-sweet smell of the ad hoc altar in front of him, and an annoying twitching muscle in his forearm. No heightened perception was forthcoming as far as he could tell, however.

Vincent floundered for something else to focus on, something that would consume his entire attention. His mind wandered backwards, wading through decades that smelled like chemicals and death. It settled into his eight-year-old self, watching a fierce lightning storm dance over the Gulf of Mexico from the window of his grandparents' apartment. The pulse of the waves and the flash and crack of the lightning absorbed him. Such raw power, just frolicking through the sky and sea. He watched the rhythm of the crashing ocean and the chaotic explosions of electricity through his bedroom window almost all night.

The grown-up Vincent felt something shift in his psyche, like a latch falling open, and the memory of the storm vanished in an instant as he rocketed back into the present moment. Vincent opened his eyes and was immediately dizzy despite the near blackness of the closet. He closed them, forced himself to breathe slowly and ready himself, then opened his eyes again. Tendrils of shimmering mist drifted around the darkness. Vincent ignored them and pulled himself to his feet by the doorknob, cursing when he realized one foot was soundly asleep. He opened the door and balanced in the doorframe, shaking the numb foot to restore circulation and squinting against the sudden change in illumination. As his eyes adjusted, Vincent lowered his still-tingling foot to the ground, forgotten, and marveled at the hallway around him. In most ways it was as boring and barren as ever, but Vincent could now see another layer of reality above that, and it was beautiful. Bright, sparkling streams flowed through the air in unimaginably complex patterns. Some of the coils bore colors, even colors Vincent was sure his eyes shouldn't be able to perceive. Magic was everywhere Vincent looked.

All of Vincent's research suggested that peering through the proverbial third eye only changed particular aspects of perception, usually small ones. You see some auras or some dead people once in a while—surely it wasn't meant to be so all-encompassing? Either the spell had worked far too well, which Vincent doubted given his inherent resistance toward this type of magic, or this place was absolutely teeming with power.

All manner of ideas flooded Vincent's mind, but he forced himself to calm down. There would be time for that later. All the time in the universe, perhaps. Now, he needed to stay focused and find Fifteen. Who knew what kind of trouble she'd gotten herself into? Especially in a place like this. Leaving his incense to smolder out, Vincent left the house and got into his car. The magic was stronger outside, and it took every iota of his willpower not to try to capture it there and then.

Tyler flipped through the rack of miscellaneous costume pieces. The problem was, no two things went together. He pulled out a black velvet cape and held it up. "There's got to be something I can do with this, right?"

Cameron looked up from the rack two sizes smaller. He gave a doubtful half-frown. "Matador?" he said, shrugging.

Tyler nodded and put the cape back. "Maybe this was a bad idea. We should have just gone to Halloween store at the mall."

"Yeah, except the mall is like an hour away, and we can't *drive*."

"Right. How does a disco cowboy sound?"

"Like you're having better luck than me."

Tyler draped the leather vest over one arm and went in search of something more appropriate than floral bellbottoms to match. Or at least something less heinous. This was the first year Tyler had shopped for his own costume. He should have known he wasn't ready to take on the town junk store. He was about to suggest they just go back to his house and shop online when a familiar face perusing the girl's section made him do a double take.

"Hey, Cam," Tyler whispered, "is that Lydia?"

Cameron looked up, and Tyler tilted his head toward the blonde with perfect curls holding a mermaid dress up to herself. Cameron's brow knit in confusion.

"It sure looks like her. But what's she doing here?"

"Your guess is as good as mine," Tyler said. Lydia Knightwood was two years older than them and had just started high school. Although she lived in town and was around their age, she had made a great show of not wanting to hang out with most of the other kids. The whole family didn't like anyone who wasn't human. They weren't too fond of humans who kept the company of other sentient species, either. Tyler had gone to school with Lydia for several years, but rarely saw her deign to set foot around town.

"Didn't Scarlet say we should keep an eye on the Knightwoods?" Cameron said, a little conspiratorially. Tyler nodded. When Scarlet issued the directive during training, Tyler had been certain he would never have occasion to do anything about it. Fate must have had other plans. Tyler sauntered over to a rack of shoes closer to Lydia, trying to act casual. He went around the back side so he would have a good view. A moment later, Cameron sprinted after him with zero stealth whatsoever. Tyler fought the urge to facepalm. Lydia glanced at Cameron as he sailed past, scowled, and went back to browsing.

Cameron skidded to a stop beside Tyler, almost crashing into him. Tyler rolled his eyes and picked up a pair of duck-foot sandals, trying to look busy for the no one who was watching. Across the way, Lydia's cell phone rang. Tinny EDM blasted from her purse throughout the store. Tyler and Cameron froze, their full attention on their target. Lydia dug her phone out of the bag, took in the name on the caller ID, and answered with a "Hey, girl!"

"I heard what happened with your dad, babe! Are you gonna be all right?" said a teenage girl on the other end of the line. Cameron tugged Tyler's sleeve, no doubt wanting to know what Tyler could hear through the phone with his superior hearing. Tyler flapped his hand in a shooing-shushing gesture.

"Ugh, I don't know," Lydia said, lifting out a red mini-dress to examine. "I guess I'll live."

"For real, I can't believe he'd do something like that," her friend said. Tyler's eyes widened. Surely not. Surely they weren't talking about *that* so casually.

"Well I can. He's so horrible." Lydia threw the red dress onto the pile of clothes in her cart. She did sound upset, though.

"What are you gonna do?"

"I have a plan," Lydia said, beginning to steer her cart toward the changing rooms. Tyler grabbed Cameron's arm. Cameron leaned so far into the rack his face was practically buried in a pair of glittery neon sneakers.

"No way is Dad going to cancel my Halloween party just because of one stupid F. Because I just checked this hellhole's return policy, and guess what? It's too late to get all his money back. That's what he gets for making me 'learn the value of a dollar.' Budgets are stupid."

They kept talking, but the boys stopped listening. They looked at each other morosely. So much for their careers in espionage.

"Do we…report all that?" Cameron asked.

"I guess," Tyler said. "At least we can say we tried."

"Yeah, I don't think it's going to be any help, though. Hey, are those, like, duck shoes?"

Mid-afternoon sunlight streamed through the thick glass windows in the large front room of Kitch Manor. Kylie lay on the soft, dark living room carpet with an algebra textbook and calculator in front of her, surrounded by sheets of printer paper covered in equations. Sally was on the floor beside Kylie, on her back with her laptop on her stomach. Beyond Sally, Joon was sitting suspiciously close to William while they watched some old black-and-white movie on the TV. It *was* about time Joon started dating again.

"I think I'm almost ready to take the test for this class," Kylie said to no one in particular, surfacing from the depths of mathematics for the first time in two hours.

"Already?" Sally's eyebrows rose. "You've only been at it a few weeks."

Kylie shrugged.

"She's always been a little math wiz," Joon said, favoring Kylie with a proud smile. "She was on the math team for a while. Until she called the coach a bitch and got kicked off."

"Well, she *was* a bitch," Kylie said.

William laughed, and Joon elbowed him in the side, but not very hard.

"She was," Joon admitted, "but you probably didn't need to tell her."

"Yeah, I did miss math team. Having any luck over th—" The words died on Kylie's tongue as she got a good look at Sally's screen. She knew Sally was delving into the latest victim of Brunswick's cotu killer. Kylie didn't want to know much about the details and was only asking to be polite, but the image in front of her captured every particle of her attention.

"I *know* him," Kylie said, pointing to the man front and center in the group photograph. He was tall and lean, maybe late thirties or early forties, with his tight ebony curls trimmed short. The slightest of beards sloped down his cheeks and covered his chin. He was surrounded by seven other people, everyone smiling. The man had his arms around the people to either side of him. One hand was missing the first two fingers.

"How so?" Sally asked, shaking Kylie free from her shock. Kylie related the story about the man Kara photographed outside her bedroom window. Having already told it to Joon and the police after helping kill her dead teacher, Kylie'd had plenty of practice.

"You couldn't say for sure that it was him, though," Sally said. "There are probably quite a few people out there missing fingers on their right hand. Even if your friend's photo could reliably narrow down the skin color."

"I guess you're right," Kylie said, a little disappointed.

"You don't think that's mighty coincidental?" William said. "Mr. Fun and Finger Free showing up before the girls were attacked and again with your, uh, murder victim." His left foot, dangling over the armrest, flexed and relaxed several times in a row.

"Oh no, I do. I just want to approach this reasonably. I'll see if—" Sally focused on the screen. "—Dr. Vincent LaMont isn't your average cellular biology professor. If there's a connection, I'll find it."

Driving this tiny town's main thoroughfares had been torture for Vincent, seeing the way the magic caressed its inhabitants like they were old friends, flowing into and through them. What did they have that Vincent didn't? There was no obvious uniting trait. He'd never seen a town with such different citizens. Since when did humans get along with other species? Or their own species, for that matter. Vincent supposed a person could put up with a lot for a slice of that power.

Following the magic as best he could follow so chaotic a force, Vincent realized it was toward the outskirts of town that it grew strongest, near the forest. He still hadn't found any sign of the magical nuclear explosion he suspected he would find in place of Fifteen. A little observation helped him see the difference between the magic in the air and that which certain individuals generated themselves, and that, he hoped, would clear things up. A cotu in human form and a witch looked the same physically, and he couldn't tell which magical signature went with which, but as he circled the edges of town he saw a faint glow that resembled one of the two emanating from the trees and knew he must be close. If not to Fifteen, at least to something interesting. He parked the car off the side of the road a few hundred feet past the neighborhood where he saw the glow and entered the trees.

Inside the forest, Vincent didn't just see the swirling currents of magic, he felt them humming in his chest. He knew that this forest was alive and aware. Should he say something?

"Um, hello," Vincent said aloud, feeling a little absurd. The trees creaked, although there wasn't any wind. "My name is Vincent. I'm looking for my student, Fif—no, Chantrelle. Her name is Chantrelle." Only the sounds of birds greeted his's ears, but he felt that whatever approval he needed had been granted. Vincent moved deeper into the forest, surprised to find that the way forward toward the bluish-white glow always seemed to be on a path. Once, he glanced behind him and saw that the path stopped a few feet back. Vincent had seen a lot of strange things in his time. Hell, he'd raised the dead so many times he'd lost count, but this was the first time in a long time that he actually felt a little lost.

As Vincent came closer, he saw that the magical signature he'd been following was actually two, swirling together: the blue-white one he'd seen in town emanating from many of the citizens and a deep purple one. Almost as soon as he made this revelation, he was upon it. The glow was coming straight up from a hole in the ground at the edge of a small clearing. The bluish glow was painfully bright which was probably why he hadn't noticed the subtler signature within from town. Vincent got down on his hands and knees by the opening in the earth. The magic dancing within showed him that it wasn't too deep. Vincent wanted to investigate, but he also didn't want to plunge into a hole he couldn't see any way out of. He did have more important tasks at hand. But, Chantrelle... Vincent inched his lower body into the hole backwards and dropped down.

Joon surveyed the scene and had to admit it had come together nicely. There were times when she had her doubts, but the three of them had pulled it off. Or they would, assuming the finishing touches were in place within the next twenty minutes. It was looking promising. The additional recruits were invaluable. Alex was in a tree hanging the projector while Scarlet ran the extra-long extension cord *very carefully* from the front room out to him. William and Jenna were gleefully putting the last of the multitudinous decorations Jenna had procured everywhere possible throughout the front yard, and Hope was helping Joon set up the refreshment table, a task they hadn't wanted to do until just before guests, the few that didn't live there, were slated to arrive.

"Are we absolutely certain that the kids are going to be able to get Sally to come out here?" Joon fretted as she poured cheese puffs in a bowl shaped like a giant spider.

"Relax, Joon, I'm sure between the two of them they can figure something out," Hope said. "I'm also pretty sure Sally is onto us, so I doubt it'll be that hard. Are you going to kill me if I sneak a bat cookie early?"

"Nah, go ahead. You've earned it. Plus Kylie and I already ate a couple. They're super good, if I do say so myself," Joon bragged. Hope just nodded, her mouth full of bat-shaped pumpkin cookie goodness. Joon giggled.

"I'm glad you like them. I just wish it wasn't so hot out. Is it supposed to be this hot in October?"

"Depends upon the year. Or the day. Welcome to North Carolina."

"Ugh. I guess you're used to it if you grew up here, though, huh?"

"Not even a little. I'm from New England. I've been here a little while, but I'm not sure you ever *really* get used to it. Just so you know, that ice cold sweet tea isn't just a Southern cliché, it's a lifesaver in the summer. Jenna makes the best."

I hope we don't have to stay here that long, Joon thought, but she didn't dare say it out loud. If she did, there was a chance Hope would break down for her just how long Kylie would be a cozy prisoner here. Joon didn't really mind, but she knew Kylie felt differently. Footsteps padded up behind her, and Joon turned around.

"The decorations are up," Jenna declared with pride. William stood beside her with fluffs of cotton spider web caught in his hair.

"They sure are," Hope said. Joon bit her lip so she wouldn't giggle. The yard looked like a Halloween store exploded in the middle of it. From what she had heard, Sally would probably love it.

"We're going inside to change into something spookier if we can be spared for a few minutes," William said.

"Sure. I think everything is almost ready."

"Why don't you go ahead too, Joon? I can probably handle pouring candy in a bowl," Hope said. "It won't take me long to change anyway."

"Oh! Okay, and try to keep an eye on those two for me, please." Joon gestured at Alex and Scarlet flailing with the electronics. "They concern me." Hope and Jenna laughed.

"As well they should. I'll supervise," Hope promised. "Now get a move on. The Drakes will be here any minute."

"No, Richard, no matter how you try, you will never be able to turn into a rock," Sally said, rolling her eyes. "I suppose you could transform into a flesh blob that looked like a rock, but why?"

"Ew, thanks for the mental picture," Kylie said, her lips twisting in disgust.

"He asked," Sally said, opening her arm toward Richie. Richie shrugged, unapologetic. The three of them sat in the basement sitting room on well-worn, brown sofas by the light of a couple of mismatched table lamps. Kylie and Richie had devised a genius method of keeping Sally distracted until it was time to take her outside: ask her a barrage of a questions. Because they both realized soon after meeting Sally that she couldn't stop herself from answering questions, even if she didn't know the answer.

Kylie glanced down at her wristwatch. 6:58, no time for more questions. They needed to get out front ASAP. She gave Richie's foot a light kick.

"Maybe that's my cue to stop asking, then," he said.

"I think it is," Kylie agreed. She stood up, thinking at top speed. They hadn't really planned this part. What would get Sally outside? "Oh, um, did you see that super cute outfit Jenna put on the gargoyle today?"

"Really, Jenna dressed Griswold? No, I hadn't seen." Sally jumped up and took off up the stairs. Kylie and Richie scrambled after to make sure she went where she was supposed to.

"You think she knows?" Richie whispered.

"Shhhh! She's at the front door." The blinds were closed, but light glowed through them. Sally didn't say anything about the suspicious illumination coming from her front yard, so Kylie had to think that Richie was onto something. She'd probably known what they were about all evening. Kylie appreciated her doing them the courtesy of not letting on.

Sally opened the front door wide. William was waiting on the porch, dressed as a very dapper Satan in an old-fashioned red suit coat over a black button-up and slacks. He twirled what appeared to be a real pitchfork in one hand. Kylie thought it was an odd choice to have white horns. Maybe that's all he could find. It was a pretty good costume piece. She couldn't even see the headband.

"Happy birthday," William said. He stopped playing with his pitchfork and leaned it against his shoulder. He smiled at his sister, and his typically guarded eyes softened.

"There's a movie screen on my front yard," Sally replied.

"Yeah. What do you think?"

"I think it's a fantastic idea," Sally said. She raised herself up on tiptoe to scan the assembly on the lawn. "And there don't appear to have been any casualties getting it up there."

"Um, well, there may have been a fern—"

"Shhh. I don't want to think about landscaping now. I believe there is fun to be had?"

"And I was promised I could light the candles, so let's get to it!" Richie said. He darted around Sally and into the party proper below.

"I was hoping he'd forgotten that." William sighed and ran a hand through his hair.

"Well, we all like blackened cake, right?" Kylie said, following Richie into a sea of jack-o-lantern string lights. She found her sister lounging in one of the lawn chairs around the fire pit. A bonfire was already roaring. They managed to keep Richie from helping with that, at least. Joon was wearing a store-bought sexy nurse costume. She was watching the scene on the porch intently.

"You can relax. I'm pretty sure she's thrilled." Kylie sat down beside Joon.

"What? Oh, good."

"Hey, Joon?"

"What?"

"There's a mosquito on your leg."

Joon swore and slapped at the insect. It left a smear of blood on her thigh.

"Not fair! I practically took a bath in bug spray," Joon said.

"Maybe this was not the best outfit for an outdoor party?" Kylie suggested.

"But I like it..."

"No you don't." Kylie rolled her eyes. "You thought William would like it, and maybe get you out of it. But nobody feels sexy covered in bug bites."

"Kylie Nicole!" Joon stared, open-mouthed, at her little sister. Kylie shrugged.

"What? I'm not a kid anymore. I know things."

"Oh like hell you do." It was Joon's turn to roll her eyes.

"I knew one thing, didn't I?" Kylie smirked.

"No," Joon said, without any conviction. Kylie laughed. Joon kicked off her heels and curled her toes into the grass. The light from the fire glittered off her red nail polish.

"You might be a *little* right, but the costume was also on sale. Not as on sale as the 'sexy black bear' costume, but I wasn't feeling that one for some reason."

"I can't imagine why not. What does that even mean?"

"You don't want to know. Do you have a costume? I'm sure it'll be a while before the first movie starts if you need to change. I know you couldn't really do that ahead of time."

"Yeah, you're welcome, by the way," Kylie said, nudging Joon's shin with her sneaker. "Nah, I didn't get a costume."

"Oh-ho, are we too cool to dress up for Halloween now?" Joon raised an eyebrow. Kylie crossed her arms and tried not to smile.

"Maybe I am. Which one of us is getting eaten alive by bugs?"

"You've got me there." Joon raised her eyes above Kylie's head. "It looks like Richie is about to light the candles whether everyone's there or not. You'd better get over there. I'll round up the stragglers."

While Richie lit the candy-striped candles one-by-one from a flame held between his thumb and forefinger, William fished a plastic tiara out of the inside of his jacket and wondered if Sally was pretending to enjoy herself for his and Jenna's sake. This was nothing like the kind of parties she went to as a girl, and there was no doubt that she loved those. Even nearly a century ago, Sally probably wore dresses to those events that cost more than they spent on this entire party. A party in her honor with twelve guests, if one was generous with the term "guest," where her indigent brother was about to crown her with a two-dollar tiara. It wasn't what she deserved, but it was better than he'd thought he could deliver, only because so many had been so willing to to help. Sally had built something special here. She had people who genuinely cared about her.

Richie finally finished the candles without catastrophe, and most of the assemblage started to sing "Happy Birthday." William crowned Sally from behind and she squealed with delight. Several of the guests lost a beat in the song. They had probably never heard Sally make such an adorable, girlish sound before. But William had. He had made sure to be there to protect her as best he was able when she had been a child, and he could remember when all it took to banish her tears was something sparkly. That was a very long time ago. These days it was hard to say who protected whom, but at least he could still make her happy once in a while.

"I hope chocolate and strawberry are still your favorites, because that's what I got," William said when the last strains of ill-harmonized song died away. "Jenna was pretty sure I was right, so I'm blaming it on her if I'm wrong."

"Hey!" a plague doctor hollered in Jenna's voice from across the table, cloak billowing out as she put hands on her hips. Sally laughed.

"You're both right. Any volunteers to cut this thing, or do I have to do it myself?"

"I've got it." William picked up the knife and sliced the sheet cake into uniform squares with almost mechanical precision in no time flat. He served Sally first, although she tried to protest, and then everyone else as they crowded around in a claustrophobic knot. They dispersed as they got their cake, though, and Alex set to work trying to start the first movie. William watched from behind the food table. He took a flask from the other inside pocket of his jacket and took a long drink. A flicker of movement outside the ring of citronella torches and jack-o-lantern string lights caught his eye. He tilted his head. He focused his eyes on the dark distance, but with all the light sources close by, it was hard to see much. The far reaches of the orchard petered out into the grassy meadow that extended all the way to the lake. Whatever it was, it had moved somewhere near that transitional boundary. He didn't see it again, though. If it were anything at all, it was probably just a deer. William took another swig and stashed the flask back in his jacket. Sally wouldn't like him drinking at her party. He found a cinnamon hard candy in the candy bowl and popped it in his mouth before wandering over toward the rest of the group.

Joon sat in the back row of lawn chairs by herself. The movie was in black and white and looked like it had been filmed on a toaster, but Sally and her original housemates, and Jason and his mom, seemed to be enjoying it. The rest had taken to talking by the fire where Alex wouldn't shush them. Joon was thinking about joining them, maybe roasting a few marshmallows, when a flash of red appeared in her peripheral vision.

"Lose something?" William was leaning over the chair beside her, dangling her baby doll heels from his fingers. A couple tiny black marks had been left on the pleather by sparks from the bonfire. Oops.

"Oh, thank you!" Joon plucked the shoes from his hand and slipped them back onto her feet. "How very Prince Charming of you."

"That's the first time anybody's said anything like that." William looked forward at the movie screen, or rather king-sized sheet.

"I don't believe you," Joon said. "You're very charming. And such a handsome devil." William gave her the side-eye.

"Been saving that one all night, have you?"

"Yes." Joon grinned in triumph.

"Absolutely terrible." He rolled his eyes. "But thank you. You look lovely yourself. I'm not too fond of nurses, but you might could change my mind." Joon felt her heart quicken. William kept his face toward the screen but his eyes flicked down at her, and he smiled. Joon grabbed his hand and stood up.

"Come with me." She pulled him towards the nearby orchard so they wouldn't have to walk past anyone.

"Wh—okay." William stumbled once. Joon scarcely gave him a second to catch his footing. He allowed himself to be led at her will. As soon as she thought they were out of sight, or at least unlikely to be noticed, Joon put her back to a tree trunk and drew William against her body. He needed no further encouragement. William pressed his lips to hers and buried his hand in her hair. Joon tasted spice and whiskey on his tongue. She worked her hands underneath his shirt, feeling his muscles move under his icy skin. The chill sent goose-bumps up her arms.

William froze and pulled back. Joon started to ask if she'd done something wrong, but he wasn't looking at her, he was looking off deeper into the trees, eyes wide and alert. Alarm sparked in Joon's chest. She tried not to think too hard about William being of a different species, but in the dark she could see his eyes reflecting the dim light and realized that he could sense things in the night she couldn't.

"What is it?"

"I'm not sure. Probably nothing." He kept peering into the darkness.

"Oh no, nothing is nothing in the woods at night." Joon's voice squeaked and her head shook.

"Maybe you're right. Go back to the others. I'm going to check it out," William said. He disentangled himself and took a step deeper into the orchard.

"What? By yourself?" Joon followed, although she stayed hidden behind his back. William glanced back at her.

"Well, yeah."

"Not a chance! Splitting up gets you killed in every horror movie ever made. I'm coming with you," Joon whispered, gripping William's arm as if her life depended on it. There was scarce a drop of light left under the canopy, but Joon could see William's reflective irises roll up and down. Whatever. He could judge her if he wanted, but she sure as hell wasn't going anywhere in those woods alone, not even the few yards back to the party.

William turned back toward whatever he had seen or heard and strode off without hesitation. Joon stumbled after him, not expecting such a carefree pace. She made herself let go of his arm so her obituary wouldn't read "Killed by forest monster trying to play three-legged race" and crept along as close behind him as possible without treading underfoot. It was still too close. When he stopped, she ran straight into his back. She let out an "Oof," and William whipped around to cover her mouth. He looked her steadily in the eye, took his hand away, and then pointed. Joon squinted in the direction indicated by the vague red shape. She thought maybe she could see *something*, a figure of some sort moving in the trees at a distance. If not for the movement, she doubted she would see it at all. And the way it moved—it seemed awkward and wrong, yet a little bit familiar as well.

I think it's hunting. William's voice, but Joon wasn't hearing it with her ears. *I'm not sure what that thing is, but I don't like it. It smells rotten.* Joon didn't know how to do what William was doing, so she had to resort to speaking out loud, as quietly as she could make herself.

"You don't think it's a zombie, do you?"

I don't know. Maybe. I've only ever seen two or three, and they're all so different.

"What do we do?" Joon watched the figure lurch slowly to and fro. It didn't seem to be coming any closer, but it was hard to tell.

If it's a zombie, I'll need to behead it, and that would be much easier with a good weapon. It doesn't look like it's going to get very far. Let's go back to the house and find something to take care of it with. William put an arm around Joon's shoulders and began to lead her back the way they came. She looked back, but she'd already lost the ominous figure between the trees.

Alex sat on the end of the front row, separated from Sally by Scarlet. *A Bucket of Blood* wasn't one of his favorite movies, but the birthday girl seemed happy, so Jenna's first choice could be counted a success. Alex did not look forward to taking the walk-in movie set-up down in a few hours when everyone who didn't live here had left, but it was worth it. Perhaps Alex had misjudged William. He no doubt cared for his sister. Not as if that was the only measure of a man.

Alex!

It took a great deal of self-control for Alex not to jump out of his chair. The telepathic missive sounded like someone whisper-yelling between his ears.

Behind you.

Alex turned and saw William, with Joon clutching his arm like a life preserver, standing behind the rows of chairs. Alex sat his bowl of popcorn on the ground and slunk out of his seat as unobtrusively as he could. No one gave him any mind. He met William and Joon behind the rest of the audience.

"We didn't want to disturb Sally, but we need some advice," William said, ever so softly. "We found something lurking in the orchard. Joon thinks it's a zombie. Do you know where Sally keeps the good beheading weapons?" Alex studied the pair before him and felt that he didn't really want to give either of them the good beheading weapons.

"What were you doing in the orchard?" Alex said, stalling while he tried to think through what to do about this. It really seemed like a Sally problem, but he didn't want to interrupt her birthday festivities, either.

Joon frowned. "That's none of your business."

Alex repressed a smile. Perhaps so, but she could be less obvious.

"All right, come with…" Alex watched past William's shoulder as a disoriented young man with gray skin shambled out of the trees, twigs caught in his beard and hair. "Is that what you're talking about?" Joon and William spun around to follow Alex's line of sight.

"Yep, looks like it," William said. There wasn't much air moving, but even without the benefit of the wind Alex could smell the stench of decay and chemicals that wafted off the creature. It was hard to say for sure, but it very well might be a zombie.

"William, you—" Alex was cut off by a glass-shattering shriek. It was Kylie. Alex's shoulders slumped. They had been trying to avoid panic. But when he looked at Kylie, she wasn't even looking at the rotting man emerging from the woods. She was standing and pointing toward the driveway with an expression of bug-eyed horror. Alex, William, and Joon swiveled their heads at once. Another zombie, much taller and bulkier, was lumbering down the drive. Behind it, a middle-aged man stood in the middle of the road. Alex could see his entire body crackling with energy. His aura was electric with it. The man stood with his hands behind his back, a small, smug smile on his face. His dark eyes darted between the two dead men, watching them with cool interest.

Alex could just see Joon in the periphery of his vision, vaulting over lawn chairs to get next to her sister. William bolted in some other direction, leaving Alex alone nearest the zombies. But only momentarily. Sally, Scarlet, and Hope soon surrounded him. Even William returned a second later, with the cake knife and serving spatula in his hands. Not great weapons, but they might be better than bare hands.

"I think you're outnumbered, Professor LaMont," Sally called to the man in the road. His eyes widened a sliver, but there were no other cracks in his composure.

"There is more to odds than numbers," the professor called. "But we don't need to fight over this. I'm here for her." He pointed past the closed ranks of the manor's finest. No one turned to look. It didn't matter who he wanted, but there could be little doubt that it was Kylie.

"Give her over to me, and I won't cause any trouble. Well, any more trouble," the professor said, a smile twitching the corners of his lips.

"No," Sally said, snorting. To Alex's left, William crouched, ready to charge. Scarlet started to growl. Alex sent Pansy and Joon a telepathic missive: *Take the kids and go inside.* He gave them quick directions to Scarlet's cache of weapons. Someone might as well use it.

The professor shrugged. The zombie from the woods veered off toward the group retreating into the house while the other stepped off the driveway and toward the task force standing between the professor and his quarry.

"Don't say I didn't give you a chance," Professor LaMont said. Alex could feel the static crackle of the man's energy. This might not be easy.

William yowled, a sound akin to the scream of a mountain lion, and charged the warlock professor with flailing cutlery. Professor LaMont took a step back and held up his hands. The air rippled in front of him, and William was knocked back a good fifteen feet. Undaunted, William rolled onto his feet again and charged the now nearer target, the zombie. He never lost his grip on the utensils.

Scarlet, having taken advantage of the warlock's momentary distraction, was on his back, sinking her teeth into the back of his neck as deep as she could before she, too, was ejected. Alex left Professor LaMont to the more magically qualified and ran to William's aid. In the half-second it took him to decide, William had plunged the spatula through the thing's eye and the cake knife into its throat farther than Alex would have thought possible. Thick, black blood oozed from both wounds as William braced one leg against the zombie's chest and attempted to free the knife with both hands.

"Give up," Alex said. He gave the zombie a quick once over. It wasn't as decomposed as he would have liked. William seemed to understand what he had in mind.

"You hold, I'll pull," William said, releasing the knife. The zombie tried to wrap its hands around his neck, and William swatted them away with mild annoyance. Alex nodded and went around back. The creature's head lolled, trying to see both enemies at once, but William slashed and punched at it with such ferocity that it was kept quite busy. Alex waited for the perfect window, then threw one arm around its neck and the other around its waist. The zombie roared, grabbing for Alex but unable to do more than pull his hair and scratch at him. William caught one of the waving limbs, leaving the other to snatch Alex bald. Alex could feel him pulling against the shoulder joint and closed his eyes against any gore-spatter. William grunted with the effort.

"Damn, he's a fresh one. Muscly, too. Hardly any give—ah-ha!" There was a thick, wet tearing sound, and then the tug at the shoulder disappeared. Cool drops of liquid hit Alex's face.

"One down, three and a head to go!" William chirped.

"We only have to get the head," Alex said, spitting as he tasted rotten, chemical-laden blood on his lips. "And probably the arms so we can get to the head."

"Fine, be like that." William somehow managed to wrestle the remaining arm away from Alex's scalp—Alex didn't open his eyes to investigate—and resumed the task.

Joon and Pansy ran through the manor as best they could while constantly checking for zombies and counting that all five kids were still there. By a Halloween miracle, the half-remembered directions brought them to a door in the basement with a black metal wolf silhouette hung at eye level. That seemed like the place, and Joon was eager to at least hide somewhere, so she barged in without hesitation. Of course, the lights were off, but Pansy found the switch and flicked it on.

The room was not very large, but it was packed with every kind of weapon imaginable, including quite a few Joon had never seen before. An array of guns were racked on the back wall. Mounted on the side walls were swords, bows, spears, axes, and all manner of other deadly paraphernalia. Joon guessed the half dozen trunks on the ground held ammunition.

"Children will not be choosing their own weapons," Joon said.

"I'm nineteen," Richie yelled, shoving past her.

Drat. Joon definitely thought he was younger. She ushered everyone inside and closed and locked the door behind them. Joon turned to tell Pansy what kind of weapons to go for, but Pansy was way ahead of her, already testing the heft of a curved sword in her hands. Ignoring Joon's order, Jason was in the midst of taking a crossbow down. His mother was literally right there, so Joon decided it wasn't her problem. She wasn't even going to think about Richie, so she turned her attention to the other three standing and staring at her in terror like good little children. Joon glanced around, picked three small daggers, and handed them to the kids. Kylie, who had thwarted zombies in the past with a pencil and a textbook, seemed satisfied, playing with it to see how it felt. The boys just stared at the little pig-stickers, and then at Joon.

"You've got to be kidding me," one of them said.

"Nope," Joon said. "Go to the back of the room and let the grown-ups do the fighting. Try not to stab each other." Grumbling, the boys did as they were told, going to stand on either side of Jason. He had found the crossbow bolts somewhere and nocked one with the utmost concentration. Joon wasn't sure how much good that would really do against a zombie. If she had her way, he would never find out. She looked around for a weapon of her own. Heavy footfalls thudded down the basement steps. Pansy moved to block the door, sword at the ready. Joon's eyes lit on the perfect choice. She wasn't sure what it was, just a metal rod with a knob of sharp edges and points at the end. But it looked an awful lot like a weaponized bedpost. Joon snatched it from the wall and joined Pansy, beside and a little behind her where she hoped she was out of the way of the blade. Despite his eagerness to play with the toys, Richie was nowhere near when the footsteps stopped at the door. The doorknob rattled. It rattled harder, then there was a snap from the other side. The inside knob fell off. Outside, the creature yelled its inarticulate frustration. Two gray fingers poked through the hole in the door around the mechanism of the deadbolt. Both women shrieked, and Pansy swiped her sword down across the undead hand. She took off both fingers, the barest tip of the sword scratching the door frame. The fingers fell to the floor, where they continued to twitch. For a moment, there seemed to be no reaction from the enemy. Then it began to pound on the door. Joon and Pansy stepped back. The wood soon began to buckle and splinter where the knob used to be.

With one last crack, the door broke enough for the zombie to push through. It spared a glance for Joon and Pansy before making straight toward the space between them. With a war cry, Pansy swung for the throat. Joon aimed for the back of the head at the same time, and the zombie's cranium collapsed in a geyser of black gore. The remnants tumbled to the ground, followed by the body a second later. At the back of the room, Kylie cheered.

"We should probably find somewhere else to hide," Pansy said after a beat. "It's pretty obvious we've been here now."

Joon nodded, shuffling her bare feet away from the widening puddle of blood around the re-dead zombie.

"Any ideas? Is there a panic room in this place?" Joon asked.

"I think we're *in* the panic room," Pansy said. "We might just have to pick a place and take our chances. Hold on to your weapons, kids."

"Not a problem, Mom," Jason said.

Scarlet dove to the ground to avoid a lawn chair flying for her head. She rolled aside a heartbeat before it plunged toward the ground, the legs embedding themselves in the earth where her chest had been a moment ago. More chairs whirled through the air, as well as any other object that could be easily levitated. It was difficult to tell which projectiles were Hope's and which were the sorcerer-professor's, so Scarlet was doing her best to avoid all of them. Her success rate was about seventy percent.

Scarlet pulled herself up into a crouch and waited, ready to dodge or dive in for another attack on Professor LaMont at any moment. She and Sally had only gotten a few good ones in, but the blood seeping through the enemy's tattered clothing gave Scarlet reassurance that they were doing their part. She wondered why Sally hadn't zapped him senseless yet, but there was no time to ask. A flurry of stones pelted Scarlet from above without warning. She yelped and darted away.

Hope seemed to be gaining ground, thank goodness. The professor's shields had been no match for her, but he had a harder time cracking hers. Scarlet watched, lying flat on the ground with her arms over her head, as Hope conjured a fiery rope from the tip of her finger and sent it flying through the air toward the professor. The rope of light wrapped itself around Professor LaMont's torso like a climbing vine. He yelled, in anger rather than pain, and indeed Scarlet could see no sign that it burned him. But several of the vindictive lawn chairs dropped to the ground.

The professor tried to brush the tendril off with his hands, presumably employing a counterspell in the process. At least, Scarlet hoped so, otherwise it was a rather pathetic display. Hope continued to cast offensive spells in his distraction. Tree roots burst from the ground and entangled the professor's legs. Scarlet leapt to her feet and made a dash at him, arriving a moment after Sally. Scarlet locked her jaws on his shoulder. Sally, the ends of her fingers transformed into large, black claws, raked the knife-like points down his back. Hope's flaming tendril was undisturbed by Sally's claws. Scarlet felt the professor send out a shield, but this time, it barely upset her balance. Sally, without the benefit of having her teeth sunk in the man's flesh, was knocked back a half step. A fuzzy, static sensation prickled Scarlet's skin, and she felt her hair begin to lift. She pulled her teeth free and backed away a few feet. She noticed that Hope was no longer casting, save for a few small objects swirling above her head. They both sensed the finish coming.

Sally put her hands on the professor's shoulders. The muscles under her skin rippled and there was an audible crack as her body released its electric charge. Professor LaMont went limp in her grip. Scarlet could still hear his heartbeat, though. Sally hadn't killed him. She wanted him for something.

The roots around his legs slithered back into the earth, leaving holes in the lawn that Alex was not going to be happy about. The last levitating objects thumped to the grass and the faint light around Hope faded. Scarlet looked across the lawn, checking on Alex and William for the first time since the fight got underway. Alex, covered in black gook, was sitting on the armless body of a bulky zombie while William tugged on the thing's head. The zombie made loud vocalizations that sounded more annoyed than anything else.

"You guys need any help over there?" Scarlet called.

"What we need is a machete," Alex said.

"I've got it." Hope waved her hand, and the zombie's head popped off in William's grasp. He fell back on his rear, looking at the head with surprise. Alex was showered anew with zombie blood. He turned, ever so slowly, to glare at Hope.

"Oops?" Hope said. Sally spotted an upright chair near where the outdoor theater had lately been and carried the unconscious necromancer to it.

"He won't stay out long," she said. "We need to decide what to do with him. I'm thinking basement? I don't know about y'all, but I have some questions I would like answered."

"This is really not how I wanted this party to go," William said, tossing the zombie head aside.

"I don't know," Sally said. She walked over to a hydrangea bush where something in the branches sparkled. She fished out her birthday tiara and placed it back on her head, along with a couple of leaves. "I thought it was pretty nice. The party crashers were a bit unpleasant, but they did bring me some lovely zombie body parts to play with in my lab, so it wasn't all bad. Speaking of such, has anyone checked on the others? That seems important." William scrambled to his feet and ran into the manor, Alex right on his heels. Scarlet began gathering up zombie limbs for Sally, since she seemed so keen on them.

"Hey, that was a great spell, Hope," she said, placing a leg under her arm. Hope smiled.

"Thanks. I realized he was drawing power from the environment, a lot of it, so if we didn't want to keep at it until Jesus comes back I'd have to keep him from doing so."

"He was drawing it from me, too," Sally added, picking the professor back up to take downstairs. "I couldn't build up a charge until you blocked him." That explained it. Scarlet was glad sometimes that she didn't wield magic. It was awfully complicated. She thought she had as many pieces of zombie as she could carry at once without dropping any, so she began to make her way toward the porch.

"Battling sorcerers is always an exercise in creativity. You never know where they're drawing power from. But that'll be a handy spell to keep in mind from now on," Hope said. "Scarlet, you are *not* touching the doorknob with that hand! Let me get it."

9

Kauai

Seventeen. Thomas still wasn't sure he believed it. They kept at it all night and into the morning, and Koni hacked up seventeen of those Swarm demons before the fever finally left him. Most of them they drowned in a bucket of holy water—a strange new experience for all present—but a few nearly escaped. Roland impaled one with a wooden cross, and Iakopa simply stamped another into oblivion with his foot. It might have been the most chaotic exorcism in history, but it worked.

A few women of the village had brought food to the stricken family in the midst of the madness, and now it was breakfast time for the exorcists. Koni was still asleep. He had been since they finished extracting the last demon, and who could blame him? However, neither Thomas nor Iakopa was willing to leave until they were sure everything was fine. Iakopa was sprinkling a mixture of seawater and turmeric from the end of a leaf throughout the home, in case any dark energies remained. Thomas and Koni's parents sat on the floor eating, clustered around Koni's bed. Mele stroked Koni's arm, watching intently for the first sign that he was regaining consciousness. Roland, for his part, had apparently decided it was time to ask Thomas the question Thomas had been hoping no one would bring up.

"Mr. Thomas, you told me you are not a priest." Roland didn't sound suspicious or accusatory, just confused. "Where did you learn so much about demons?" Thomas bit into a mango to buy himself some time to think about his answer. Maybe they deserved the truth. He chewed, swallowed.

"Well, when I was still young and much too reckless, my wife and I had a son, the sickliest little thing I've ever seen." Thomas studied the fruit in his hand, trying not to remember the image of his thin, listless infant. "He wasn't even old enough to crawl, and he was dying.

So I made a deal with a devil. Not *the* Devil. A servant of Hell named Daemonicus. A low-life, really, on their totem pole. But what I was saying—"

"Daemonicus?"

For a moment, Thomas didn't even realize who had spoken. The quiet, melodic voice was the absolute antithesis of the raspy growl he had heard before. Then Mele shrieked his name and threw herself onto him in the most desperate embrace Thomas had ever seen, and it became abundantly clear that Koni was awake, and had just said aloud the name of the devil that owned Thomas.

"I'm fine," Koni assured his mother while she hugged him to death. He never took his eyes off Thomas, though. "But, I thought I heard you say 'Daemonicus.' Who are you?"

"I brought him here to save you," Roland said, taking his son's hand. "I owe him more than I could ever possibly repay."

"Don't mention it," Thomas said. "Now, Koni, how do you know that name?"

"I—I'm not sure. I think that word is one of the last things I can re-member...before now. What happened? And where are Kai and Kap?" Koni's parents lowered their gazes. Before they could break the news to him, Iakopa intervened, handing Koni a cup of an herbal concoction.

"Here, drink this. It'll help you regain your strength," Iakopa said. Koni made a face. He probably wasn't too keen on drinking anything after vomiting up a hive of demons, but he did as he was told.

"Now, son," Iakopa said, "we don't know exactly what happened to you and your brothers, but I'm afraid the news is not good."

Thomas watched a line of ants marching across the ground in front of him and thought about what he would do. Practically speaking, he should run as far from this situation as possible. For all he knew, Dae-monicus was still on this island. The right thing to do, though, would be to try to find Daemonicus. There was a chance that the middle brother, Kai, was still alive—a good chance, in fact. Daemonicus was a businessman first and a Satanist second. If he kidnapped Kai, there was a reason. He wanted Kai alive for something. To sell him, prob-ably, or some part of him. If Thomas went looking for Kai *right now*, he might be able to bring the boy back to his family in one piece. Or, he might just get himself captured, and then neither of them would make it home. Not that Thomas had a home to go to.

Thomas heard the front door swish open and thump shut. Iakopa squatted beside him, following Thomas's gaze to the dusty insects.

"What are you going to do now?" Iakopa asked without looking up.

"I'm going to go find their other son," Thomas murmured.

"Me as well. How do we start?"

"We start at the last place he was seen. We see what we can find."

"The men have already searched there. That's where we found Kapena's body."

"I haven't seen it yet."

"I'll take you, but I really don't think it will help much."

Iakopa wasn't completely wrong. There really was very little to see. Iakopa and one of the villagers who first found the scene took Thomas on horseback to the base of a nondescript hill surrounded by a few trees and lots of grass and dirt.

"This was where we found Kapena." The townsman dismounted and stood by the spot. A few clumps of torn grass spoke to the struggle that had taken place. Thomas walked over, and then around, looking intently at the ground like he knew what he was looking for. He didn't. There were some vague footprints in the patches without grass, but nothing that just screamed "I'm a clue!"

"And you don't know what killed him?" Thomas asked, glancing up at his companions. They shook their heads. "Well, at least tell me what this looked like." He swung his arms in a wide gesture. "I need a mental picture."

The witness did his best to explain. They went looking for the two older boys after the arrival in town of Koni and the horse. Their parents knew where the three had gone, so it wasn't hard to guess where to search. When they got to the base of Kawaihoa, the ground was splattered with fresh blood. Kai was nowhere and Kap's body was in the spot indicated, eyes open, sprawled on his back, a gaping hole ripped in his throat.

"Kapena was strong," the man said, finishing his tale. "I don't know any animal on the island that could have beaten him, and no man would have done this."

"Well, yes and no," Thomas said. "He's not a man exactly—oh, hello!"

What's this?" A glint in the dirt had caught his eye. Thomas bent and picked up the lustrous rock. It was just a big hunk of quartz, nothing spectacular at first blush, but as he rubbed his fingers over its surface Thomas could feel shallow lines carved into the cool, white gem. He tilted it and watched the sun catch the facets. Sure enough, the lines formed curves and symbols. Thomas recognized some of the sigils from Hope's spell books.

"It's a token," Thomas said. "Witches use them to increase their powers. Is there anyone on the island it might belong to?" The two Ni'ihau men glanced at each other, then shook their heads.

"Are you sure? Yeah? Well, good, because this may be able to lead us to Kai." Thomas caressed the token beneath his fingers and closed his eyes. He couldn't feel much power left in the token, but the island around him practically sang with natural energy. Thomas opened his mind and let it seep inside of him and to the stone in his hand. The quartz warmed against his palm. Thomas opened his eyes. He could feel the others staring at him, but he ignored them in favor of the rock.

"Now that you've recharged your batteries, how about you take me to your leader?" Thomas asked. A thin ray of white light shot out of one of the crystal's vertices and way off into the distance in front and to the right of Thomas. He squinted but couldn't see any obvious destination.

"I suppose we follow the white light, then?" Iakopa said somewhere behind Thomas. He glanced over his shoulder. Iakopa's tense body language made it clear that he wasn't at all comfortable with this turn of events, but he was holding up better than the other man, who was clearly poised to bolt any second.

"Yep. It'll lead us back to the token's last owner, wherever they may be." Thomas turned until his body was aligned in the direction of the light. Was that the ocean peeking between the hills? "I have a sneaking suspicion that we may require a boat."

Thomas, Roland, and Iakopa followed the laser-like guidance beam of the token mostly along the margin of the two-lane road, the sun shining through a light mist of rain. After meeting up with Roland, they followed the token's lead off Ni'ihau, as Thomas had thought they might have to, and then to port on Kauai. Now they were trekking along the roadside headed toward Koloa. It had been a long time since anyone said anything, and Thomas would have been happy to keep it that way, but he wasn't going to get a break from uncomfortable questions any longer.

"Thomas, how is it you can do this?" Iakopa asked. "I have seen magic before, but not like this. Are *you* a witch?" Thomas recognized that sharpness, that electricity in his voice. He didn't want Iakopa to be afraid of him. But he understood.

"I'm not a witch. You have to be born a witch. I'm a sorcerer. I get my powers from outside myself." Thomas kicked a stick out of their path.

"Is that, uh, better?" Iakopa said.

"What, do you mean 'Am I less evil?'" Thomas laughed with a hint of bitterness. "Witches and sorcerers are all just people. You tell me."

"As long as he can find Kaimana, I don't care if he's the Devil himself," Roland said.

"You've got to be careful talking like that," Thomas replied in warning. "Someone might be listening." The ray of white light he'd been following winked out, and the token started to hum, more a vibration than a sound.

"I think we're here, whatever that means." The three men looked around. They were still outside the city, so there wasn't much: a tiny row of souvenir shops on the far side of the road, and a small bed-and-breakfast on the nearer.

Thomas looked at the building. "I'm going to bet on the Aloha Inn here."

"They could be in the forest," Iakopa said. Thomas shook his head.

"Not Daemonicus's style. He hides in plain sight. It's classier. Now, I have an idea how to approach this, but Iakopa, I'll need you to do a tiny bit of acting." Thomas looked over at the older man, thinking there was maybe a fifty-fifty chance of him agreeing to trust a sorcerer if it might save a child.

"What? Why me?"

"Daemonicus and his people definitely know who I am, and they might recognize Roland, too. I'm not sure how much recognizance they did on their target," Thomas said. "But I'm pretty sure they won't know you. You're the ace up our sleeve today."

"Oh, good?"

"Relax. I'm giving you the easy job. It'll be safer than selling Boy Scout popcorn. Probably."

Where is it? Where is it? Kell dumped the contents of her duffel bag out on the bed. Nothing. The piece of quartz was nowhere to be found. She had searched the whole room. There was only one explanation—she had dropped it on Ni'ihau. Daemonicus might come any minute to ask for it back. They were leaving in a couple of hours, maybe fewer, as soon as he "tied up some loose ends" and arranged a meeting with Jasmine to hand off the Guardian. He charged more for murder than kidnapping, and Jasmine couldn't afford an assassination. She had plenty of magic, but not a lot of money.

"All right, all right, I can fix this. How can I fix this?" She could teleport back to Ni'ihau, but then how would she find it? The token was probably near where they caught the boys. She could easily have dropped it during that chaos. Could she find the spot again? Maybe. If she could get a clear picture in her head, she could get there. She would need to be fast, though, or Daemonicus might notice she was gone. *Should I just tell him?* A trio of brisk knocks came at the door to Kell's room. *There he is!* Kell sucked in a more-or-less calming breath and went to answer. *It'll be all right. I'll just tell him what happened, and then I'll go take care of it, and everything will be fine.* Kell gathered her courage and flung the door open before she could change her mind and try to run. The caller was not Daemonicus. It was an older, bronze-skinned man with soft eyes, holding in his hand the very thing Kell was afraid she would never see again.

"Excuse me, miss, but I found this, ahem, this rock in the lobby, and I was trying to find out who it belonged to—"

"Thank the spirits, you've found it!" Kell snatched the token from him and hugged it to her chest. "You have no idea how glad I am to have it back! Thank you!"

"Y-you're welcome," the man mumbled, looking perplexed. Kell thanked him again, wished him all the best, and closed the door. She rubbed the token against her face, feeling it purr. Maybe fate was going to be kind to her after all.

"That's not Daemonicus, in case you were wondering." Thomas and Roland came around the corner and joined Iakopa in the hall in front of room 107.

"Who was she?" Iakopa asked.

"Probably just someone working for him. She can lead us to him, though, and that's where we'll find Kaimana. We need to follow her whenever she leaves."

"What if she doesn't go back to him?" Roland asked.

"Daemonicus doesn't like loose ends," Thomas assured him. "He'll call her back, for one reason or another. Let's wait in the lobby. We look suspicious standing around here."

"My family doesn't have any money. They can't pay you. Just let me go. I won't tell anybody," Kai said.

"I already have my payment secured," his captor responded, "as long as I bring you to my client. You want some more water?"

Kai nodded, and Daemonicus, the gentleman kidnapper, obligingly refilled the glass for him. It was a weird setting. Kai had woken up on a couch in this room. He wasn't tied up or handcuffed. The only thing keeping him in was this man, Daemonicus, who would simply herd Kai away anytime he got close to the door or a window.

"What does your client want?"

"That's not my problem." Daemonicus picked something up off the coffee table. Kai had only seen a smart phone twice in his life, but he guessed that's what it was. Daemonicus pressed a few buttons.

"Jasmine, your majesty, we're almost ready..." Daemonicus was looking at the floor, focused on his conversation. Now was Kai's chance. He couldn't bolt for the door, of course. That would be entirely too obvious. But there was something he could do, a little trick he had spent most of his life trying not to use. His parents—well, Koni and Kap's parents—had told him to keep it a secret, for his own good, but if ever he needed to break cover it was now. A touch was all it took, and Daemonicus had touched Kai's arm when he pushed him back from the door. Kai already knew what Daemonicus wanted most to see. He held out his hands and willed the image to come to life. Kai couldn't see it himself, not with his eyes, but in his mind he knew what picture Daemonicus would find when he looked up: Kai with a roll of parchment in his hand.

"I will see you shortly then." Daemonicus clicked off the call. "All right, young Mister Guardian, your new owner will be here to pick you up soon. I trust you won't try anyth—what's that?"

"It's a gift," Kai hedged, forcing a smirk, "from our father below. I think He likes me better than you." Kai could feel each irresistible word rolling off his tongue like smooth, gleaming pearls. Whenever he turned on his trick, people couldn't help but listen and believe what he said. Kai enacted the motions of unrolling the imaginary scroll. He glanced down at it. "I see it has your name on it, right there at the bottom, in your own blood. I can hardly read it. You blood seems to be white. How strange." Daemonicus's eyes widened so far Kai thought they might drop out of his head and plop onto the floor.

"Why do you have that?" Daemonicus rasped.

"I have it because you want it," Kai said, the only true part of the tale he was spinning. "Our master has big plans for me, you see, and He is willing to let me trade you your contract for my release. It would be insulting to turn down such a generous offer, don't you think?" Kai turned the paper around to show his kidnapper and then rolled the parchment up slowly, leaving the part with the signature for last so Daemonicus could get a nice, long look at it, and believe. He grasped the contract in one hand and crossed his arms, waiting for Daemonicus to make a decision. Kai was confident which decision he would make. All Daemonicus said he would get from handing Kai off to his client was money, and that wasn't what he desired above everything else. What he wanted was to escape his destiny. Nothing else was more important.

Daemonicus licked his lips—nervousness, perhaps, or just the raw hunger for what Kai held in his hand. This could still go wrong. If Daemonicus tried to take the contract by force, he would quickly discover that it was an illusion. Kai had to hope that the power he was pretending to have would be enough to keep Daemonicus at a distance.

"And He will protect me from any...consequences?" Daemonicus looked Kai in the eyes. Kai held his gaze steadily, determined not to break character. His life might depend on it.

"He guarantees it."

"Then it's a deal." Daemonicus raised his right hand and bit into his palm, to Kai's amazement. Then he extended his arm for a handshake. Kai moved to grasp Daemonicus's hand, then realized he, too, would be expected to seal the deal in blood. Kai put his hand to his mouth and tore the flesh at the base of his thumb with his teeth, fighting not to show any sign of the pain it caused him. He proffered his hand and Daemonicus took it, mingling Kai's blood with the liquid like milk that seeped from the wound in his own hand. The sting of Daemonicus's blood in his ripped skin was far worse than the bite had been, but Kai managed to keep a straight face. Daemonicus pulled out of the handshake. With a nod, Kai set the scroll down on the glass coffee table between them and stood to leave. He walked toward the door as fast as he thought he could without raising suspicion. He couldn't be sure that the image of the contract wouldn't dissolve the moment Daemonicus reached out and touched it. He opened the door, just inches from escape, to find a young woman outside, her fist ready to knock. Kai felt like his heart jolted to a stop. Was this the client, here to take him? She seemed equally surprised to see him, her mouth drawn in a little "o." They stared at each other.

Behind Kai, Daemonicus screamed a string of vitriol in a language Kai didn't recognize. From his tone of voice, though, Kai guessed he had discovered the trickery. Kai and the girl outside the door regained their senses at the same time. He dashed forward to push past her as she held up her hand to stop him. A pulse of something like a wall of energy hit Kai and knocked him flat onto his back. In an instant, Daemonicus grabbed him up and pinned him to a wall, fangs protruding beneath his curled lips.

"What is going on here?" the young woman demanded, her long hair flying as she rushed to put her arm between Daemonicus's teeth and Kai's throat.

"This little *imp* tried to fool me, and I won't let him get away with it," Daemonicus growled, glaring at her. "Your queen wanted to kill him, did she not? Now I'll do it for her, free of charge. It would be my pleasure." The woman edged away from Daemonicus and his vengeful fury but didn't move her arm yet.

"I'm not sure she would be okay with that..."

A battle cry roared in the hallway, and Roland charged right into Daemonicus. Caught off guard, Daemonicus stumbled, and Kai squirmed out of his grip. Daemonicus turned his attention to Roland, fully prepared to tear him apart, until a new assailant, this one wielding something in one hand, hit him from the back and latched on. Kai moved to help his father, but the girl who had come to his rescue only seconds before grabbed his arms and twisted them behind his back. Kai kicked her in the shin. She lost her grip. Another, gentler set of hands took hold of him.

"Come on, Kaimana," urged Iakopa. "Your father will be right behind us." Short of his family, Kai trusted no one more than his pastor. He allowed himself to be ushered out of the room and down the stairs. They exited through a side door. Kai was assaulted by a rush of sights and sensations he had never experienced before. A cacophony of noise surrounded him, and great monoliths of brick and stone rose on each side as Iakopa guided Kai into a quieter place hidden between two buildings.

"Where are we?" Kai panted, leaning against one of the walls for support.

"Koloa," Iakopa said. "But you'll be home soon."

"Kai!" Roland appeared at the mouth of the ally and raced to hug his son. Over his father's shoulder, Kai saw the tall *haole* man who had helped Roland fight Daemonicus. The weapon he'd had in hand when he entered the hotel room had vanished, but smears of white blood on his skin and clothes suggested it had served its purpose.

"We need to get back to Ni'ihau right now," the stranger said. He ushered them all further back from the street and through a maze of alleys and side streets to lead them out of the city.

Kell lay flat on her back on the hotel carpet and blinked at the ceiling, trying to process what had just happened. Clearly, she was not meant for the chaos of a fight. She sat up. Daemonicus was on the floor a few feet away, grunting and struggling to pull an iron cross out of his abdomen as it burned every part of his flesh that it touched.

"Hold still." Kell crawled over and wrapped her hands around the cross. Daemonicus put his hands over hers and together they yanked it out.

"Holy Lucifer, that hurt! Get me a bottle of blood from the fridge, girl."

"Who is Lucifer?" Kell clambered to her feet and retrieved the blood for Daemonicus.

"You don't know who—you know what, I am not in the mood to explain." Daemonicus put the bottle to his lips, and after only a few gulps the hole left by the cross began to close. Kell settled onto her knees by his side.

"Can we go over what just happened?"

"We've been swindled, that's what happened," Daemonicus muttered, licking a smear of red off his lips. "I thought we had the upper hand, but they were ready for us. The Guardian knew exactly what to say to throw me off. How did he even know what it looks like? None but I and the Devil himself have ever seen that contract. Oh, it doesn't matter. What matters is taking the boy back. This isn't just a job anymore. I have a score to settle." Daemonicus's visage contorted with rage. Kell scooted away to a safer distance.

"What's your plan now?"

"I don't have a plan," Daemonicus said. "There's no time for that. You stay here and wait for Jasmine. She'll be here any minute. I'm going to go do what vampires are made for, and hunt."

"I don't know what they wanted with me," Kai said, shaking his head. He winced as Thomas, the stranger who orchestrated his rescue, wrapped gauze around his bitten hand. The wound had widened in the past hour, but Thomas promised that it was only the aftereffects of contact with Daemonicus's blood, and it would heal well enough as long as it didn't become infected.

They were headed back to Ni'ihau in a motorboat lent them by the family who owned the island. Kai was in shock, but not from his cut hand—Iakopa had explained to him what transpired after his kidnapping. And the only thing keeping him grounded was the questions Thomas kept asking.

"He didn't want money from us," Kai said. "He told me he was selling me to someone else, and then later he said his client wanted to kill me. I have no idea what that was about. Kill me? Why? What did I do to them? And he called me something strange…um, 'little mister guardian,' I think."

"*Guardian?* That's what he called you?" Thomas looked up from Kai's palm to his eyes. Kai nodded.

"This may be worse than I'd thought." Thomas tied off the bandage and sat back on his heels. "If you're a Guardian, and Daemonicus is sided against them, then he may never stop trying to find you. We'll have to kill him."

"I can accept that," Roland said.

"It isn't that easy. Daemonicus is from a superior breed of vampire. Only werewolf venom could kill him, so unless you happen to know someone who is a werewolf, I doubt we can win that battle. Even if we could find a werewolf to help us, Daemonicus is allied with the forces of Hell. He might not die even then."

"What would you have us do then? We can't just wait for him to come back and slaughter my children again," Roland said. Kai felt his insides tighten.

"No, you can't. There's really only one place I know of where Kai might be safe."

"I don't understand," Kai interrupted. "What do you mean? What does Daemonicus want? *Why is this happening to me?*"

"Is it, perhaps, his…trick?" Iakopa suggested meekly.

"What trick? Do you mean something he can do that others can't?" Thomas glanced from Roland to Iakopa and back again. The two Hawaiian men only stared at each other, neither willing to speak first.

"Yes, that is what he means," Kai whispered. "I can make people see what they want to see."

"Now I don't understand."

"I'll show you. Can I show him?" Kai looked to his father and his pastor. They hesitated, then agreed. Kai called up the image of that which Thomas wanted most in his mind: his son, a thin blond child with golden-green eyes. He cast the illusion for only a moment. These visions caused people pain more often than pleasure. However, it was enough. Thomas rocked back, stunned by the lifelike vision.

"How do you *know?*"

"I just do." Kai shrugged. "When I touch someone, I know. It's been that way since I was a small boy."

"Well, that is some trick," Thomas replied, "and I dare say it is exactly why Daemonicus and his 'client' are out for your blood."

"It's not his fault," Roland said. "He was born that way."

"I know. My son Jason is a Guardian as well. It isn't something you choose. It simply happens. You can call it fate, or bad luck, or whatever you want, it doesn't matter. But your life, Kai, that does matter, and we must protect you at any cost."

"I hate to do this to you, but it is absolutely the only way I know of to keep you safe."

"I'm not coming with you for myself. I'm coming because of Kapena." Kai fixed his eyes on Thomas's. Both the fires of anger and the blackness of grief entwined his words. "If I stay, Daemonicus will continue to hurt my family. If I leave, I may get the chance to hurt Daemonicus back. But I'll need time—and werewolves—to do that.

And that's what you offer me. Safety, yes, but revenge, that is what *I* want most."

"Well, if you want to kill Daemonicus, I must caution against it," Thomas said. "On the other hand, I would be happy to assist you in any way. Until Daemonicus is dead, I can't see my family again, either. All right, the portal is ready." Kai eyed the swirling disc suspiciously. He thought he trusted Thomas, but he wasn't sure he trusted this magic.

"You just have to walk through. It might make you dizzy, but it won't hurt. I guess you can hold my hand if it'd make you feel better," Thomas said. Kai hesitated, but fear got the better of his pride.

"Um, yeah, okay." Kai grabbed Thomas's hand, which felt like more bones than flesh. Thomas ducked through the portal and gently tugged Kai behind him. Kai resisted for a second, then followed him through. A cold tingling melted through Kai from his skin to his core, and then abruptly vanished. Kai stumbled out of the portal on the other side, head spinning, a little nauseated, but in one piece. He was still cool, though. A chill breeze streamed past, competing with the warmth beaming down from the sun. They were standing by the roadside on a little strip of weedy ground, thick forest pressing in on the other side of the asphalt.

"Where are we?"

"Pretty much the middle of nowhere, North Carolina," Thomas answered. "I have somewhere in mind for us to stay, but we have a ways to walk. Come on."

It had been years since Daemonicus hunted like this, subordinating the businessman to the predator. He followed Kai's scent like a bloodhound, but the men who had taken the Guardian were smart. They went out of their way to pass through every church and heiau they could find en route to where they had stored their boat. They knew Daemonicus couldn't set foot on sacred ground, regardless of whether it was dedicated to Christ or to the ancient Hawaiian pantheon. Treading on consecrated soil was difficult for many vampires, but impossible for one in league with the Prince of Darkness. Daemonicus picked up his prey's trail on the other side of the temples, time after time, but the delays cost him precious minutes.

When Daemonicus reached Ni'ihau at last, he followed the smell of Kai's blood first to his home, but when the Guardian wasn't there he found a fresh trail that led, once again, to the grounds of a church. Whoever had planned this escape was clever. Daemonicus's initial thought was to wait outside for them to leave the church, but when he came right to the edge of the property he realized that he was too late. Static charged the air and the faint burnt stench of a hole torn in the fabric of space wafted from the open church door. Someone had taken the Guardian through a portal. It could be anywhere. Daemonicus roared in frustration and punched the earth.

"He told me you would come," said a gruff voice from behind, and downwind, of Daemonicus. He turned to find a small, weathered man brandishing a homemade crucifix. Daemonicus smiled darkly. At least he would get a little blood out of this failed venture. The human stood his ground, face set in stony determination, without the slightest hint of fear.

"That won't stop me, little man," Daemonicus chuckled, advancing.

"It doesn't have to," he said coolly. He threw something with his other hand. Daemonicus caught it easily. For a split second, he laughed at the absurdity. It was only a ball of wet clay. Then it melted in his hand and began to run down his arm, scorching like fire. His laughter turned to screaming. He tried to rub the mud off, but it clung wherever it touched his skin. Staggering backwards, Daemonicus tripped over a low stone wall and fell into the churchyard.

Iakopa watched the last blobs of flesh crumble into ash. It was hard to believe that the charred remains before him could still somehow be alive, but after all that he had seen lately, Iakopa was willing to trust Thomas's warning. He had been right about the soil from the church grounds: that hunk of clay had just let him turn one of the host of hell into a pile of blackened bones. However, Thomas said that a few drops of blood could be enough to make the demonic vampire whole again, if the bones were allowed to remain in one place. They had to be separated, permanently. The pastor already knew how to accomplish that. The place known as Lana had some of the roughest surf to be found in Hawaii. Iakopa packed the bones in a sack and emptied them into the ocean at Lana, to be scattered and broken among the rocks and waves.

10

Brunswick

Sally read and reread the gilded numbers, waiting for the motel door to open. She wasn't sure how she felt about the whole situation. There was a suspicious tint to the whole affair, and Sally was somewhat doubtful that the note came from Thomas. It might be a trap. In a way, she almost wished it would turn out to be a trap, because she was better equipped to deal with that than with facing Thomas. If it were true, she was certainly glad that another Guardian was safe, if indeed the young man Thomas had found was a Guardian. She would be relieved to know that Thomas was all right. But she was not looking forward to talking with him. He had looked up to her once, and she mostly just taught him her faults and a few of her illicit connections. He became a skilled sorcerer, yes, but also a criminal, a black magician, and now an absent father. How much did he still blame Sally for leading him down the wrong path?

The door swung aside. Thomas looked just like she remembered: tall and skinny as a bean pole, blond curls framing his pale, angular face. Only a few shallow wrinkles around the eyes indicated how long it had been since they last met. Thomas's cotu blood was letting him age rather gracefully. Behind him, a long-haired, caramel-toned young man sat on a dingy sofa, staring blankly at the carpet, tearstains on his cheeks.

"Thomas."

"Sally." He stepped aside and gestured for her to come in. She did, hearing Thomas's handwritten letter crinkling in her coat pocket. The Guardian hadn't registered her entry at all. It was beginning to look like he might be the most traumatized of them yet.

"How did you find him?" Sally craned her neck to see Thomas's face while they talked. He told her the wild story, with demons and a magic treasure map and all manner of strangeness. In the course of the explanation, he also told her something she wasn't sure he would ever admit to.

"I knew Daemonicus's methods because I've been evading him for a long time. You see, I bartered with a demon I should've let alone, with Daemonicus as a middleman. He's since come to collect."

"Thomas!" Sally didn't even consider trying to hide how incensed she was. "You said you wouldn't—"

"I know what I said!" Thomas snapped, fire sparking in his eyes. "I promised Pansy I would leave black magic behind when I married her! But I had to. Jason was dying. You couldn't save him. There was no other choice."

Sally recoiled as if she'd been struck across the face. She was acutely aware that she had failed Jason and his parents without being reminded of it. Thomas shut his eyelids, and Sally could imagine him counting to ten to calm himself.

"If I can manage to turn the tables on Daemonicus, maybe I can come home," he said at last, with forced coolness. "In the meantime, I'm entrusting Kai to you. He's had a hard time of it. I know it's not your forte, but try to be gentle with him."

"So...what has Thomas told you about me?" Sally asked, expertly weaving the black sedan she took on errands through the winding mountain roads. She wanted to answer any questions Kai might have, but she also couldn't help wondering what light Thomas would have painted her in.

"Um, he said you know a lot about magic and medicine, and your job is to protect Guardians. That's it."

"Well, that's a pretty short summary. Did he at least explain what Guardianship is?"

"Yeah, yeah he told me," Kai said. Sally glanced over at his morose form in the passenger seat.

"Good Lord, what happened to your neck? Looks like a vampire bite." Sally took her foot off the gas and gently pulled down Kai's shirt collar to get a better look at the two red punctures. Kai flinched but allowed the intrusion.

"I don't know what it was," Kai replied. "I didn't see it."

"You didn't see a fanged person bite you almost on the front of your neck?"

"Whatever attacked me was…invisible." Kai looked out the window, a little red coloring his cheeks. Admitting to an assailant that cannot be seen probably struck him as an embarrassing thing to say. Sally simply found it interesting.

"Hmm. Invisible vampires. That's not something you see every day. No pun intended. Do you mind if I photograph that bite when we get to my house?"

"You want to *what*?"

"I want to document the bite. I keep a database of vampire bites. It's almost as good as having a picture of the culprit. Better, even, because bite patterns are fantastic for identifying vampires based on the crimes they commit. The location of the bite, whether they bite with four fangs or two, et cetera, it's all very important for linking vampires to exsanguinations. If the one who bit you is an enemy of the Guardians, I would very much like to find him, and possibly put a stake in him; I'll have to see. But only if it's all right with you."

"Well, I guess it's all right with me, um, if you need to. You know, I don't think I've ever had my picture taken before." Kai absently rubbed the mark on his throat.

"Try not to touch it, dear, you might mess up the shape," Sally said. "Never had your photo taken? You are most fascinating. I hope I can get along better with you than the others."

"The others?" Kai repeated.

"The other Guardians. Did Thomas not tell you anything?"

"He said that his son was one of them, but, how many are there?"

"Including you, we know of four, but there are supposed to be twelve. You have a lot to learn, Kai, but we'll get there. And you have two new brothers and a sister to help you out."

"Right. Yeah. Okay." Kai closed his eyes and leaned back against the seat. Sally let the conversation die. She was relieved to drive in silence.

It was morning in the Kitch Manor, and for the moment it was quiet. In a little while, the rest of the household would start to stir and madness would ensue. The house, though huge, was originally built for just four people. The breakfast nook was not prepared to accommodate nine. Until then, however, William had the place to himself. After so many years on his own, observing a rather random sleep schedule, William had forgotten that he was actually a morning person when he wasn't hungover. It was nice, all this silence. If only it would be that peaceful inside his head, as well.

The shrill cry of the telephone broke the relative tranquility. William considered ignoring it, but no, that probably wouldn't be the nicest thing to do. He laid aside his book and answered the infernal ringing machine.

"M'hello?"

"Well you sure sound chipper," Sally responded.

"Isn't it a little early for sarcasm?"

"It's never too early for sarcasm. Are you doing all right?"

"Not too bad, I guess. Just didn't sleep real well. Where are you anyway?"

"I'm on the highway, headed back home," Sally said. "An old friend just found us a Guardian."

"*Another* one, already?" This was the second Guardian in a month. Kylie and her sister were just barely getting settled in, and here was number four come to join in the fun.

"Yep. They're just falling in our laps these days."

"Who is this 'old friend' you speak of? Anyone I know?"

"Yeah, actually. Are you alone?"

William lowered his voice. "Yes."

"Okay, good." Sally took a deep breath. "It was Thomas. But he doesn't want everyone to know that, because apparently he's in hiding. Which is why he's missing in action. It's complicated."

"Really? I suppose he did kind of have an on-the-run thing going. What's he hiding from?"

"A powerful *primum* vampire sent to kill him by a demon, or something to that effect," Sally answered. William made a few inarticulate noises of surprise, but Sally talked over him. "He didn't give a whole lot of details, but it's not that far-fetched. You know what kind of lives we live. Anyway, I just wanted to make sure somebody knew I was bringing company. I'll be home in twenty."

"And that's how Kai got here," Sally finished. Alex, Hope, Scarlet, Jenna, and William surrounded her in the basement sitting room, listening to her story. Now that she was done, she surveyed her audience, trying to see what they thought. Her gaze lingered on Hope. It was important that Hope understood Thomas had done this on his own, not at Sally's bidding. Sally found herself increasingly unwilling to argue with Hope about such things. With Guardians living in her own house, Sally felt the stakes far more keenly, and infighting seemed less attractive. Thankfully, Hope appeared calm, if a bit confused.

"I still don't understand that map Thomas made," Scarlet said. "Can we do that?" She looked over at Hope.

"I...I don't know," Hope admitted. "I've never heard of a spell that does that. Maybe he made it up. And, you know, he's a sorcerer, not a witch. He has to use external sources of power. We know he sometimes tapped into really dark sources of magic. That's how sorcerers can sometimes do things that witches can't."

"It sounds like becoming a sorcerer is a pretty good deal, then," William said.

"It isn't that simple," Hope explained. "Sorcery is potent, but dangerous, and the magic can be unpredictable. Thomas nearly killed himself several times when he first started practicing."

"If he weren't part cotu, I doubt he would be here," Sally said. "But could we *try* to replicate his spell? And by 'we' I mean 'Hope.'"

"Haven't you practiced sorcery before, Hope? Maybe I'm mistaken, but I thought that was something you were into when we first met," Jenna said.

"It was. You're right. But it started causing more problems than it was worth, so I stick to what I was born to do these days. I'll try to recreate the map, but even if I resorted to sorcery, without knowing the first thing about his spell, I can't guarantee I'll get anywhere."

"Should we even let Thomas keep using his map, if it's so dangerous?" William asked.

"I don't think there's anything we could do to stop him," Alex said.

"If his motivation is to protect his son, then there may not be any force in the world that could dissuade him."

"I agree with Alex," Sally said, "and I think we should let Thomas keep going. Maybe we could even help him out. He's a bit reckless, but we already trust him to a certain extent, and he's going to do whatever he wants anyways. So I propose we just accept his assistance. If no one objects…" This time, everyone except William looked right at Hope.

"That sounds fine," Hope said, looking Sally in the eye. Sally nodded. This, at least, they could agree upon. It was almost cause for celebration. After a few more questions, Sally's colleagues began to disperse, but William kept hanging around. Finally, when everyone else was gone, he got up off the floor and came over to Sally's chair.

"Can I talk to you for a minute?"

"Always."

"Maybe it's none of my business, but I was just wondering why you didn't go ahead and tell them that you have other people helping us search, too," William said, brow furrowed.

Sally exhaled a puff of air. She probably shouldn't have let her brother see so much of her operations, but she was always afraid to leave him alone. He might hurt himself, or someone else, if left unsupervised.

"Since I told you about that, I suppose it is your business," Sally said. "All right, well, you have to know that Hope and I have had a disagreement from the beginning about how many people to include in our network. She doesn't trust anyone. Frankly, I don't either, but I do trust that people are able to be manipulated. I would hire others to assist in our endeavor, but Hope refuses to put any faith in strangers.

"I shouldn't hold it against her. Her own fiancé was willing to burn her at the stake, after all, so I know from where her trust issues stem. Still, you know I'm not a patient woman. And this has taken so many years, I…the longer it's taken, the more Hope and I have fought. If Hope found out that I had done what I wanted all along behind her back, she would consider it a betrayal. The whole group could break down. It's a fragile ecosystem we have here."

"So, then, it's really important that Hope never finds out about, you know, them," William concluded, speaking slowly as if to weigh the meaning of each word.

"You could say that."

"But what if one of them does find a Guardian? What then? Will you just say it was Thomas again?" William sat down on the arm of Sally's chair. Without really thinking about it, Sally took his hand.

"I don't know. Maybe. I'll think of something. I'm pretty good at improvising. It's one of the reasons I've managed to survive this long." She forced a smile. "Don't worry about me. I can take care of myself."

Kylie was in the process of muddling through online pre-algebra when Jason landed on the sofa beside her. She smiled warmly and took off her headphones. She only saw Jason every couple days, but he had a sweet, unassuming friendliness that she liked immediately. He was a very different kind of friend from those she had at home.

"You ready to hit the library today?"

"Sure," Kylie replied, "and Richie says he wants to come, too. But I think there's someone else we should ask, eh?"

"Oh, right. Alex told me about him. Where is he?"

"Upstairs. His room is across from ours. I don't know if Kai will come with us, though," Kylie said. "He's barely left the room since he got here. When I introduced myself to him, he told me his brother had just been killed, and he wanted to be left alone."

"Oh, wow, okay." Jason's eyebrows rocketed upward on his forehead.

"Yeah, I totally get it. I was a mess after our parents died, and I don't know what I'd do if something happened to Joon. Kai's allowed to be weird. I still think we should offer to take him with us, just so he knows we're here for him, you know? Nobody should be alone for too long."

"I guess not, but I'm not going to try to make him socialize with us."

"Yes, I'll come." Kai sighed. "I need to do something, or I really will lose my mind." He closed the door behind him and waited with Kylie for Richie and this other boy, Jason, to join them from down the hall. Kai was still wearing the pajamas Sally had bought him, even though it was almost four in the afternoon, and his long black hair looked like a tangled clump of seaweed. He wasn't in any shape to meet his other Guardian 'brother'—the very *first* new Guardian, they'd said—

but it would have to do. Richie's door opened and he came out into the hall, followed by a tall, skeletal person with golden curls and a sharp, angular face.

"Is that Jason?" Kai asked. Kylie nodded. Kai was a little surprised. He had been building up in his mind a heroic, Herculean image of his Guardian forebear, but this boy hardly looked like he could withstand the force of gravity.

"Hello, Kai," Jason said in greeting, reaching Kai and Kylie in a few long strides. Richie caught up several seconds later. Jason's smile was warm, his voice deeper and smoother than Kai would have expected for a boy four years his junior.

"Hey," Kai said. His tone sounded dull and hollow even to him. Jason just nodded, his expression full of sympathy.

"I'm sorry you've had to go through this," Jason said. "We're all here for you, whatever you need. Come on, the library's in the basement."

Several flights of stairs down, Jason turned his copy of the key in the lock, shoved open one of the heavy, wooden double doors, and ushered his fellow Guardians into the library. It was easily the largest and most beautiful room in the house. Kylie gasped. Kai's jaw dropped open. Richie didn't look especially impressed, but two out of three wasn't bad.

"How do you even *find* anything in here?" Kylie said, a few of her soft, high-pitched echoes tossing about the room.

"I really don't know. I only know where the Guardian-related stuff is. If I ever want to look up anything else, I have to ask Sally," Jason told her. "I think she has the whole place memorized." Jason led the way to a particular spot on the first through fourth shelves, on the wall to the right of the door, where the books and documents they cared about resided. It wasn't hard to find, because of any collection in the library this one was most-used and thus the least ordered. Some books were lined up side-by-side, others stacked one on top of the other, and all interspersed with folders, piles of loose paper, and a couple well-worn binders. Sally kept the rest of the library neat and organized, but here there was too much activity to maintain her preferred impeccably ordered state.

"These," Jason said, grabbing a stack of papers off the third shelf, "are copies of the Guardian prophecies. I thought we might all have a look, if anyone else is interested."

In short order, the prophecies were strewn across a swath of the library floor and the four Guardians were avidly reading and discussing them, along with the notes on their margins.

"This one has your name on it, Jason," Kylie pointed out.

"Yeah, we think that's me," Jason said, "especially now that we know my gift is for languages. 'Silken tongue,' and so forth. Not that we can be totally, one hundred percent sure."

"Maybe you should be glad about that," Richie said. "I don't know what 'torn from within' means, but it sounds bad."

"Oh, I've already got that part covered," Jason said. The other three looked up at him with blank confusion and varying degrees of concern.

"Well, it's hard to explain if you don't know much about cotus," Jason continued. "It's just, I have this disease that cotu hybrids get, that causes ulcers and internal bleeding, and other un-fun things. So, I'm already pretty tore up. Oh, Kai, can you hand me that one under your hand there? I wanted to show it to Richie." Kai gave Jason the prophecy, eyeing him kind of strangely. They were all looking at him like that now. This was why Jason hated talking about his TTS. People always thought differently of him afterwards.

"Mahalo. So, Richie, I wondered if this one was about you." Jason handed the paper off to Richie, who read it out loud for the benefit of Kylie and Kai.

> *"Fire and Ice*
> *With unlimited sight,*
> *Through closed eyes—*
> *A fierce warrior*
> *To know the path,*
> *Frost blackened*
> *Flame bitten."*

"You see, Sally underlined 'sight.'" Jason pointed to where a line of magenta ink emphasized the key word. "That's what they call the ability to see the future, or auras, or anything else that only a select few can see: the Sight, usually with a capital 's,' but who knows what language this was translated from. And you do see through closed eyes, because you only see the future when you're dreaming."

"You see the future?" Kai blinked at Richie.

"Yeah, sometimes," Richie said. "I don't recommend it. I don't know, you could be right, Jason. And it mentions fire a lot, which makes sense because I am, apparently, a fire cotu."

"And you came here with an ice cotu," Jason reminded him.

"I guess Sally agrees with us, because there's my name at the bottom of the page. At least my prophecy isn't that creepy one with the snakes."

"Well, what about me?" Kylie said. "Do I have one, too?"

"Yeah, somewhere," Jason answered. "The question is 'which one?' Most of them talk about the Guardian's powers. Do you know what yours is?" Kylie shook her head, appearing a little disappointed.

"If it's any consolation, I didn't know what mine was for a long time," Jason said. "Hopefully yours will be more useful, though."

"What about you, then, Kai? What's your so-called gift?" Richie turned his gaze toward the newest arrival. In answer, Kai placed the prophecy he'd been reading in the middle of the little circle they had formed on the floor. The other three leaned over to read it.

The sea in his blood,
The Siren's song in his touch,
Knows what you want
When you want it too much.
He plays on love, lust, greed,
And the desires of the heart.
You see what you need,
Though it may tear you apart.

"That's a dark way to say it, but that's me," Kai said. "With a touch, I can tell what you want most, and I can make you see it. It might be an object, or there might be more than one thing you need that I can choose. Sometimes it's a person, someone you've lost or who you want to hear say something. Whatever it is, I can show it to you, make you believe it's real, right in front of you." Richie whistled. Jason had to concur. It was a potent talent.

"But what if the thing I want most isn't a thing?" Kylie asked. "What if I really want, like, world peace or something?"

Kai shrugged.

"I've never met anyone who didn't want something or someone I could show them." Kai picked up the prophecy and set it by his side, out of view. "This poem has to be about me."

"We should let Sally know, then," Jason decided, then thought about it. "Except, not right now, because I think she's still working."

"Working on what?" Richie's voice betrayed more than a little worry.

"You mean you haven't heard yet?"

"Okay, now you're scaring me. Heard what?"

"There's been another murder," Jason told him. "Another cotu with her Stone ripped out." Richie's face turned ashen.

"What?" Kai asked, glancing from one Guardian to another. So Jason explained, as efficiently as possible, about cotus and their Stones and the first body they'd found.

"So is it a serial killer?" Kylie whimpered.

"I think you have to have three victims to call it a serial killer," Jason said. "Besides, if it is a serial killer, you're in the clear. It's just those of us with Stones that have to worry."

"Does this kind of thing happen often here?" Kai asked, his thick, dark eyebrows pulling a crease in his forehead.

"No, it doesn't, I swear," Jason said. "The Brunswick Codes keep crime pretty well under control. It's usually really peaceful. Well, until Jasmine discovered I was a Guardian. I guess now all hell has kind of broken loose." Jason looked down at his tennis shoes, thinking about all the carnage the Black Dog left behind when it came searching for him.

"Hey, that's not your fault," Richie said. "None of us wanted this."

Kylie nodded. "You can say that again."

"Jasmine...who is she? Sally says she's one of our enemies, but why?" Kai stared pensively at the prophecies around his feet, perhaps thinking the answer might be in one of them somewhere.

"We assume she works for the Infinites, but we don't actually know why," Jason answered. "Genies are normally harmless, mischievous at worst, or at least that's what I've been told. The only one I ever met tried to kill me."

"I wonder what they've promised her," Kai mused, his fingers tapping his shin rhythmically as he considered whatever possibilities might be in his head.

"If you go up and poke her, maybe you can tell us," Kylie joked.

"Ha, no. I don't think I'm that curious." For the first time since they'd met, Jason saw Kai smile, just a tiny bit.

So far, it was looking much like the last time: nothing major to go on. The victim was a mature light cotu with no identification. Sally took down a detailed description of her appearance, down to the positions of moles on her skin and the color of her nail polish, to put out on the wire, but she doubted it would help any more than it had to date. Asking around for people to identify shapeshifters by how they look is often ineffective. The perimortem story was much the same, although the cuts looked a little cleaner. As Sally poked around the bottom of the rib cage, she saw something glinting embedded in a vertebra behind where the Stone had once been.

"Hello, what are you?" Sally grabbed a pair of tweezers from the tray of instruments on the counter behind her and pinched the shiny thing with them. It wasn't very deep in the bone, but she didn't take any chances. She worked the object out at a glacial pace. When she finally got it free, she held it out and examined it. A smile crossed her face.

"Small metallic object, likely a broken scalpel blade, found lodged in the L1 vertebra," Sally said aloud, leaning toward her audio recorder. "There is a gelatinous smear of a purple substance on one edge, in addition to the victim's blood. Possibly the blood of an individual of another species." The only species Sally could think of off the top of her head with purple blood were merfolk and water nymphs, both of whom seemed unlikely perpetrators for a couple of terrestrial crimes, but there was a sure way to find out.

"I'm storing the sample to take to my friends at Pedigree." Sally set the snapped blade on the tray for a moment, changed gloves, and retrieved a small glass tube and a plastic bag from one of the upper cabinets. Pedigree Sequencing was a laboratory that made most of their money testing the bloodlines of pedigreed dogs and cats, over the table, anyway. Sally had used their genetic services several times over the last six or seven years, and she wasn't the only one who asked them for unorthodox tests. How else would she have made their acquaintance?

Sally gently placed the sliver of metal in the glass tube and affixed the lid. Then she placed the tube in the bag and sealed it. Taking a permanent marker off the counter, she quickly scrawled the appropriate information in the blanks on the front of the bag. The lab probably didn't care whether she attempted to follow protocol or not, but she liked to think they thought better of her for the effort. She put the bag in the refrigerator in the corner beside other samples she had already taken during this session. She closed the door and closed her eyes for a moment. She prayed it wasn't just paint or grape jelly or some other unhelpful purple thing. She couldn't test for the presence of blood when the metal was already covered in the victim's blood. Sally prayed it was purple blood. If it was purple, it couldn't be his.

Please, God, don't let it be him.

11

Brunswick

"**A**re you sure this is okay?" Kylie fretted. "I thought Scarlet usually, you know, supervised. Isn't that what you said?" Kylie wasn't sure how Jason and Richie's training regime was. This whole concept of her and the boys being made battle-ready seemed a bit outlandish to her, but Joon said it was a good idea.

"Scarlet can't always be here," Kai said, "and we need to keep ourselves sharp."

"Speak for yourself," Kylie replied with a snort. "There's nothing sharp about me, and I'm fine with that."

Beside her, Richie snickered.

"Richie, come on now," Jason said.

"What?" Kylie blinked at the boys, clueless.

"Nothing," Jason said. "Let's just get to work. Kylie, do you want to join me, since you haven't done this before?" Kylie looked longingly at Richie for a moment, then nodded to Jason. Jason raised an eyebrow at her, but said nothing.

"I'm fine alone," Kai said, heading off any suggestions to the contrary. With a stuffed target under one arm and a bag of throwing knives tossed over the other, he headed off at a brisk trot to the opposite side of the dance hall. The idea of Kitch Manor having a dance hall was also weird to Kylie. Sally didn't seem like the ball-throwing type. Jason did say her parents built the house, though, so maybe they were the partyers. Regardless of why it was there, the hall was pretty, with polished hardwood floor and paneled walls. Kylie would hate to put a dent in it. But the torrential rains outside prevented training outdoors, and where else could knife-throwing, fire-starting, et cetera be safely done inside?

"Richie, what are you up to?" Jason asked.

"William tried to teach me to pitch fireballs the other day," he answered. "It...didn't work, but I'm going to keep trying."

"Inside?" Kylie burst out.

"I keep a couple fire extinguishers in here," Richie said. He pointed toward two sat on the floor at the head of the room. Kylie didn't find that entirely comforting, but she supposed it was Sally's house to let Richie burn down if she wanted. Richie the Ticking Time Bomb wandered off to find a corner to set fire to. Jason tapped Kylie's shoulder and inclined his head toward a blue wrestling mat on the floor. Kylie shuddered a little inside. This was not something she wanted to try, and it was a far cry from the normal life she wished for, but again, Joon was right. They were lucky to have made it out alive when the zombie horde descended. They needed to be prepared for the next crisis. She would rather be taking lessons from Scarlet, but Scarlet was spending the three nights of the full moon out in the woods werewolfing, and the sun set early this time of year.

"I did karate for a few months when I was a kid," Kylie offered, following Jason's lead. "Will that help?"

Jason shrugged.

"I don't think what Scarlet's been teaching me is karate." He slipped his sneakers off and stepped onto the mat, then beckoned with an index finger. Kylie groaned. She shed her shoes and joined him. She spaced her feet apart and took a stance that she thought might have been something like the once she learned from Master Lowry forever ago. Kylie balled her hands into fists, trying to look tough. A smile played at the corners of Jason's mouth, but he had the good grace not to laugh out loud.

"So, maybe you haven't noticed, but I'm not much of a bruiser," Jason said, stretching an arm behind his head. "I haven't got the muscle you'd find on a carrot. Scarlet had to figure out something else. I'm not sure I like it, but, hey, I'll do what I have to."

"Me, too," Kylie agreed. "So what's this magical technique she's been teaching you?"

"It's, uh..." Jason cleared his throat and looked down at his feet. "It's how to hurt people. Strategically, I mean. I can't take anybody out with force, but a few quick jabs in the right places will do the trick instead."

"That's what they're telling you to do." Kylie's fists fell forgotten at her sides.

"That's what they're telling *us*," Jason said, correcting her and meeting her gaze for a split second. "It's not something I'm proud of, but as many times as I've had to be rescued, and one time it was completely my fault, I don't want to be a victim anymore."

Kylie nodded, biting her lip.

"What the hell," she replied, smiling grimly. "I stabbed my math teacher in the neck with a pencil. No going back now."

"A pencil?" Jason's eyes widened, and Kylie felt a tingle of pride. "You've got to tell me that story later. Now, one of the first things Scarlet taught me was to go for the eyes. Please be careful practicing this."

"What are we doing?"

"We're running errands, Richard. It's a thing people do," William said, teasing.

"Yes, I know that, but *why* are we doing it?" Richie, exuding an atmosphere of general grumpiness, trudged along beside William as they browsed the aisles of Brunswick's only grocery store. In theory, getting out of the Manor for a while with William had seemed like a good idea. Richie was under self-imposed house arrest, to make sure William was always around to protect him. Between that and the gory future Richie experienced on an almost nightly basis, he was going slightly crazy. Now that he had been out of the house for a while, though, he realized that the air was cold, he was tired, and the errands were tedious.

"You said you were bored. Flour, check." William tossed the flour in the cart and crossed it off Sally's list. "And I kind of needed a break from, uh, well, you know. Shortening, check."

"Huh? No, I don't know. Enlighten me."

"From Joon. That was the last thing on the list. Let's go." William turned the cart around and headed for the register.

"What about Joon?" Richie thought William and Joon were getting along fine. They sure seemed to spend a lot of time together. Since Richie was now spending a lot of time with William, he couldn't help but notice.

"Is she trying to flirt with you or something?" Richie guessed.

"Um, yeah, a little," William said. "The problem is, it's working."

"What? Really? I thought girls weren't your thing."

"I never said that. I'm not *just* into men," William said. They had reached the front counter by now, and the cashier, a middle-aged woman in an apron, gave them an odd look, but started scanning their purchases without a word. "Right now, I'm feeling *really* attracted to Joon," William continued, "and I don't like it."

"Well, why not? She is pretty," Richie pointed out. He'd thought about trying to win her himself, but she related to him more like a child. Maybe it was because he was on the short side. People did tend to think he was younger than he actually was. Either that, or he just wasn't quite the Don Juan he liked to fancy himself to be.

"Most of my relationships haven't gone very well," William said, ducking his head in embarrassment. "Especially the ones with women. I just don't think it's a good idea. I'm trying to stay away from her until I get over it." They hefted the bags of groceries and went out into the parking lot. The sleek plum-colored car Sally had lent them sat waiting, frost spotting the edges of the windows. The frozen air bit right through Richie, but William didn't even have a coat on over his t-shirt.

"What if you don't get over it?" Richie asked as they loaded the wares in the trunk.

William sighed. "I don't know. I don't want to think about it." He slammed the trunk. shut Richie took the hint and stopped talking about it, for the moment.

Scarlet led the way, weaving through the Brunswick forest as easily as she navigated her own home. The woods were always changing—meadows would close in one place, appear in another, and the course of trails and streams would shift. Even the openings to the underground caves would move. Only the werewolves really knew the woods, because they spent more time in them than anyone else in town. Last night, a group of them had found a shallow ravine where there hadn't been one before. It wasn't just a split in the ground, though. Scarlet thought the forest made it on purpose, to show them. Some species of werewolves forget their nightly escapades, but pack wolves like Scarlet have better memories. So as soon as she regained human form, Scarlet went straight home and brought Sally to see what they'd discovered. They reached the edge, and Scarlet pointed down into the bottom, where the bodies were.

"Dear Jesus..." Sally murmured. "Do you know how many there are?"

"At least twenty," Scarlet answered, "but they're all piled on top of each other, and we were afraid to disturb them." Scarlet had feared that they might either damage evidence or unearth restless spirits. Either way, not a good move.

The corpses were in varying states of decay. Some still had a covering of skin left; others were reduced to bones. They spanned many races and represented both sexes. Most appeared as young adults, although one small skeleton was clearly a child. The denizens of the mass grave had something in common, though: all were cotus with their Stones cut out of their bodies.

"That's...damn. Okay, I don't know if this is serial murder or genocide, but this is bad," Sally stated, a note of shrillness in her voice the only sign of how deeply this atrocity horrified her. Sally was a stoic woman, but Scarlet knew that this hurt her, far more than she would ever let on.

"Well, I guess there's one good thing here," Sally added. "I'm now absolutely sure that the killer isn't who I was afraid it might be."

"Why? Who did you think it was?" Scarlet tilted her head to the side. She didn't remember Sally ever naming a suspect.

"I was worried it might be my brother," Sally said, after looking around to be sure they were alone. "It doesn't seem exactly like his kind of murder, so I wasn't sure..."

"William?" Scarlet exclaimed. "I know he's a little troubled, but would he really do something like that?" Sally had told Scarlet a thing or two about her brother before. He was probably the only living family member she liked, but he had issues stacked to the rafters. Scarlet had seen him in passionate conversation with no one. She never even told Sally about that one time she found him passed out on the sofa and carried him to his room. To Scarlet, William just seemed broken.

"He's done it before," Sally said, "although I don't think ever on this scale, and not just cotus. But it couldn't have been him, because I can see at least three down there that are too old. They have to have been there at least a year. He hasn't been in Brunswick that long. And unless it's a matter of defense, he only kills women."

"Sally, you know I love you, but you knew that your brother kills people, and you thought it was a good idea to leave him alone with the Guardians?"

"Well until recently, all the Guardians were boys! Besides, don't think I'm not watching him. He's trying to be better, and I'm giving him the chance to prove himself, under close supervision. And I have every confidence that you, Alex, or Hope could and would take him out if he ever got really dangerous. But I didn't want to make all that public knowledge, especially since Hope doesn't trust me any farther than she could throw the Statue of Liberty." For a while, neither woman said anything. They stared at the death in the earth below them, trying to process through the shock.

"What do we do now?" Scarlet finally asked.

"First, we don't let anyone near this place. You stand guard. I can't have a panic while we're trying to work this out. The DNA results I'm waiting on should come in the mail in…" She looked at her watch. "…in about forty minutes. We'll move from there."

"Have you at least *talked* to Joon about it?"

"Richie…" William examined the jar of pickled cactus in his hand, wondering what on Earth Hope needed this for and trying to think of something he could tell Richie to make him give it up. William certainly couldn't tell him the truth.

"It couldn't hurt just to talk, right?"

"Yes, it could," William insisted, fighting his frustration. "Look, Richie, I've spent most of my life going in a really, just, really *dark* direction, and every girl I've ever gotten involved with has made it worse. I. Can't. Go there. Again." William plonked the jar in their shopping basket and started scanning the shelf above his head for a very particular kind of dried spider.

"Fine, then." Richie put his palms up in mock surrender. "Spend the rest of your life alone. See if I care." William stopped what he was doing. He closed his eyes and inhaled deeply, trying to calm his racing heart and whirling thoughts. When he felt a little saner, he opened his eyes to catch Richie's gaze.

"I'm sorry. I know you're trying to be helpful but, please, don't make this any harder for me. I can barely cope as it is, and this is how it has to be. It's safer that way."

"What could some woman have done to you that was so terrible?" Richie asked. William swallowed and looked away from Richie. It felt like everything inside him was seizing up. He could try to change the subject again, but it would be impossible to evade the point indefinitely. William looked around. There weren't any other shoppers, the shopkeeper was in the stockroom. They were, for the moment, alone. The opportunity might not come again. William stared down at his feet while he tried to find the words to explain.

"It's not just about what they did to me; it's about what I've done to them," William choked out. He bit into his lower lip and tasted blood. "Women bring out the worst in me, and my worst is…pretty bad. I, well, I know you've heard about it. I…I—I'm the Ripper." William could feel himself shaking. This was the deepest, blackest secret he had, and telling it to Richie felt like having his own body ripped open.

"You're a what?" Richie wasn't stupid. He knew what William meant, William was sure of it. He just didn't want to believe it. William was still looking at the ground but could feel those chocolate-brown eyes on him, begging for him to take it back, to make everything the way it was two minutes ago. But it was too late for that.

"Not 'a,' 'the.' You know, that was my street name: Jack. The Ripper."

Since Brunswick didn't appear on any map and was only sometimes accessible to the world around it, the postal service didn't run there. Sally paced the length of the post office in the nearest small town that occupied this plane. It was a tiny building in a tiny town, but the staff were kind enough to devote one of the four walls to P.O. boxes for Brunswick.

The bell on the front door tinkled cheerfully, and the postman, actually an older, silver-haired woman, came in with a sack of letters. Sally stopped pacing and stood by the counter, arms crossed, clenching and unclenching her hands, while the boxes were filled at a glacial pace. *Why is everyone else so relaxed whenever I'm in a hurry?*

At last, all the mail was delivered. As soon as the mail carrier walked away, Sally dashed to her box and opened it with one stabbing motion of the key. She shuffled through the stack of mail. Bills, spam, *Pseudoscience Monthly*, ah, there! A simple white envelope from the lab. She tore the top of it open with her fingernails. Sally scanned the pages until she found what she was looking for.

"Genie blood," she mumbled. "Jasmine, what the hell are you doing now?" Sally's phone buzzed in her jeans pocket. She checked the caller ID. It was William.

"Everything all right?"

"Sally, I can't find Richie," William yowled through the phone, in the voice of abject panic. "He ran off, and I've driven up and down Main Street, but I can't find him. I think he might have gone off in the woods."

"Goddammit, William, don't tell me that!" Sally closed her eyes and pressed her fingers against them. *Genies are cutting the Stones out of cotus, and Richie is missing.* Sally's first thought was to ream William out for losing the Guardian, but that wouldn't make anything better. "Okay, where are you?"

"Uh, um, parked in front of Mario's Pizzeria," he said.

"Stay right there. I'm going to send help your way, and then I'm coming myself. Try to stay calm. It'll be fine."

Richie didn't remember running away. Everything was a blur from the moment William said "Jack the Ripper" until now. He found himself in a part of town he didn't recognize, a place full of crumbly brick buildings and trash in the streets. Unlike a city slum, the ramshackle houses were built far apart, and the icy wind swirled between them. Richie sat on the cracked sidewalk, arms wrapped around his torso for warmth, his mind galloping in circles. He couldn't accept that his best friend was the most infamous serial murderer in the world, yet he couldn't deny that he had seen William—Jack—kill without remorse. The loyalty and friendship the ice cotu had shown to Richie didn't mesh with Richie's concept of the cruel, bestial Ripper. At the same time, why would William admit to something so horrible if it weren't true? Could it be a delusion? Maybe William just *thought* he was Jack the Ripper...

Ultimately, it was the cold that forced Richie to slow down and think more practically. Numbness was beginning to creep up his extremities. He didn't want to go back to the Manor, where he would have to live under the same roof as the Ripper, but there was really no other choice. How to get back was another matter. Richie didn't know for sure where he was or how he had gotten there. There was a phone in his pocket. He had put it on silent after the first hundred frantic texts and calls from William. If William was already looking for him, the fastest way to get home would be to call him for a ride, but Richie couldn't do it. William had saved his life many times, and part of Richie still believed that William would protect him to the very last, but even so he could not make himself dial that number and ride in the car with that man, not now.

With half-frozen fingers, Richie took out the phone and punched in Sally's number instead. He didn't like her, but at least he was confident that he could trust her. As he was about to hit "send," a prickly, itchy feeling on the back of his neck distracted him. He slapped at the presumed spider but didn't find one. He didn't have time to think about it before he was overtaken by unconsciousness.

"When the Queen assigned me to this, I thought catching cotus would be hard, but they're so arrogant! Even after they found two of the dead ones, this idiot was just sitting out in the open, all by himself! It's like shooting fish in a barrel." Maryam, a muscly, amber-toned genie, wrapped her arms around the torso of their latest acquisition. Despite the chilly weather, he radiated an intense heat. A fire cotu, perhaps, or maybe a light cotu. Maryam's partner took his legs, and together they lifted him up and carried him off the street. Safe under the cover of a weak cloaking spell, the two genies lugged the cotu a few yards to the forest margin. There, they dropped him on their sled and dragged him into the dark mouth of a cave hidden within a thicket.

"We'll need to tell Jasmine we found an entrance so close to the town," Maryam commented. "It might not be here for long, so we'd better take advantage while we can."

"Richie *what?*"

Jason looked up from his homework, eying the other Guardians around the sitting room. Kylie and Kai mirrored his own concern. For Alex to be yelling into the telephone about Richie didn't bode well.

"Should we ask?" Kai said.

"Do you think anyone would tell us?" Kylie replied, a little bitterly. She had a point. They might, they might not. Jason shrugged and listened harder.

"All right, I'm on my way. Call William back and make sure he stays put," Alex said and hung up. He went straight to the coat closet and put on his jacket.

"Is Richie okay?" Jason asked.

"I hope so," Alex said. "When I find him, I'm gonna kill him." He went out the front door and left the Guardians staring at each other.

"Richie's missing?" Kylie said. "What should we do?"

"As you so astutely suggested earlier, I doubt we'll be allowed to do anything at all," Jason said, although he wanted to help as well. Kylie tapped her fingernails against the edge of her laptop.

"What about the professor?" she said after a moment. "He has a habit of trying to kill Guardians. Maybe he knows who else is in that business around here. And he's conveniently located in the basement if we want to ask him."

"What?" Kai said.

"You really think *we* can get something out of him?" Jason asked. "That hasn't worked yet, and people much more experienced than us have been at it for a while."

"What?" Kai said.

"Well, they haven't been trying our best secret weapon, have they?" Kylie said, pointing at Kai with her toes.

"What?" Kai said again, sounding even more worried. Jason gave him his most disarming smile.

"Kai, what do you say to interrogating an evil sorcerer to see if he knows where Richie might be?"

Kai sighed and closed the book he had been reading.

"Might as well. Won't somebody try to stop us if they catch us?"

"Don't worry. I have an idea," Jason said.

Kai followed Jason down to the basement, a realm with which he was still unfamiliar. Though he wouldn't like to admit it, the Manor's lowest reaches made him uneasy. He wasn't fond of basements in general. He had only been in a few and found them oppressive. But there was something else about the labyrinth under the Manor, a dark and unkind atmosphere that made Kai shiver. Perhaps the inexplicable fact that a prison cell had been built into one of the chambers had something to do with it.

Although Jason was the one who didn't live there, he led the way through the baffling array of halls with perfect confidence. Kai ran his hand along the cool, stone wall and peeked into rooms as they passed them. Many were empty or almost empty. Kai recognized an exam room. They passed a room full of things preserved in jars of fluid. A tiny, winged human stared at Kai from its watery tomb with pale, dead eyes. He shuddered and looked away.

"We're almost—crap," Jason whispered as Hope walked out of a door not ten feet in front of them. She saw them and blinked in surprise.

"What are you doing back here?" she asked. Her tone didn't sound suspicious, maybe a little worried. Kai allowed himself to breathe.

"Trying to find a responsible adult," Jason answered without hesitation. "The toilet in the bathroom right upstairs keeps flushing by itself, and I don't know if it's possessed or trying to cough up a fluke monster, but I thought someone ought to know." Jason looked Hope right in the eye, his posture relaxed and open. If Kai didn't know he was lying, he couldn't have told it by looking at him. That wasn't a skill he expected from the meek, younger boy.

"And it took all three of you to come tell me this?" Hope said, glancing at Kai and Kylie.

"I've seen those videos of snakes crawling out of toilets," Kylie said. "We don't wanna be anywhere near that thing. Just in case." Kai just nodded. Hope rolled her eyes.

"Someone needs to pay more attention to what you kids are watching," she said. "All right, I'll go make sure the bathroom hasn't flooded." The three Guardians watched Hope until she disappeared around a bend. For a moment longer, nobody moved or spoke.

"I think it's the room she came out of," Jason whispered, breaking the silence.

"Let's find out." Kai took the lead this time. Jason closed the door behind them. A recess in the back of the room about six feet on a side was enclosed on the front with thick, vertical iron bars. A door of the same was mounted in the middle. Inside the simple cell, a man in a white t-shirt and sweatpants sat on a cot. His entire body was entwined in threads of yellow-white light, even his head. He looked up at the sound of the latch and snorted.

"They're sending the children in now? Even the girl. I can't *wait* to see this plan," said the prisoner, one Professor Vincent LaMont. He tilted his head, expectant. Jason and Kylie, in turn, looked at Kai.

"I can't reach him," Kai said. "The cell's too deep. We wouldn't happen to have a key, would we?"

"We might not need one," Kylie said. She crossed the room and knelt to examine the inset lock on the cell door.

"This doesn't look too nasty." She pulled a few pins out of her hair. "But you two need to be ready for him to make a run for it, if he can with all that glowy crap on him."

Professor LaMont declined to comment, leaving his mobility a mystery. Kai assumed a boxing stance. Jason came up beside him. They stood there several minutes while Kylie picked the lock with great care and no hurry. Professor LaMont began to examine his fingernails. At last, Kylie got the lock open with a satisfying clunk. She tore the door open and ran behind the boys. Professor LaMont only sat there, smirking.

"Doesn't look like he's going anywhere," Jason said.

"Stay with Kylie, just in case," Kai said. He entered the cell with his eyes trained on the professor. Jason and Kylie had told him what they knew about the man, and Kai didn't think Professor LaMont was someone you would want to turn your back on. The professor didn't show Kai the same attention, but his quick, covert glances told a different story than his air of nonchalance. This man had raised the dead, and now he was afraid of an unarmed sixteen-year-old. Maybe he should be.

Kai reached out and put his hand on Professor LaMont's shoulder. He flinched from Kai's touch. The professor was one cracked up cookie. Kai knew what he had to do. He didn't like it, but he thought about Richie, lost and probably in danger, and about how this man had hurt Kylie. Kai could find it in himself to hurt him back. Kai watched as the expression of mild confusion on Professor LaMont's face morphed into pure shock.

"There's my baby," Kai cooed. He moved his hand to the professor's head, stroking his hair lovingly. The professor's mouth gaped open and closed twice before he managed to form words.

"Y-you can't, you aren't, it's not possible!" he stammered. He jerked away from Kai's touch, for which Kai was grateful but had to act offended. He put his hands on his hips.

"Oh, so I guess you're the only one who can bring back the dead, then?" Kai said.

"But I *tried*," Professor LaMont sputtered. "I tried everything! Why would you be here now if you wouldn't talk to me then?"

"Oh, Baby Bug," Kai said, trying to think fast. "I wanted you to let go. You needed to move on."

"You called me Baby Bug," Professor LaMont murmured, eyes so wide Kai could almost see his unchanged reflection.

"Oh, I'm sorry, I know you asked me to stop calling you that—"

"No, no." The professor stood up. "It's okay. I just can't believe it's really you." He laughed, tears forming in his eyes. Kai smiled and opened his arms. The professor dove into the comforting embrace of his dead mother.

Kai held him for what felt like an eternity, rubbing the grown man's back and wishing he were anywhere and anyone else. Finally, the professor pulled away. Kai plastered the warm smile back on.

"But, why *are* you here now?" Professor LaMont asked. Kai let the smile fade slowly, working up a serious expression that much more suited his mood.

"Vincent, there's something we have to talk about," he said. "Your behavior lately concerns me."

"What do you mean?" Professor LaMont appeared genuinely baffled. Kai could have laughed. Did he really think he had done nothing reprehensible?

"Well, I know I was a bit of a, what did that teacher call it, a helicopter mom? I was a bit of a helicopter mom when I was alive, so I've tried to let you find your own way since I died and had time to think about things, but I'm very alarmed to see you endangering children!" Kai did his best to sound disappointed. The professor looked away.

"It's not like that, Mom," he said. "Well, I guess it is, but the Infinites are going to build a whole new world. You know, good of the many and all..." Professor LaMont risked a glance up. For the first time during this charade, the expression on Kai's face matched his actual opinion on the matter: are you serious right now?

"They're children, Vincent," Kai said. "You tried to feed that poor girl to pigs. Do you really want to start a new world by killing babies?" Okay, none of them were exactly babies. Richie was already an adult. But it got the point across. The professor shrank away from his mother's harsh words.

"There's nothing I can do about it now," he said. "I've failed. I won't get another chance. I'll probably be killed. It's not like I can change my stripes now." Kai shook his head and took Professor LaMont's hands in his.

"There's still time," Kai said. "You're not the only one trying to hurt the children, are you, Baby Bug?"

The professor shook his head slowly.

"That's right, you're not," Kai said, "and the others have one of them babies right now. You might be able to help before it's too late."

"I don't know all the others!" the professor said. "I know where the ones that live right here are, but that's it. They don't have us work together." Kai fought not to look surprised. Right here? He could see Jason and Kylie exchanging frightened looks out of the corner of his eye.

"Maybe that will be enough," Kai said. He squeezed the professor's hands. "I have to go now."

"What? No! Don't leave!" Professor LaMont's wails tugged at Kai's heartstrings despite everything the man had done, but of course Kai couldn't keep this up indefinitely.

"This boy needs his body back," Kai insisted. "Don't worry, baby, I'll see you again someday."

"Promise?" the professor asked, but Kai was already letting the illusion go. No promises. For a moment they stared at each other, then suddenly both remembered they were still holding hands. They let go of each other. Kai wiped his hands off on his jeans. When Kai looked up, Professor LaMont's eyes were fixed on Kylie. She met his gaze evenly and angrily. Kai had no doubt that the other Guardians appreciated that comment about "the good of the many" as much as he did. Everyone seemed to want them to do something for the good of the many. The professor would prefer that they died for it. Unless Kai had changed his mind. They only needed him to doubt himself for a moment, long enough to give them an idea where Richie might be. Kai stayed in the cell, watching the professor watch Kylie.

"There's a bunch of witches living in tunnels in the forest," Professor LaMont finally said. "I only know where to find one entrance. If you'll get me something to draw with, I'll make you a map."

As of right now, Richie was Alex's least favorite Guardian. Sally was sitting beside William on the sidewalk, stroking his head to calm him down. Alex was sitting in the backseat of the car, trying to block out William's blubbering and the general madness of downtown in order to search for Richie. In retrospect, it might have been easier if he had just stayed at the manor and done this in his quiet, little tower, but when Sally called and told him that Richie was missing and her brother was having a nervous breakdown, Alex didn't really think, he just got on his motorcycle and came as fast as he could.

"Shhh, William, it's not your fault," Sally soothed.

Like hell it's not. William told them what happened. It was news to Alex that William was Jack the Ripper, but he took it in stride. He figured his body count was a lot higher than good ol' Jack's, so who was he to judge? But William should have known that Richie couldn't handle such a revelation. *Don't be angry, be zen,* Alex ordered himself. Outside, he heard Sally's cell phone ring. Alex growled in frustration. About thirty seconds later, Sally opened the car door. Alex opened his eyes a sliver.

"Forget it. I think you need to look somewhere specific," Sally said. She promptly ducked away, talking on the phone again.

"What? How?" Alex climbed out of the car. Sally held up a finger. Alex glanced at William. William sniffed and shrugged.

"Text it to me," Sally said into the phone, and hung up. She turned to the men. "The other Guardians have some explaining to do when this is over."

"They know where Richie went?" William scrambled to his feet. Sally's phone chimed, and she studied the screen as she answered him.

"They got Professor LaMont to tell them where there's a genie nest near town," Sally said. "Not that we have any reason to think they have him other than paranoia, but Alex can check, and then we can either panic more or less." She held her phone out to Alex. He took it. On the screen was a picture of a hand-drawn map of part of the town with a star inside the area labeled "woods." Star marks the spot, he supposed. There weren't many landmarks on the map, but it did tickle something at the back of Alex's mind. He focused on the image in front of him until the phone went to sleep. Then he closed his eyes and sent his consciousness drifting. It soon found the place that matched the map. He searched the energetic landscape for the familiar amber glow. He almost missed it, but a faint aura did catch his eye, seeming somehow far away. How could that be?

"I found him." Alex came back to his body as fast as he could, leaving himself a little dizzy. "He's in the woods, up past Panther Street, and I think he might be underground."

"How did he get all the way over and under there?" Sally asked.

"It doesn't matter," William said. "Let's just go find him before he gets hurt. I'll drive."

"No, you won't. You're too frazzled," Sally said. "William, you can keep an eye on the phone in case there are any updates. Lead the way, Alex."

As soon as Alex parked on the street nearest where he had seen Richie's aura, he began to get a sinking feeling. He knew he had been here before, months ago, when he had spotted that strange energy signature in the forest. But he hadn't found anything. It seemed he had been too quick to dismiss his concerns because here they were, running to Richie's rescue exactly where Alex had entered the forest then.

Sally's car swooped up to the curb and parked within three inches of it. William jumped out before it stopped moving. Alex began to hurry between the houses toward the tree line. He stopped just inside the woods to quickly, but politely, state their business and ask permission. Sally held William still for him to do so. The forest voiced no objections, so they rushed on, Alex at the head of the pack, until they reached a clearing that struck him as familiar. This was the place. But just like the first time, there was nothing to be seen but a clearing.

"I saw him here, I swear," Alex said, gesturing at the ground, "right beneath our feet."

"There has to be an entrance to the tunnels around here somewhere. They're all over the place." Sally parted her jaws to taste the air with the scent glands in her mouth.

"Already found it!" William hollered. Alex and Sally looked behind them to see him leaning against a tree several feet deeper into the forest. He was gazing down into a black opening, about two feet across, in the leaf litter.

"That wasn't exactly what I had in mind," Sally said, coming to William's side. "Those little holes go straight down, and the floor can be a loooong way yonder. Trust me. I've fallen through a couple." Alex was about to suggest they find another, less hazardous opening, but without warning William stepped forward and right into the hole. Alex and Sally knelt at the edge, peering into the black. After a a heart-stopping moment, there was a thump.

"I'm okay," William yelled up at them. "Come on down!" Alex looked to Sally. She shrugged.

"Down the rabbit hole it is, then," she said, swinging her legs around into the gap. She pushed off and soon disappeared. A moment later, she called for Alex. He lowered himself in backwards and let go, landing in a crouch on the cool, stony ground. It was a significant fall—the soles of Alex's feet stung from the impact—but not too bad for a cotu or a vampire. He looked up at the circle of greenish light above him that represented where they had come in.

"I hope you have a plan for getting back out," Alex said. He surveyed their surroundings. A human would be nearly blind, but the dim glow from the hole was plenty for the three of them to see by. They were in a small, low-ceilinged cave rimmed by gray-blue stalactites that dripped tiny, plinking drops of mineral water. A few dark blotches in the walls marked where tunnels or recesses might be.

"Not really," Sally admitted. "I'll figure it out once we find Richie. I bet he fell through that hole, or one like it."

"I don't smell him…" William said. Alex could hear him shuffling his feet.

"I can't say it's him, but I do smell cotu," Alex said. It was a rusty smell, like human blood, but it also had a harsh, chemical taint. Sally caught his eye, and Alex gave a minuscule nod. There would only be one reason that he could smell a cotu when two other cotus couldn't detect the scent. A vampire could sniff out as little as a few drops of freshly spilt blood at quite a distance, even if the animal it came from was too far away to smell otherwise.

"This way," Alex directed, walking toward a tunnel that branched off on his right.

Richie blinked open heavy eyelids and saw the glaring white lights above his head. Cold metal cuffs around his wrists and ankles locked him to the table, but another force, invisible but immovable, held his head and the rest of his body flat to the table. He curled the ends of his fingers and was relieved to find that he was capable of that much motion, at least. He could twist his head, but he strained his eyes to see what was around him. Unfocused humanoid figures moved at the edge of his vision. He could hear their voices whispering, but only snatches of their conversation were anywhere close to clear. Richie didn't need to listen to know what was about to happen, though. His heartbeat throbbed violently in his neck, and he was breathing too hard and fast to really get any air. The figures moved closer and encircled him. The brightness above them cast their faces in shadow, but Richie could see the bluish surgical masks over their mouths and the shine of their eyes.

Without a word, a pair of hands came into view and then vanished again beneath Richie's line of sight. A blade tip pierced Richie just underneath the sternum, and he pressed his eyelids shut. The knife ran over the same line again, and again, and again, slicing deeper and deeper, until the wound went far enough for another hand to slide one of the scissor blades under his skin. Richie's throat constricted, but his paralyzed vocal cords couldn't scream. Searing hot tears streamed from the corners of his eyes as he felt his abdomen cut open, and he prayed for the dream to be over. What he couldn't know was that this time, it wasn't just a nightmare.

12

Brunswick

Alex turned a corner, and the scent of cotu blood smacked him in the face. A more muted whiff of genie accompanied it. At the end of a short corridor in front of him there was, inexplicably, a door, fitted in a low, square opening carved from the stone. Sally and her brother came up behind him. William hissed as the scent washed over them, too.

"That's Richie's blood," he growled. Sally grabbed his arm to hold him back a heartbeat before he lunged for the door. He was bigger than her, but she knew just where to snag him to catch him off balance.

"We don't know what's through there," she said, pulling him back. "We need a plan."

"I'm not waiting for them to cut his Stone out," William told her, trying to squirm free of her grasp.

"All right, I'll go straight for Richie, and y'all two can take care of whatever else in is there," Sally said. She let go of William and held up a hand, bidding him to stay put for just another second. She padded quietly up to the door, flung it open, and then stood out of the way as William charged headlong into the room, Alex following more cautiously in his wake.

Of course, their entrance caused complete chaos, and Alex had only a moment to take in the scene. William's fears were not unfounded. The room was only a cave, but two shelves set into the walls at the level of a genie's hands were laden with surgical tools. Two gurneys in the middle of the room each bore a bloodied cotu surrounded by four masked and gloved genies. Alex didn't pause to see if one of them was Richie. William had already pounced on one of the "surgeons" and her coworkers were rushing to her aid, metal implements clattering to the floor as they abandoned their projects. Alex could see the glittering magic gathering around them, but he had no intention of giving them time to reach William. Bearing his teeth, he stormed into the throng and latched onto the carotid of the first genie to come into his grasp.

When Sally followed Alex into the room, she immediately saw a flaw with her plan. She should have considered the possibility: there were two victims in the room. The choice was already made for her, of course. If Richie died, the entire multiverse would be put at risk. She skidded to a halt at the table on the right. To her horror, Richie's eyes opened a sliver. She put her hand under the back of his neck and sent a pulse of electricity into his brainstem. Unconsciousness was immediate. She hesitated half a second, then ran to the other table and did the same for the woman there. If she didn't have time to save her, at least she could stop her pain.

Sally returned to Richie's side. One of the genies snagged her shoulder and tried to pull her back. Sally charged her entire body like a human-sized electric eel, and the genie was thrown back into the cave wall. She slumped to the floor and didn't get up, so Sally disregarded her. One good look at Richie, and she wasn't sure there was any hope of putting him back together, but she pushed the doubt aside. The genies had pulled his skin and abdominal wall aside like they were dissecting a frog. The full extent of the internal damage caused by their artless rummaging was unclear. They hadn't removed the Stone entirely, that much was certain. Sally would need more time to figure out what they *had* done. That was a luxury she didn't have at the moment. Rendering Richie unconscious had slowed his heartbeat drastically, but she needed to get him to the Manor *now* if there was any chance to keep him from bleeding to death. Sally drew a portal as fast as she could and wheeled the gurney through. Sally took one last look at the other gurney before following Richie.

Alex surveyed the destruction around him, satisfied that he and William had done their jobs. His stomach was full of genie blood, his clothes soaked with it. All eight genies were dead. Four had fallen to Alex, and four to William—a perfect division of labor. Alex's kills were marked by torn throats. William's kills were a lot gorier. He could see where the name Ripper came from.

Sally had taken Richie, but the other eviscerated cotu remained. Alex went to the head of the table to break her neck as a final act of mercy, but there was no need. He felt William come up behind him and stop short of joining him at the side of the gurney.

"I feel bad just leaving her here like this," Alex said. William didn't say anything, but after a moment of odd noises he appeared beside Alex with the bloodied lab coat of one of the genies in his hand.

"Oh. Um, thanks." Alex took the coat and wrapped up as much of the she-cotu as possible in it and hefted the bundle into his arms. She was tiny.

"What are we going to do with her?" William said at last.

"If we can't figure out where she came from soon, I guess we'll have to bury her in Brunswick somewhere," Alex answered. "Anything is more respectable than leaving her to the genies down here in this hole, wouldn't you think?"

"I wouldn't have thought about it at all."

"You and Sally are definitely related." Alex picked his way through the minefield of corpses and carried the she-cotu through the portal Sally had left open for them, William trailing after.

William stood up. Sat down. Stood up. Tramped the length of the basement den. Stopped in a corner. Glanced at the door. He thought operating rooms were supposed to be whitewashed with observation windows and antechambers and a label on the door. This one used to be a wine cellar. The door was plain and wooden and behind it his sister was working furiously to piece Richie back together. William had seen him, though, and he didn't think Sally could do it. But he hoped to God, if there was one, that she could.

It's my fault. It's always my fault. He's going to die, and I did it. I've killed him and I didn't even touch him.

Well, of course. You destroy everything you love just by existing, Jack.

Shut up! I don't need this from you. There's got to be something I can do...

Killing yourself would probably help.

That's not going to save Richie, you idiot.

It's still a good idea.

Get out of my head.

You get out.

A light touch on his shoulder startled William out of his inner dialogue. A short, sharp hiss escaped before he realized it was only Joon, trying to be of comfort. As if she could. Pity was all in her eyes and her aspect. William tightened his crossed arms and flicked his eyes downward.

"Are you all right?" she asked.

"Do I look all right to you?"

"Okay, stupid question. I'm sorry. I didn't know what else to say. It's just that when I came down here and saw you...I don't think you should be alone," Joon explained, her voice down-feather-soft. "I've been here, and I—"

"You have never been here," William said and then laughed humorlessly.

"Oh-kay, not *here*, exactly." Joon took her hand away and leaned her palms into the back of an armchair. "I *have* spent my fair share of time in a hospital waiting room not knowing what the news would be."

"Did you put the guy in there?"

"No, and neither did you," Joon said, with a touch of sharpness this time. "I ran into Alex. That's why I came down. I learned *way* more than I ever wanted to know about what happened out there. I get why you're blaming yourself, but it isn't fair." It took a couple seconds for William to process what Joon had said in his distracted state of mind. Once he did, his heart did a double somersault and started racing to beat the band.

"What did Alex tell you?" William wasn't sure how much of his panic came through in his voice. Something changed slightly in Joon's face when he asked, a narrowing of the eyes, a bit of a frown, but what emotion it reflected he hadn't a clue.

"Just that you and Richie got into a fight, and he ran off because teenagers don't think before they do. And then, tunnels, and fighting, and blood, and gross things...you know."

"Oh." William barely restrained himself from sighing out loud. "Yeah, that sounds about right." So Joon still didn't know. *Best keep it that way.* "But, you don't understand. I'm the one that, uh, started the fight. If I'd just kept my mouth shut, Richie would still be—"

The creak of hinges cut William off midstream. He and Joon both swiveled to look at the operating room door. It wasn't Sally, but Hope, who had been assisting her, slipping out the door.

"She's almost done stitching him up," Hope reported, "and everything is back where it's supposed to be, so now we just have to wait." William swore and began pacing the room. Hope glanced quizzically at Joon. "He'll be fine. I think."

Joon frowned. "What are we waiting for, exactly?"

"Sally is keeping him in a medically-induced coma for a couple hours to give the wounds time to start healing," Hope said. "Normally cotus heal faster than this, but the damage is pretty extensive. If he's doing well after that, she'll try to bring him out. We'll just have to see if she can wake him up and go from there." William grabbed a table lamp and hurled it against the far wall as hard as he could. The explosive crash of shattering glass behind them made both Joon and Hope jump, but it did nothing to calm the unbearable riot of emotions. William leaned into the cool, stone wall behind him and sank into the floor, curling into himself as his breathing came faster and faster.

It was cold—nose-numbingly, bone-achingly, unbearably cold. Richie whimpered, and started to curl up into his core, desperate to conserve any warmth he might have. A hand touched his shoulder, a warm hand, so warm against his icy skin that it burned, and he was glad for it.

"Don't move any more than you have to. You'll pull your stitches," a woman's voice told him. The voice was familiar, but Richie couldn't quite put a name to it. He stopped moving, frightened by the thought of torn stitches, and the hand retreated, taking its heat with it. Richie forced his eyelids apart to see where that warmth had gone.

The first thing that came into focus was Sally, arms crossed, leaning her shoulder against a wall for support. Her entire demeanor had a limp, exhausted aspect. She was sideways, which seemed weird until Richie realized he must be lying down. Normally, Richie would find an appearance from Sally annoying at best, but now he was quite relieved to see her, instead of the dark surgeons.

"I'm cold," he whispered through dry lips.

"I know," Sally said, blinking sympathetically. "I've turned the heat in this room as high as it will go, and I've got you under every electric blanket in the house. Your body temperature is still a lot lower than I'd like, but until your Stone heals this is the best we can do."

"It wasn't a dream this time," Richie guessed, turning his head to stare at the ceiling.

"No, I think not," Sally said. "Whether this was the event you were predicting remains to be seen, I suppose. Alex and William really did a number on their operating room, such as it was, so maybe no one else will have to go through this."

"William…" There was really nothing else he could say to express the tangle of thoughts and feelings that broke over him.

"I know what happened. He told me. Well, he told me that he told you. I already knew." She anticipated his reaction, for once, and put her arm over his chest to hold him down right before he started to jolt upward in surprise.

"You *knew?*" Hitting Sally's arm was like running straight into a steel bar, but the pain that spread through his trunk as a result of the sudden motion was worse. Richie lowered himself back down, gingerly, doing his best to keep his eyes on Sally until she came up with an excuse. It had better be a good one.

"Of course I knew," she said, pulling Richie's blankets up to his chin. "That's why he came here. He realized, finally, that he was out of control, and he wanted help. I've tried to convince him to see a psychiatrist. I know of a few who are most discreet. He won't do it. He spent time in asylums back when they were a very special kind of hell, and now he won't have anything to do with the mental health establishment, even on an outpatient basis. But he needs the help, there's no denying that, and the world would be a better place for it, so if I'm the only person he'll go to, then I am not going to refuse."

"So, you're containing him," Richie paraphrased. Sally nodded. "But what about the rest of us who live here?"

"You were never in danger with him, Richie," Sally said, meeting his gaze evenly. "You're the closest thing he has had to a friend in a very long time. He wouldn't hurt you. Besides, he only ever hunted women, and the last time I checked, you are not a woman." It occurred to Richie that the last time she checked would have been earlier that day when he was naked on an operating table. He blushed and burrowed further under the covers. Sally didn't seem to notice. She just kept talking.

"When he first came, there was *no one* here to be threatened by him," she continued. "Everyone was either strong enough to fight him or, you know, not female. Even now the only ones who might be at risk are Joon and Kylie, and I think Kylie's a bit too young to catch his eye, so really it's just Joon—"

"Oh, God, Joon." Richie wanted to smack himself, except he was afraid to move his arms.

"What about her?"

"We were talking about her," Richie said. "That's why he told me that he's...we were talking about how much he digs her, and he was trying to tell me that he needed to avoid her so he wouldn't hurt her, and I was arguing with him 'cause I didn't know any better...ah, goddammit."

"Hmm, that could be a problem. Perhaps it's about time that Scarlet and Joon became real good friends...right now he's too busy worrying about you to cause any trouble, though."

"Has he been here?"

"He only just left. He helped us rescue you. He stayed around the whole time you were in surgery, and he was in here with you for over an hour. He would still be if I hadn't had to crank the heater up. It's much too hot for an ice cotu in here. I had to drag him out before he fainted." Richie wasn't sure how he felt about that. Part of him was touched that William was so concerned about him, but he was also appalled to have had a serial killer at his bedside while he was sleeping. Sally had sworn that William wouldn't hurt him, though, and so far she had been right. They had been under the same roofs for over a year now, and William had never been anything but kind—if strange. Richie closed his eyes, more conflicted than he'd been since he decided to leave his family for their safety.

"Technically William is still assigned to help watch over you and the other Guardians when Alex is in school with Jason, but if you want, I'll tell him to leave you alone," Sally offered.

"No." Richie opened his eyes and looked over at her. Her face was suitably surprised.

"You said he won't kill me," Richie said. "We don't want him upset. We don't want him out unsupervised. We don't want him near Joon. So I'll keep him busy. Containment."

"My, you *are* a brave little toaster," Sally replied, smiling. Richie wasn't sure how she meant that, but he took it as a compliment.

This time when Richie woke up, he was finally warm, but he was also looking right at William, so it was still somewhat unpleasant. He closed his eyes immediately, hoping William wouldn't notice he had opened them at all. Richie hadn't decided yet how to handle the situation with the Ripper. Unfortunately, for once, William was being observant.

"I don't know about you, but I'm having one of those 'where do we go from here' moments," William drawled. "First things first: how are you feeling?"

Richie sighed and sat up as much as he was able, now that the conversation was unavoidable.

"I feel a bit like I've been carved for a Christmas turkey," Richie said. "What about you, though? Sally said you were 'having a coronary.'"

"Oh yeah, they got tired of listening to me, I guess," William said. "Hope finally gave me something to help me calm down." That made more sense. William was almost never this mellow sober, at least not that Richie had seen. He was just lounging in a chair, head back, staring at the ceiling, completely limp. Richie found he was relieved that William wasn't in possession of all his faculties. There seemed less reason to be afraid.

"Hope drugged you to get you to shut up?" Richie knew the witch to be a little impatient, but still, that seemed harsh.

"To be fair, I was sort of, um, throwing breakable things at walls and such."

"You what?"

"I don't cope well with stress, or anything, really."

"I'm beginning to realize that." Richie fiddled with the blanket on top of him. He had that sort of dream feeling, like he did when he first told William—Jack, then—that he would go with him to find Sally. It was that this-isn't-real, watching-one's-self-in-third-person sensation. He didn't like it, but right now he thought maybe he needed that defense mechanism.

"I don't know where we go from here, Will. I have no…point of reference, no idea what to do when you find out that your best friend guts women for fun."

"I-I'm your best friend?" William sat up straight, a hint of a smile on his face.

"I think you missed the point." Riche rubbed his forehead in exasperation.

"No, I heard you." The smile faded, and a darker expression emerged. He flopped back into the chair. "I never kill for *fun*, Richard. I kill out of desperation, although I don't expect you to understand. I thought my sister would be able to help me, she *is* helping me, to learn how to avoid that need. And she's not the only one."

"You mean me," Richie said.

"Who else would I be talking about?"

"William, what do you want from me?"

"I want you to live. More than that, I want you to thrive. And, you see, that's the amazing thing, because you are the first person I have met in so long that I really, truly want only the best for." He leaned over the arm of his chair and fixed Richie in his intense, though glassy, gaze. "That's kind of a big deal. I didn't think I could do that anymore."

"You are so high."

"Sure, that too. But I needed to tell you, because Sally said you aren't going to make me leave. Maybe, probably, it's not for my benefit, but I wanted you to know it might work."

"Work how?"

"I mean you might make an upstanding citizen of me yet," William said.

"That sounds…sort of horrifying," Richie said. "I mean, it's better, but it doesn't seem like you, you know?"

"Isn't that what we want?" William asked, sounding genuinely confused. "Don't we want me to be less me? Because the real me is pretty bad. You of all people should know that by now."

"I don't know…you did save me." Richie reminded him. "More than once. And the first time, I was a stranger. You rescued me from being werewolf chow, and you didn't even know why you did it. For you to do something so selfless…there must be a part of you that's better. I think that's the only reason I can sit here in the room with you and talk like it's a perfectly normal thing. There is a part of you, however small, that I still sort of trust."

"I don't understand that."

"Yeah, I'm not sure I get it myself. I guess I've just quit trying to understand."

"What do you mean you're leaving?" Jason squeaked. He couldn't believe what he was hearing. Alex couldn't just leave Brunswick! Alex cleared his throat, keeping his head down to dodge the gazes of the half dozen people he'd gathered for this announcement. The movements of the Earth could have been heard in the den of the Manor.

"I'm taking the search farther," Alex continued. "If T—our friend hadn't been looking, then Kai would be dead. Everything we've worked for would be lost." He glanced at Sally, then Hope. "We need more people searching, *and* it needs to be people we trust. You don't need me here anymore." Alex's voice broke, and he had to take a breather before continuing. *We* do *need you,* Jason thought. *I need you.* He looked at Sally where she sat beside Alex. Surely she would tell him that he was being stupid. Alex would listen to her. Sally's hands were cupped over much of her face, hiding most of her expression, maybe on purpose. But Jason could see the shock and hurt in her eyes. Still, she didn't say anything.

"You have William in the manor, and all of Scarlet's werewolves patrolling the town," Alex said. He raised his head. "Where you need me is out in the field. I know a Guardian when I see one. That's something I can do that no one else can. The best thing I can do is leave."

"But…" Jason never finished his sentence. Tears misted over his eyes, and he buried his face in his mother's shoulder. She immersed her hand in his curls and rubbed his head to comfort him.

"Who's going to watch over Jason at school if you go?" Pansy asked. There was a moment of silence, and Jason turned his head to see what was going on. Everyone was looking at Sally, expecting her to assign the task.

"I guess I will," Sally said, sounding faintly surprised. "Alex…how long do you plan to stay gone?"

"I don't know," he admitted. "I guess when I find a Guardian, then, I'll come home."

But for how long? Jason wondered. Whoever their old friend was that delivered Kai hadn't so much as stayed for dinner.

"When are you leaving?" Hope asked.

"As soon as I throw my crap in a suitcase, I guess," Alex answered. "So, probably a couple days. Then I'll go to the airport and see where the planes are going."

"So soon," Jenna murmured.

"I only just decided I was doing this," he said. "But I'll have my phone, and if any of you ever need anything, or want to talk, call. Especially you, Jason. You're my favorite, you know. Don't tell the other Guardians." Alex smiled mischievously, and Jason couldn't help but smile back. There was quiet for a moment, and then without warning Scarlet pounced with a hug attack.

"I'll miss you. You have to talk to us every week, and your dad, too, so we don't worry. And if you don't come back, I'm coming after you, you hear?" Scarlet licked his chin, and Jason tried not to let the disgust show on his face. She really had been a werewolf too long. But she'd shaken everyone of their stunned paralysis, and everyone had to take a turn hugging Alex. Sally nearly cracked his ribs.

Sally was sitting on the porch when Jason arrived. She wasn't waiting for him this time, though. She was in the swing, head resting on gloved hands. Jason trudged up the steps and came to sit beside her. Her eyes were red, but whatever tears they'd shed were dry by then.

"He's gone already, isn't he?"

"Yes," Sally said. She sniffed. "I caught him on the way out, but we couldn't think of much to say. And then he left."

"Are you okay?"

"No," she answered. Jason hadn't expected her to be honest with him, but he was glad of it.

"Me neither," Jason sighed. He began to rock the swing gently. It reminded him of when he used to sit on the porch swing at his grandparents' house, shelling peas with his grandmother while she rocked the swing. It made him feel just the tiniest bit better.

"It's not the first time," Sally said. "He's left the Manor before, even for months at a time. I always knew he'd come back when he got too lonely. But this time he isn't just running away. I don't know if he'll want to come back to—to the way things were."

"He'll be back." Jason nodded, staring off at the frost-dusted forsythia bushes at the end of the porch.

"Sometimes I really wish I had your faith in people." Sally chuckled without humor. "I've come to expect the worst."

"That sounds miserable."

"At least no one can disappoint me." She shrugged, crossing her arms over her chest. Jason stopped swinging and studied her for a long while. He wondered what kind of disappointments she must have faced to make her so keen to avoid them.

"Try to put a little trust in Alex," Jason said at last. "He's doing this for us, after all. I don't think he'll leave us hanging forever." Sally crushed a dried leaf under the toe of her boot.

"Well, I guess I can try."

Kell, Jasmine, and five of their sisters held hands around a table on which a pile of charred, ashy bones was gathered in a shallow metal baking pan. They'd done it. They had really done it. It was probably the most difficult, weirdest, most complicated spell she had ever tried to weave, but it had worked.

"Is that all of them?" Kell marveled, releasing the hands of the genies on either side of her.

"We'll know soon," Jasmine said, "if we're successful. All right, hand me that pitcher, dear." One of the genies dutifully gave her Queen the plastic jug full of purple blood.

"Are you sure it shouldn't be human blood?" Kell fretted. "Wasn't he human to begin with?"

"If this doesn't serve, then we'll go find some human blood," Jasmine said. "Our blood was more readily available." She tipped up the pitcher and poured the blood into the pan of bones. It washed ashes and bits of seaweed from the bones, then pooled beneath them.

"I know I'm asking a lot of questions," Kell said, "but how is he going to reconstitute in a cookie sheet? That seems a bit…small."

"I'm sure he'll think of something," Jasmine said. "He's probably done this before."

"In a cookie sheet?" Maryam reiterated. Jasmine glared at her, and she looked down to avoid her Queen's reproachful gaze.

"If Daemonicus wants to live again, then yes, he will do exactly that. I couldn't just have his bones rolling around all over the floor, could I? We had to put them in something."

"I think it's working," Kell said. The blood was soaking into the bones and crawling across their surfaces, coating them in a grape-jelly layer. Globs of muscle and tendon began to form along the most intact bones, and the parts of broken ones gravitated together. An eye orbit was coalescing in one corner. A section of spine floated into the middle. Unidentifiable fragments somehow found their place in the mending skeleton. Several of her sisters closed their eyes or looked away, unable to endure the grotesque spectacle, but Kell and Jasmine kept their gazes riveted. This was a momentous occasion, not just because they wanted Daemonicus for their cause, but also because no genie had ever done this before. That was mostly because religious law forbade it. Jasmine promised that they would be forgiven, as the laws were not designed for the war they presently fought. Their foremothers couldn't have imagined it.

As Kell and Maryam had suspected, the skeleton soon outgrew the cookie sheet. The few muscles that were available arched the spine and lifted the skull over the edge of the pan, onto the table, so that the process could continue. Striated tissue enveloped the skeleton. Organs blossomed in the confines of the rib cage. After mere minutes, skin encrusted the rounded part of the skull as a lichen blankets a rock. Flesh filled in, skin grew to cover it. Lids draped over the eye sockets and the globes grew in behind them. Finally, fuzzy, infantile hair grew from the tender flesh, and with a watery gasp the reborn Daemonicus filled his undead lungs.

"I am a bit surprised, your Majesty. Kell gave me the impression that you wouldn't accept failure on my part so graciously. Why have you brought me up from the depths?" Daemonicus tied the belt of the bathrobe Jasmine had gifted him, waiting calmly for her response. He was somewhat grateful to her for bringing him back, although he couldn't stop himself from thinking that spending eternity scattered across the bottom of the ocean, too disjointed to really think, was a much more peaceful existence than he would have to look forward to, now that he was whole and once more able to be properly sent to the afterlife.

"Alone, both of us have come tantalizingly close to killing one of the Guardians, but we haven't succeeded," Jasmine said, leaning back with both hands against the table Daemonicus had regenerated on less than an hour before. Smears of genie blood and tiny pieces of vampire flesh sullied the wood. Jasmine didn't seem to notice.

"I think, together, we can do what neither of us quite managed on our own," Jasmine continued. "My masters want results immediately. I asked, and they agreed to offer whatever you may wish, if you will join with me."

"That sounds promising," Daemonicus said. "May I ask what they offered you?"

"Vengeance." Fury simmered behind Jasmine's dark irises. "Humans have nearly destroyed my species. Only a few nests remain. I want their kind gone from this world, and the Infinites will make it so."

"Ambitious." Daemonicus raised an eyebrow. "I like that. But you'll find that my goals are much less lofty."

"You can tell us in a moment. One of my masters is on the way."

"Excellent. I look forward to meeting him."

Meri Elena

Meri Elena is a North Carolina native and lifelong bibliophile. She started writing "seriously" in fourth grade, and her first published story, the horror novelette *Anew*, came out as a Kindle e-book in the summer of 2012. The e-book short story collection *These Four Walls* followed in October, 2013. Her short fiction has also been published in the *Off the Beaten Path* anthology series by Prospective Press.

She has won a Figment.com short story contest and been a finalist for another. Her essay on vampire mythology and the psychology of fear was selected for print in Teen Ink magazine. Her current project, first begun in fifth grade, is the Brunswick Prophecies series.

Meri graduated from North Carolina State University with majors in Plant Biology and Genetics and a minor in Creative Writing, and is currently a graduate student in Journalism at Indiana University Bloomington. In addition to literary and academic pursuits, she spends her time in used book stores and with *Buffy the Vampire Slayer*. She collects Bay City Rollers memorabilia and as many cats as she can reasonably keep up with.

www.ingramcontent.com/pod-product-compliance
Lightning Source LLC
Chambersburg PA
CBHW071153180726
48291CB00007B/2444